JAMES HADLEY CHASE

"the king of all thriller writers" – *Cape Times*

"master of the art of deception" – *New Statesman*

"has many imitators but he alone is monarch"
– *The Sun* (Sydney)

James Hadley Chase

Strictly for Cash

Panther

Granada Publishing Limited
Published in 1966 by Panther Books Ltd
Frogmore, St Albans, Herts AL2 2NF
Reprinted 1966, 1973, 1975

First published in Great Britain by
Robert Hale Ltd 1951
Copyright © James Hadley Chase 1951
Made and printed in Great Britain by
C. Nicholls & Company Ltd
The Philips Park Press, Manchester
Set in Intertype Times

Contents

1. Double-cross   7
2. Fog Patch   44
3. Flash-back   81
4. Fade-in   117
5. Curtains   169

PART ONE

DOUBLE-CROSS

I

WE hit Pelotta around nine-thirty at night, after a four-hour run from Kern City. Packed with stores, souvenir stands, cafés and filling-stations, it was like any of the other small towns along the Florida coast.

The trucker, whose name was Sam Williams, pointed out the places of interest as we drove along the main street.

"That's the Ocean Hotel," he said, jerking his thumb at a gaudy affair of chromium, neon lights and bottle-green awnings that stood at the intersection that led across the town and to the sea. "Petelli owns every brick of it. Come to that, he owns pretty well the whole town. He owns the stadium too. That's it up there."

I peered through the windshield of the truck. Aloof on a hill, overlooking the town, was a circular concrete building, open to the sky in the centre, and roofed in on the rear stands. Above the roof were vast batteries of lights strung together on big steel frames, and which could be focused down on the ring.

"There must be a pile of jack coming out of that joint," Williams went on. He wiped his red, fleshy face with the back of his hand and spat out of the window. "Petelli promotes a fight programme there every Saturday night."

He swung the truck to the right, away from the bright lights of the main street, and drove down a narrow road, flanked on either side by wooden buildings. At the far end I could see the water-front: the ocean glittered in the moonlight like a sheet of silver paper.

"Tom Roche's place is on the corner, facing the sea," Williams said, slowing down. "I'm behind schedule or I'd come in with you. Tell him I sent you. He'll fix you a ride to Miami. If he won't play, talk to his wife: she's a good kid."

He pulled up, the nose of the truck facing the dimly lit water-front. I opened the cabin door and slid to the ground.

"Well, thanks for the ride," I said. "I hope we meet again."

7

"I'll look for you. So long, pal, and good luck."

I stepped back and watched the truck move off along the water-front, then I turned and walked over to Roche's Café.

It was a two-storey building made of salvaged lumber and painted white. The double swing-doors stood open, and music from a juke-box ground out into the night.

I mounted the three wooden steps and paused to look in. There were tables dotted around a fair-sized room, a counter on which stood three steaming urns, half a dozen wooden stools up at the counter, and a big electric fan in the ceiling that churned up the hot air.

Two men in singlets and dirty canvas trousers sat at a table by the door. Near the juke-box to the right of the counter at another table was a big, heavily built man in a white tropical suit and a yellow and red hand-painted tie. Seated opposite him a short, fat man in a brown suit and a panama hat gazed emptily into space. A truck driver, in a leather wind-breaker and breeches, sat on a stool at the counter, his head in his hands. Behind the counter a slim, white-faced girl, I guessed was Alice Roche, was putting two cups of coffee on a tray. At the far end of the counter, polishing an urn, was Tom Roche, a dark, skinny little guy with a hard, bitter mouth and a shock of wiry black hair.

For a few seconds I stood in the darkness, watching. No one noticed me.

I watched the girl take the cups of coffee across the room to the big man and his fat companion. She put the cups on the table, and as she did so the big man grinned up at her and his hand gripped her leg below the knee.

She stiffened, nearly dropped the cup, and tried to back away, but his thick fingers retained their grip while he continued to grin up at her. I expected her to slap him or scream, but she didn't do either. Instead, she looked hurriedly over her shoulder at Tom Roche who was concentrating on the urn and not noticing what was going on. The look on her face told me she was scared to make a scene because she'd be pulling Roche into something he wasn't big enough to handle, and I felt a sudden cold knot form inside my chest. But I didn't move. It would have been simple to have walked in there and socked the big fellow, but that wouldn't have taken care of Tom Roche's pride. No man likes another to protect his wife when he's there to do it himself.

She leaned down and tried to prise the big fellow's fingers off her leg, but she hadn't the strength.

His companion, the fat man in the brown suit, tapped him on

8

the arm and whispered to him imploringly, nodding at Roche who was standing back to admire the shine on the urn.

The big fellow gave the fat man a shove with his free hand; the kind of shove you'd get from a steam-roller if you walked into it without looking where you were going. It left the fat man gasping.

The hand slid up above the knee, and the girl in a kind of desperate frenzy hit the big fellow on the bridge of his nose with her clenched fist.

The big fellow cursed her. Then Roche looked their way, and his pale face went the colour of mutton fat. He took four lopsided strides that brought him out from behind the counter. He had on a surgical boot that built up his shortened right leg, but it still gave him a limp like he had stepped into a hole every time he took a stride with his right foot.

The big fellow let go of the girl and shoved her aside, sending her reeling across the room into the arms of the trucker who had slid off his stool and was gaping, without making any move to help.

Roche reached the table. The big fellow didn't bother to get up. He was grinning. Roche's right fist swung up and round towards the big fellow's head. The big fellow weaved inside the swing and Roche's fist hit space. He lost balance and came forward, and the big fellow gave him a dig in the belly. Roche was flung across the room and thudded into the counter. He slid to the floor, and lay gasping.

The big fellow stood up.

"Let's get out of here," he said to the fat man. "I'm sick of this joint."

He walked over to where Roche was struggling to get up.

"Take a swing at me again, you little rat, and I'll smash you," he said, and drew back his foot to kick Roche.

I was across the room in three strides and pulled him away from Roche. I spun him around and smacked his face, hard enough for the smack to sound like a ·22 going off at close range.

That smack hurt, as I meant it to hurt, and water spurted out of his eyes as he staggered back.

"If you must kick someone," I said, "kick me. I'm a better target."

If he hadn't been half crazy with rage he wouldn't have thrown the punch he did. It was a round house swing that started from his ankles and telegraphed itself all the way. The kind of punch you'd throw at someone who didn't know the first thing about fighting. The kind of punch that would have flattened an elephant if it had landed, but it didn't land.

I moved inside it and socked him with my special right hook that travelled about four inches and had my whole weight behind it. It exploded on his jaw with a devastating impact and he went down as if he'd been pole-axed. I didn't wait to see if he were going to get up. I knew he wouldn't. When they go down like that, they stay down.

I stepped back and looked at the fat man.

"Get this hunk of garbage out of here before I really go to town on him."

The fat man was staring at the big fellow, spread out on the floor, as if he couldn't believe his eyes. As he knelt beside him I went over to Roche and helped him to his feet. He was breathless, but he could stand, and he had still a lot of fight left in him. He made a move towards the big fellow as if he were set on hitting him again, but I held him back.

"He's had enough," I said. "You don't want to break your hands on a lump like him. Take it easy."

The girl came over and put her arms round him. I left him to her and joined the two men in singlets and the trucker who were staring down at the big fellow.

The fat man was trying to bring him round without much success.

"Bust his jaw," the trucker said, and drew in an excited hiss of breath. "I've never seen a punch like it! Didn't travel an inch – and socko! Well, the bum certainly asked for it."

"Get him out of here," I said. "Come on, boys, hoist him up and get him outside."

The fat man looked up. He had eyes like pools of beer, and from his expression I thought he was going to burst into tears.

"You've broken my boy's jaw," he said, "and he's fighting on Saturday."

"I should have broken his neck," I said. "Get him out of here before I change my mind and finish the job."

The big fellow opened his eyes, groaned and sat up. The lower part of his jaw sagged hideously, and an ugly red patch showed on his right cheek where I had slapped him.

The two guys in singlets hauled him to his feet and supported him. He went with them without looking at me, his head on his chest, his eyes glazed and his legs like rubber. The fat man brought up the rear. He looked as if he were following behind his mother's hearse.

The trucker turned to gape at me as if I were the miracle boy come down from the sky on a cloud of fire.

"Well, for crying out loud!" he exclaimed. "Do you know who that was – the guy you socked? That's Joe MacCready, the local champ. He's fighting the Miami Kid on Saturday, and there's a load of dough spread on the fight. Take my tip, brother, and get out of town. When Petelli hears what you've done to MacCready, he'll blow his top. I'm not kidding. Petelli's as dangerous as a rattlesnake. Get your skates on and beat it!"

II

I pushed back my chair and reached for a cigarette, but Roche beat me to it. Everything was on the house this night. I had just climbed outside the best meal I had eaten in years, and while I ate Roche and his wife, Alice, kept me company. I liked them. They were the kind of folk I could get along with, and we were on first-name terms before I had finished the meal.

They had done most of the talking while I was eating, and now I knew it was my turn.

"Maybe you're wondering what I'm doing here," I began, when Roche had lit my cigarette. "Well, I'm from Pittsburgh. My old man ran a café bang opposite the Carnegie Steelworks. You'd have thought a café situated outside the biggest steelworks in the world would have paid off, wouldn't you? But it didn't. Don't ask me why. I never got around to figuring it out myself. There was damn-all when he died. A good thing or I might be still there. As it is I had to sell up to pay what he owed, and that left me without a home. So I thought I'd take a look at Florida, and boy! am I glad I did."

Roche scratched the side of his jaw and squinted at me.

"What's so special about Florida?"

"Ever been to Pittsburgh? Soot, dirt, noise and fog – that's Pittsburgh. That's what's so special about Florida."

"Maybe you're right. I've lived here all my life. I get sick of the sun sometimes."

"Brother, you don't know when you're well off! I've had the finest three weeks of my life riding trucks this far. This country's terrific." I leaned forward. "And that reminds me. I got a ride off a guy named Williams. He told me to come here. You know him?"

"Yeah: known him years."

"He said you could fix me a ride to Miami. Can you do it?"

"That's easy. Josh Bates is on the Miami run. I keep his mail for him. He'll be in tomorrow morning. I'll fix it for you. So you're going to Miami?"

"You bet."

"Hey, Alice," Roche said, "how about some more beer? Can't you see this fella's dying of thirst?" While she was in the kitchen getting the beer, he went on, "That's the finest hook I've seen outside anything Dempsey threw. You in the game? I guess you must be. That late shift of yours and the way . . ."

"I've been in it, but I'm through now. It's too much of a racket."

He eyed me over.

"With that build and that hook you could be sensational. Who have you fought?"

"I had three rounds with Joe Louis when he ran out of sparring partners during his Army exhibition tour. Nice guy, Joe. He said I had a good right hand."

"Joe said that?" Roche seemed impressed.

"The best scrap I ever had was when I deputized for Abe Linsky. I put Jack Weiner away in the second."

Roche gaped at me.

"You mean – *Jack* Weiner? The Californian champ?"

"That's the fella. He wasn't champ then, but he was quite a scrapper. I was lucky to hang one on his jaw. I guess he was a shade too confident."

"Jeepers!" Roche said. "Well, that's something. What made you quit?"

"I guess I like to keep my face the shape it is, besides, I've got other ideas."

"Sounds like a waste of talent to me," Roche said, shaking his head. "If you could take Weiner . . ."

"That trucker told me to get out of town. He said Petelli would have something to say about MacCready."

"You don't have to worry about Petelli. Solly Brant will tell him what happened. Besides, the Miami Kid is getting Petelli's backing. If it had been the Kid you hit, then you would have had to get out fast, but Petelli hasn't any time for MacCready."

"This Solly Brant you just mentioned. Is he the fat guy with MacCready?"

"That's right. He owns MacCready, and I bet he wishes he didn't. He's not a bad fella, but what can you do with a bum like MacCready?"

Alice returned with two pints of beer.

Roche had insisted that I should stay the night at the café, and I welcomed the suggestion. For the past three weeks I had been sleeping rough, and the thought of a night in a bed was tempting.

After we had talked a while, I pushed back my chair.

"If it's okay with you I'd like to turn in now. I've been truck riding for eight hours, and I'm about asleep on my feet."

"Go ahead. Alice'll show you the room," Roche said, and stood up. He offered his hand. "And thanks again for what you did."

"Forget it," I said, shaking hands. "Thanks for the meal. It was great."

Alice took me upstairs to a small room that looked on to the water-front.

"If there's anything you want . . ."

"Not a thing. That bed sure looks good."

"You can take a bath if you want to. It's right next door."

"I'll do that. You know this is pretty nice of you."

"We're very grateful for what you did, Johnny. That brute might have hurt Tom badly. He's not very strong."

"But he's got a lot of guts. I guess you're pretty proud of him."

"Oh, I am." She put her hand on my arm, and her eyes were shining. "He's been through some bad times, but he's always been good to me. But if you hadn't come in when you did . . ."

"Forget it. I was glad I was around."

"I just want you to know I think you're splendid," she said, and went away, leaving me a little hot and flustered.

I took a bath, lying in the hot water for half an hour or so. I could hear them talking downstairs, and when I got into bed, Roche came up and put his head round the door.

"All set?" he asked, edged his way in and stood at the foot of the bed looking at me.

I grinned at him.

"You bet."

He shifted from one foot to the other, rubbed the end of his nose with the back of his hand while he stared seriously at me.

"Anything on your mind?" I asked, seeing he wanted to say something but seemed at a loss for words.

"I guess so. Me and Alice have been talking about you. I have a proposition to make you. How would you like to come in with us? We're doing pretty well, but we could do better. With you to help us, we could expand. I don't say there's a fortune to be picked up, but if it interests you I can show you the figures. I don't mean I'm offering you a job. I'm offering you a third share in the business. It could be a nice living. What do you say? Alice and me would like to have you."

I stared at him, scarcely believing I had heard aright.

"Why, you're crazy!" I exclaimed, sitting up. "You don't know a thing about me. You can't go offering me a third of your business just because I punched a fella in the jaw. What's the matter with you?"

Roche sat on the edge of the bed.

"We need help, Johnny. We need a guy like you. You know the trade, for one thing. Then you're big and can scrap – I can't. We get some tough characters in here, and there's not a lot I can do about it. We like you. We reckon you'd be worth every nickel you take out of the business."

He was probably right, but the job was no good to me. I didn't want to hurt his feelings, but I had to tell him.

"Look, Tom, let's get this straightened out," I said. "Don't think I'm not grateful for the offer. I am, but it can't be done. Don't get me wrong about this, but frankly I've been in small-time too long. All my life I've wanted money: not a few paltry dollars – my old man had that and they got him nowhere – but a roll of money you could choke a horse with. Maybe it's because my old man kept me so short when I was a kid. The only thing he ever paid for was my food. My clothes, movies, candy and all the other things kids spend dimes on I had to earn, and it meant earning them the hard way: working after school, running errands, delivering newspapers, cleaning windows, and never having any time to play. My old man reckoned it would make me value money, but he was wrong. It made me determined to get a pile somehow and have a glorious blow with it. I've got to make money. It's become a thing with me, and when I've got it I'm going on the biggest bender ever. I thought my chance had come when my old man died. I figured I'd be able to sell the café and go a bust on the proceeds, but there were debts and there weren't any proceeds. Right now all I've got are the clothes I stand up in and forty dollars from my army gratuity. So I'm going to Miami where the dough is, and some of it's going to stick to me. Big dough, Tom, not little stuff. I have a feeling in my bones if I can get to Miami I'll hit the jackpot."

Roche sat listening, his face expressionless.

"Why Miami, Johnny? Why not New York or any big city?"

"Something I heard," I said. "I know it sounds cockeyed, but I met a guy who's been to Miami. He reckoned there was no place like it on earth. He said there were more millionaires to the square inch out there than any other place in the world, and they go there for a vacation, and they throw their money around like drunken sailors. If you're smart you can catch some of it. But don't get me wrong. I don't intend to work any racket or get into trouble. I'm going to collect this pile legitimate. There're all kinds of jobs going in Miami where you can pick up big dough. Know what this guy told me? He said lifeguards make up to two hundred bucks a week. He knew one of them who saved the life of a movie star, and they gave him a thousand bucks and a job in Hollywood. This guy himself was a chauffeur, and his boss kicked off and left him five grand. He'd only worked for him for three years. Think of that! I don't see why I shouldn't muscle in on that kind of luck. That's all it is. The money's there. It's just a matter of being on the spot when these guys throw it around."

Roche rubbed his knee while he looked thoughtfully at me.

"Your pal didn't tell you about the con men, the gamblers, the grafters, the whores and the mobsters who are all in there like a wolf-pack trying to separate your millionaires from their rolls, did he?" he asked quietly. "He didn't mention the cops who hound a guy unless he's well dressed and keep him on the move? I've been to Miami, Johnny. Before I bust my leg I used to drive a truck from Pelotta to Miami every week. It's a fine town for millionaires, but if you're short of dough, it's tougher than a jungle full of wild animals. Take my tip and forget Miami. You're living in a pipe-dream. Stay with us and you have a chance to make a reasonable living and you'll keep out of trouble. When a guy goes after the kind of dough you're talking about, sooner or later he's going to get into trouble. Use your head, Johnny. The only way you could break into big money is by fighting. I don't know how good you are, but if that punch is a sample, then I'd say . . ."

"Don't say it," I broke in. "I've quit fighting. I'm not finishing up half blind and my brains leaking blood. That's out. You say Miami is tough. This guy says it's a soft touch. I guess I'll go and find out for myself. Maybe I'm crazy, but I'm going. Sorry, Tom, but that's the way it is. And don't think I'm ungrateful."

Roche lifted his thin shoulders.

"Okay, if that's how you feel about it, then go to Miami. Have a look around. Then come back here. I can do with you. I'll give you three months before I look for someone else. Think about it, Johnny. A third share and a free hand, and only Alice and me to bother you. Think about it."

I didn't have to think about it.

"Don't wait for me, Tom," I said. "You fix yourself up. I won't be coming back."

III

I had just finished breakfast when Roche put his head round the door.

"Solly Brant's outside. He's asking for you. Want to see him?"

"Why not, or shouldn't I?"

Roche shrugged.

"Please yourself. He wouldn't say what he wants."

"Well, shoot him in."

I pushed back my plate, and, as I reached for a cigarette, Brant came in. His panama hat was pushed to the back of his head. There were dark rings under his eyes, and he looked as if he hadn't slept for days.

"I'm sorry your boy can't fight," I said before he could open his mouth, "but he got what he deserved. It's no use coming moaning to me. It's something I can't do anything about."

"Yeah, don't tell me, I know," Brant said, and pulled up a chair. He sat down. "He's a bum, always was; always will be." He rubbed his face with his hand and groaned. "That punk's put years on my life. The trouble I've had with him." He leaned forward and poked a fat finger at me. "Where did you learn to punch like that?"

"I've done a little fighting. If I'd known he had a glass jaw I'd have hit him some other place."

"He ain't got a glass jaw. Guys have been hanging punches on his jaw for years, and up to now he's liked it. I've never seen a punch like that. It would have dented a tank." He absently picked up a piece of toast and began to nibble at it. "But never mind him. If I'd some other boy to fight the Kid I'd be waving flags to be rid of him. But I haven't another boy, and this is the first major fight I've collared in years. The take's seven-fifty, and that's a lot of beer to a guy like me." He gnawed at the toast, then asked, "Who have you fought?"

"Oh, no, not me," I said. "Never mind who I've fought. You're not getting me to fight for you. I quit the game years ago, and I'm not going back to it."

The small brown eyes roved hungrily over me.

"With that build and that hook you're a natural. How long have you been out of the game?"

"Too long. I'm not interested. If that's all you've got to talk about let's part while we're still friends."

"Now wait a minute. Roche tells me you put Weiner away in the second. Is that right?"

"It's no dollars in your pocket if I did."

"Heading for Miami, aren't you?" He put down the toast and hitched forward his chair. "Now, listen, soon as I saw you I knew you were a killer. Use your head, Farrar. What do you think you're going to do in Miami dressed like that? How far do you think you'll get before some bull tosses you in the can? Even if you keep to the back streets you won't last ten minutes. If you haven't a good front, you're out in Miami."

"That's my funeral: not yours."

"I know." He took off his hat and peered inside it as if looking for something he had lost. "But I'm not talking because I like the sound of my voice. How would you like to arrive in Miami in a tropical suit and all the trimmings and driving your own car? Okay, it's not much of a car, but it goes. And how would you like to have five hundred bucks in your pocket to give you a start?"

He was dangling a nice fat worm on a sharp hook before me, and I knew it, but I listened just the same. I knew I shouldn't make much of a showing in Miami in the clothes I had on, and this had been worrying me. A tropical suit, five hundred bucks and a car sounded about right to me.

"Go on talking," I said. "It won't hurt me to listen."

"That's a fact," he said, and grinned, showing six gold-capped teeth. "That's my proposition. Deputize for MacCready, and that's what you'll get. How does it strike you?"

"Not bad. What makes you think I rate that high?"

"I don't know you do. If you've got anything beside that hook, then you can't be so bad. Suppose you come down to the gym and show me just what you can do?"

I hesitated. In a couple of hours Josh Bates would be pulling out of Pelotta for Miami. I could either go with him and travel as a bum or stick around here for four more days and then travel in my own car with money in my pocket. But before I got the car and the money I had to fight a heavyweight I'd never seen or heard of, and I wasn't in anything like strict training. I might even land up with a broken jaw myself.

"Just how useful is this guy you want me to fight?"

"Not bad," Brant said. "He's fast and pins his faith on a right cross." He stood up. "But you don't have to worry about him. I don't expect you to beat him. All I want you to do is to stay with him for a few rounds and make a show. The dough's all on him.

But if he gets too hot for you you can always do an *el foldo*."

"That's something I've never done, and don't intend to do."

"Just a suggestion," he said blandly. "Suppose we go over to the gym. We can talk better after I've seen the way you shape."

We went over to the gym. It lay at the end of a dark, evil-smelling alley off Pelotta's main street. It wasn't much of a place: one big room, equipped with two training rings, punching bags, some dirty mats scattered over the floor, a row of changing booths and a few shower cabinets, most of which didn't work.

The place was deserted when we got there.

"Waller, Joe's sparring partner, will be along any minute now," Brant said. "He's a good trial horse and you can hit him as hard as you like. If you don't he'll hit you. Let's have three rounds with all the action you can cram into them."

He went over to a locker and handed out some kit. While I was changing Waller came in. He was a big, battered Negro with sullen, bloodshot eyes. He nodded briefly to Brant, gave me an indifferent glance and went into one of the booths to change.

When I had stripped off, Brant looked me over critically, and whistled.

"Well, you ain't carrying any fat. You look in pretty good shape to me."

"I'm all right," I said, and ducked under the ropes. "But if I'd known this was going to happen I'd have laid off smoking. It's my wind I've got to watch."

Waller climbed into the ring. He was built like a gorilla, but in spite of his size I noticed he was eyeing me thoughtfully.

"Listen, Henry," Brant said to him, "let's have a fight. I want to see how good this guy is. Don't pull your punches and keep after him."

The Negro grunted.

"And that goes for you, too, Farrar," Brant went on. "Well, if you're ready. Okay? Then come out fighting and make a meal of it." He touched the bell.

Waller came forward like a gigantic crab, his head hunched down into his heavy shoulders. We moved around the ring, feeling each other out. I got in a couple of quick jabs and swayed away from a vicious looping right he threw at me. I managed to pin him with another left. None of my punches had any steam in them. I wanted to test my timing. I knew it wasn't sharp. Every now and then Waller caught me with a dig that hurt. He kept shuffling away from me, making me come to him, and countering every time I landed on him. Suddenly he stopped in his tracks and let fly a right that landed high up on the side of my head. I was rolling by the time it landed, but it was a good solid punch, and it shook me.

As he rushed in I let go a left: the first punch I'd thrown with any steam in it. He went back as if he had run into a brick wall. I could see the surprise on his face.

We moved around. He was more cautious now. That left had startled him. I got in two jabs and collected a dig in the body that made me grunt.

I was now having trouble with my breathing. You've got to be in strict training to take the heavy bangs I was taking and not worry about them. If I was going to keep out of trouble I'd have to stop him, and stop him quick.

He saw my wind was going and began to pile on the pressure. He was a difficult target to hit, and for the moment all I could do was to jab away at his face and head and hope for an opening. I smothered most of the punches he was throwing, but some of them landed and they hurt. I was glad when the bell went and I could flop on the stool and take a breather.

Brant sponged the blood from my nose, his fat face thoughtful. "You've been out of training too long," he said. "You're not timing your punches right. Better take it easy in the next round. Box him this time and keep away from him."

I didn't say anything. I had my own ideas what to do. I'd have to finish him in this round or I wasn't going to last.

Waller hadn't bothered to sit down. He lolled against the ropes, looking bored.

"Okay?" Brant asked as he reached for the gong-string.

"Yeah," I said, and came out slowly.

Waller moved in, set to nail me. He slung a left. I shifted so it slid over my shoulder and hit him three times to the body. I heard him gasp as he went into a clinch. His weight sagged on me. I tried to shove him off, but I couldn't do it. He hung on desperately, and didn't pay any attention to Brant's yells to break. He was hurt and worried. We wrestled around, and finally I got clear of his hugging arms. I caught him with a right upper-cut as we broke. Snarling, he fought back, and for a second or so we slung lefts and rights at each other. He was flustered now. I was timing them better, and they were sinking into him. A left prepared the way. His guard dropped, and I whipped over the right hook. It caught him flush on the jaw and down he went. I moved away, wiping the blood from my nose and breathing heavily. I wasn't worried. He wasn't going to get up in a hurry.

Brant climbed into the ring, beaming from ear to ear. Together we dragged Waller to his corner and propped him up on his stool. We were working on him when a voice said, "I like this boy. Where did you find him, Brant?"

Brant started as if someone had goosed him with a red-hot poker.

Three men had appeared from nowhere and were standing near the ring. The one who had spoken was short and square-shouldered. His face was as uncompromising as a hatchet and as thin, and his black eyes were deep-set, still and glittering. He had on a bottle-green linen suit, a white slouch hat, and his pencil-lined moustache looked starkly black against his olive skin.

The other two were the kind of muscle-men you can see in a Hollywood movie any day of the week. Two Wops, pale imitations of their boss, tough, dangerous, and more at home with a gun or a knife than with their fists.

I didn't like the look of any of them.

"Hello, Mr. Petelli," Brant said, his grin fixed and his eyes scared. "I didn't see you come in."

Petelli let his eyes slide over me. I had a feeling there wasn't a muscle, mole or freckle missed in that one searching glance.

"Where did you find him?"

"He's the guy who bust MacCready's jaw," Brant said, and nervously took out his handkerchief and mopped his face.

"I heard about that. Is it your idea to match this boy against the Kid?"

"I was coming to see you about it, Mr. Petelli. But first I wanted to find out how he shaped."

"The nigger seems to think he shapes all right," Petelli said with a thin smile.

"He's a little out of training . . ." Brant began, but Petelli cut him short.

"Come down to my office in an hour. We'll go into it." He looked at me. "What do you call yourself?"

"The name's Farrar," I said curtly, and ducked under the ropes.

"You look a good boy to me," Petelli said. "I can give you some fights. Have you signed with Brant?"

"I haven't signed with anyone," I said, "and I'm not signing with anyone. This is strictly my one and only appearance."

"You'd better come down with Brant, and we'll talk this over," Petelli said. "I can give you a fight a month."

"I'm not interested," I said, and walked across the gym to the changing booths in a sudden silence you could hang your hat on.

IV

I got back to Roche's Café in time to see Josh Bates driving his six-wheel truck along the water-front towards the Miami highway. I watched him go with mixed feelings. I had a sneaking idea I should have been on that truck.

Roche was polishing an urn when I walked in.

"So you changed your mind," he said. "Josh waited around for you. What happened?"

"Sorry, Tom. I got hung up." I told him of Brant's offer. "With a car and five hundred bucks I'll be set. It means hanging around for four days, but when I go I'll move on my own steam."

I went on to tell him about Petelli.

"You want to keep an eye on that baby," Roche said. "He's got a bad reputation."

"I can believe it, and I intend to keep out of his way. I've got to do a little training. There's not much time, but I figure I can get into some sort of shape before Saturday."

"You'll stay with us, Johnny. Don't argue. We'll be glad to have you."

I didn't argue. I was glad to be with them.

Later, Solly Brant came into the café. He slumped down at a corner table as if he had completed a ten-mile run.

I went over and joined him.

"Well, it's all fixed," he said heavily. "It took all my time to convince Petelli this was your last fight. I think you're making a mistake, Farrar. Petelli could make you a sack of dough."

"I'm not interested."

"That's what I told him, and I finally convinced him, but you've still time to change your mind."

"I'm not changing it."

Brant shifted uneasily.

"It'll make a difference."

"How's that?"

"Well, look, if this is going to be your last fight, you can't expect Petelli to take much interest in you, can you?"

"I don't want him to. The less I have to do with him the better I'll like it."

"But he's got his money on the Kid, so the Kid's got to win."

"Well, all right, if the Kid's all that good, he probably will win."

"He's got to win," Brant said huskily. "It's orders."

I stared at him.

"Are you trying to tell me you've arranged for me to take a dive?"

"That's it. Petelli's giving you a big build-up. The betting will switch, and he's spreading his dough on the Kid. My instructions are for you to take a dive in the third."

"I told you: I've never taken a dive, and I don't intend to take one now."

Brant mopped his face with a none-too-clean handkerchief.

"Look, Farrar, you're getting five hundred bucks and a car out of this. For the love of Mike don't make it difficult."

"If the Kid can't win by beating me, then it's his funeral. I'm not taking a dive!"

"You haven't any choice," Brant said, beginning to sweat. "When Petelli says a thing it sticks."

"Well, let's take that a step further. Suppose I don't take orders from him – what then?"

"You're up to your neck in trouble. I'm not kidding. Petelli's poison. There was a boy who lost him a lot of money a couple of years back, not doing what he was told. They laid for him and smashed his hands so he never fought again. They bashed his knuckles with a steel rod until they were pulp, and that's what'll happen to you if you don't do what he tells you."

"They'll have to catch me first."

"They'll catch you. The other boy thought he was smart. He ducked out of town, but they caught up with him. It took them six months to find him, but they found him. He was picked up with a cracked skull and broken mitts, and he's never been any good since."

"You don't scare me," I said, getting angry. "This is going to be a straight fight or I quit!"

"Use your head, Farrar," Brant pleaded. "If Petelli says you take a dive, then goddamn it, you'll take a dive. Ask anyone. Ask Roche. You just don't fool with Petelli. What he says goes."

"Not with me, it doesn't." I stood up. "This is my last fight, and I'm not getting mixed up in a dive. Tell Petelli that from me."

"You tell him," Brant said hurriedly. "It's your baby now."

"Oh, no, it isn't. You fixed this: you unfix it. I'm going over to the gym to loosen up."

He must have rushed around to Petelli the moment I had left

22

the café, for I was just getting warmed up in the gym under Waller's supervision when Petelli's two muscle-men came in.

Later I was to learn their names were Pepi and Benno. Pepi was a slick-looking Wop, wearing a pencil-lined moustache like his boss, while Benno was fat and blue-chinned and vicious.

They marched in like they owned the place, and Waller froze at the sight of them. All right, I admit it, there was something about those two that made my flesh creep.

"Come on," Pepi said, jerking his thumb at me, "get your clothes on. The boss wants you."

"I'm busy," I said. "He'll find me here if he wants me that badly."

I heard Waller catch his breath. He was looking at me as if he thought I was crazy.

"Don't give me that stuff," Pepi snarled, his pinched face vicious. "Get your clothes on and come!"

He was a head shorter than I was, and I didn't want to hit him, but hit he was going to be if he didn't change his tone.

"Get out of here!" I said. "Both of you, before I toss you out."

"Toss us out," Benno said, and a blue-nosed automatic jumped into his hand. "You heard us the first time. Get your clothes on or you'll stop a slug with your belly!"

His still glittering eyes warned me he wasn't bluffing.

Without moving his lips, Waller mumbled, "Don't be a fool, Farrar. Go with them. I know these two."

Pepi smiled.

"Wise guy. Sure he knows us. He knows Benno's been mixed up in three shooting accidents already this year. Better not make a fourth."

I got dressed while they stood around and watched me, then we went down the alley to where a big Cadillac was parked. Benno kept the gun in his hand. There was a cop standing on the edge of the kerb right by the car. He looked at Benno, looked at the gun, then hurriedly walked away. That told me faster than anything that had yet happened just what kind of a jam I was in. I got into the car and sat beside Pepi who drove. Benno sat at the back and breathed down my neck. It took less than a minute to reach the Ocean Hotel. We went in by a side entrance and rode up in a gilt-painted elevator. Neither Benno nor Pepi said anything, but Benno kept the gun pointing at me. We walked down a long corridor to a polished mahogany door marked *Private*. Pepi tapped, turned the handle and walked in.

The room was small, oak-panelled, and fitted up like an office.

A blonde sat pounding a typewriter, and chewing gum. She glanced up, gave me a swift, indifferent stare, seemed to think nothing of the gun in Benno's hand, and jerked her blonde head to the door behind her.

"Go on in," she said to Pepi. "He's waiting."

Pepi scratched on the door panel with his finger-nails, opened the door and glanced in. Then he stood aside.

"In on your own steam," he said to me, "and behave."

I walked past him into one of those vast rooms you rarely see outside a movie set. The enormous expanse of bottle-green carpet was thick enough to cut with a lawn-mower. A couple of dozen lounging chairs, two big chesterfields, a number of lamp standards and an odd table or two scarcely dented the space they were supposed to fill. Around the walls hung gilt-framed mirrors that caught my reflection as I moved forward, and reminded me how shabby I looked.

At a desk, big enough to play ping-pong on, sat Petelli. He was smoking a cigar, and the white slouch hat he had worn when he had come to the gym still rested at the back of his head. He waited, sitting forward, his elbows on the desk, until I was within a yard of him, then he stopped me by pointing his cigar at me.

"I'll do the talking; you do the listening," he said, his voice curt and cold. "You're a good fighter, Farrar, and I could have used you, but Brant tells me you want to stay out of the game. Right?"

"Yeah," I said.

"The Kid is a good boy, too, but I don't think he's got the punch you carry. Well, if I can't have you, I'll have to make do with him. This will be his first fight as far north as Pelotta. It wouldn't look good for him to get licked, so he's got to win. I've ten grand spread on the fight, and I don't intend to lose it. I told Brant you're to take a dive in the third round. Now I'm telling you. Brant says you don't like the idea. Well, that's your own private grief, not mine. You've had your chance to come in with me and you've passed it up." He paused to tap ash on the carpet. "This happens to be my town. I run it, see? What I say goes. I have an organization that takes care of guys who don't do what I tell them. We'll take care of you, too, if we have to. From now on you'll be watched. You're not to leave town. On Saturday night you'll fight the Kid and you'll put up a convincing show. In the third round the Kid'll catch you, and you'll go down and stay down. Those are my orders, and you'll obey them. If you don't you'll be wiped out. I mean that. I don't intend to lose ten grand because some bum fighter is too proud to take a dive. Double-cross me and it's the last double-cross you pull. And don't bother about police protection. The police do what I tell them. Now you know the set-up, you can please yourself what you do. I'm not arguing about it. I'm telling you. Take a dive in the third or a slug in the back. Now get out!"

He wasn't bluffing. I knew unless I obeyed orders he'd wipe me out with no more hesitation than he would have squashed a fly.

There wasn't anything I could think of to say. He had put the cards on the table. It was now up to me. Come to think of it, there wasn't anything to say. I turned and went out of the room, closing the door gently behind me.

The blonde still pounded the typewriter. Pepi and Benno had gone. Without pausing or looking up, she said, "Sweet type, isn't he? Can you wonder he hasn't any friends?"

Even to her I hadn't anything to say. I went on out, down the long corridor to the elevator. When I reached the street I spotted Benno across the way. He strolled after me as I made my way back to the gym.

V

For the next four days and nights Benno or Pepi followed me wherever I went, not letting me out of their sight for a moment. I played with the idea of slipping out of town and making my way to Miami as best I could, but I soon discovered there was no safe way of doing it. Those two stuck to me like an adhesive bandage.

I kept the set-up to myself. It was only when Tom Roche told me he was going to bet his shirt on me that I gave him a hint of what was in the wind.

"Don't do it, and don't ask questions," I said. "Don't bet either way."

He stared at me, saw I meant it, started to say something, but changed his mind. He was no fool, and must have guessed what was brewing, but he didn't press me.

I didn't tell Brant that I had seen Petelli, but he knew all right. He avoided me as much as he could, and when we did run into each other he seemed nervous, and didn't appear to like the way I was working to get into some kind of shape.

Waller didn't ask questions either, but he did everything he could to get me fit. By the evening of the third day I was picking my punches, and my breathing no longer bothered me. I could see both Waller and Brant were impressed by my speed and hitting power.

Petelli certainly made a swell job of the advance publicity. He had the local papers working on it, and a string of loud-mouthed guys going around the bars shouting my praise. This concentrated drive soon began to influence the betting, and by the morning of the fight I was a four to one on favourite. With ten thousand on the Kid, Petelli stood to pick up a bundle of money.

Neither he nor his muscle-men had anything further to say to me. Our little talk in his office seemed to them to be enough. Well, it was. I had to dive in the third round or it'd be curtains, and I had made up my mind to dive. An outfit like Petelli's was too big and tough to buck. If I obeyed orders I was set to make a good start in Miami, and that was what I really cared about. Anyway, that's the way I tried to kid myself, but below the surface I was seething with rage. I was thinking of the little mugs who were putting their shirts on me. I was thinking that after Saturday night I'd be just another crooked fighter, but what really bit deep was taking orders from a rat like Petelli.

On the morning of the fight, Brant and I went down to the gym for the weigh-in. There was a big crowd to welcome me, but I didn't get any kick out of the excited cheers as I pushed my way through the double swing-doors. I spotted Tom Roche and Sam Williams, and gave them a feeble grin as they waved to me.

Petelli stood near the scales, smoking a cigar. Pepi stood just behind him. Near by a fat, hard-faced man in a fawn suit propped up the wall and grinned at anyone who looked at him. He turned out to be the Miami Kid's manager.

I ducked the back-slappers and went into one of the changing booths. By the time I had stripped off the Kid was on show. I looked curiously at him. He was big and powerful, but I was quick to spot he was a little thick around the middle. As I joined him he looked me over with a sneering little grin.

I was four pounds heavier than he, and had the advantage of three inches in reach.

"So what?" he said in a loud voice to his manager. "The bigger they come the harder they bounce."

The crowd seemed to think that was the most original and witty thing they had ever heard, to judge by the laugh it got.

As I stepped off the scales, the Kid, still with his sneering grin, reached out and grabbed my arm.

"Hey! I thought you said this guy was a puncher," he cried. "Call these muscles, chummy?"

"Take your hands off me!" I said, and the look I gave him made him take two big, quick steps back. "You'll know whether I've got muscles or not by tonight."

There was a sudden silence, then as I walked away, a babble of voices broke out.

Brant came running after me, and as I went into the changing booth, he said excitedly, "Don't let him rattle you. He's a great kidder."

I didn't have to be a mind reader to know what he meant. He was scared the Kid had opened his mouth too wide and I'd sock him for it when we got into the ring. He wasn't far from the truth, either.

"Is he?" I said. "Well, so am I."

The first instalment of Brant's pay-off arrived in the afternoon. He brought it himself.

"Thought you'd better look smart, Farrar," he said, looking anywhere but at me. He took off the lid of a box and showed me a white linen suit, a cream silk shirt, a green and white tie, and white buckskin shoes. "You'll knock them dead in this outfit," he went on, trying to be at ease. "Better see if it fits."

"Shove them back in the box and get out," I said.

I was lying on the bed in the little room Roche had lent me. The curtains were half drawn, and the light was dim. I had seven hours before I entered the ring: seven hours that stretched ahead of me like a prison sentence without parole.

"What's the matter with you?" Brant demanded, flushing. "Isn't this what you want?" and he shook the suit at me.

"Get out before I throw you out!"

When he had gone I closed my eyes and tried to sleep, but I kept thinking of Petelli. I thought, too, of all the little mugs who were betting on me. I tried to convince myself there was nothing I could do about it, but I knew I had walked into this with my eyes open. I had kicked around in the fight racket long enough to know just how crooked it was. That was why I had quit, and yet the first offer that came along had tempted me back. If I hadn't had big ideas about getting to Miami in a car with money in my pocket this wouldn't have happened.

Suppose I double-crossed Petelli? What chance had I of avoiding a bullet? Petelli wasn't bluffing. He couldn't afford to let me double-cross him and get away with it. If he did, his grip on the other fighters would be weakened, and, besides, he wasn't the type to allow himself to be gypped out of forty thousand dollars without settling the score.

I was hooked, and I knew it, and I cursed myself. I lay on the bed in the half light and sweated it out, and the hands of the clock crawled on and on. I couldn't make up my mind what I was going to do. I was still at it when Roche put his head around my door.

"Seven-thirty, Johnny; time to be up and doing. Are you okay?"

I got off the bed.

"I guess so. Will I get a taxi?"

"I'll drive you there myself. I'm just going to have a wash. I'll be ready in five minutes."

"Fine."

I splashed water on my face, combed my hair and then put on the clothes Brant had brought. They fitted me all right, but I didn't get a kick out of them. If my own clothes hadn't been so shabby I wouldn't have worn this outfit.

A tap came on the door, and Alice looked in.

"Why, Johnny, how smart you look."

"I guess that's right."

I wondered what she would have said if she knew the price I was paying for this rig-out.

"Tom's getting the car. Good luck, Johnny."

"Thanks. I'm glad you won't be there."

"Tom wanted me to go, but I don't like fights. I'll have my fingers crossed for you."

"You do that. Well, so long. Thanks for all you've done."

"But you'll be coming back, won't you?"

Would I? I wished I knew.

"Why, sure, but thanks all the same."

"Put this in your pocket. It's brought me luck, and I want it to bring you luck, too."

I looked at the silver medallion she placed in my hand. It showed the head of some saint, and I looked at her, surprised.

"Thanks, Alice, but maybe I'd better not have it. I might lose it."

"Put it in your pocket and forget about it. It'll bring you luck."

And that's what I did. I put it in my pocket and forgot about it.

As I ran down the steps to the street, Petelli's big Cadillac pulled up. Benno was at the wheel, and Brant was sitting at the back.

"Thought we'd pick you up," Brant said, leaning out of the window. "Feeling okay?"

"Yeah. I'm driving up in Roche's car."

"You're driving up in this one," Pepi snarled, coming up behind me. "We're not losing sight of you until the fight's over."

Roche hadn't appeared. There was no point in making trouble.

"Tell Tom I've gone with the boys," I called to Alice, who was watching from the café door.

I got in beside Brant. We drove rapidly through the deserted streets. Practically the whole of Pelotta's population had turned out for the fight. As we neared the blazing lights of the stadium, Pepi said without looking round, "The third, Farrar, or it's curtains."

"Save your breath," I said. "I heard it the first time."

We drove up the broad concrete drive-in. It was already packed with cars, but Benno weaved his way through without reducing speed.

Brant said in an undertone, "As soon as it's over I'll have the dough for you in cash. The car's parked at the back. It's full of petrol and rearing to go. Okay?"

I grunted.

Benno swung the Cadillac into the vast parking-lot, and we all got out. We walked quickly across the tarmac to a side door. As Pepi pushed it open, a blast of hot, sweat-stinking air came out to meet us.

"It's packed solid in there," Brant said. "Not a seat to be had."

We climbed a flight of concrete steps, meeting people as they moved to their seats. Some of the guys recognized me and slapped me on the back, wishing me luck. At a gangway I paused to look into the arena. One of the preliminary fights was on. The ring, under the dazzling white lights, looked a mile away, and the roar of the crowd seemed to shake the whole building.

"Some house," Brant said. "Better get changed, Farrar."

There was the usual mob of pressmen and hangers-on waiting outside my dressing-room, but Brant wouldn't let them in. He got the door shut with difficulty, leaving Pepi outside to talk to them.

Waller was waiting to take charge of me.

"Don't wait," I said to Brant. "Henry can do it all."

"Now, look . . ." Brant began, but I cut him short.

"I don't want you around, and I don't want you in my corner. Henry can do all that's necessary."

Brant shrugged his fat shoulders. His face turned crimson.

"Well, okay, if that's the way you feel. But there's no need to get sore at me. I can't help it."

"Maybe you can't, but you got me into this, and I don't want you in my corner."

As he turned to the door, he said, "Don't pull anything smart, Farrar. You're in this now up to your ears, and there's no out for you."

"Dust!"

When he had gone I began to strip off. Waller stood around, a worried expression on his ebony face.

"You relax, Mr. Farrar," he said. "This ain't no way to go into the ring."

"Okay, okay, don't bother me, Henry," I said, and stretched out on the rubbing-table. "Lock the door. I don't want anyone in here."

He locked the door, then came over and began to work on me.

"Are you going to win this fight?" he asked presently.

"How do I know? Your guess is as good as mine."

"I don't think so." He went on kneading my muscles for a while, then he said, "Mr. Petelli's been around too long. I reckon he's done a lot of harm to the game in this town. Is this another fixed fight?"

"You know it is. I should have thought the whole damned town knows it by now. What else can you expect when Petelli lays ten grand on the Kid? I've been told to go in the third."

Waller grunted. We didn't look at each other.

"You shouldn't get sore with Mr. Brant," he said. "He's a good guy. What can he do against Mr. Petelli? If Mr. Petelli says for you to dive in the third, what can Mr. Brant say? If he says no, those two gunmen will fix him. Mr. Brant's got a wife and kids to think of."

"Lay off, Henry. Maybe Brant can't help it, but I'd just as soon not have him around. You can take care of me, can't you?"

"If you're going in the third, you don't need taking care of," Waller said sadly.

There was some truth in that.

"Suppose I don't take a dive?" I said. "Suppose I fight the Kid and lick him? What chance have I got of getting out of here alive?"

Waller looked uneasily around the room as if he feared someone might be listening.

"That's crazy talk," he said, his eyes rolling. "Get that idea out of your head."

"No harm in wondering. Where's that window lead to?"

"You relax. There's no sense talking this way."

I slid off the table, crossed the room and looked out of the window. A good thirty feet below me was the car-park. I leaned out. A narrow ledge ran below the window to a stack pipe, leading to the ground. It wouldn't be difficult to get down to the car-park, but that didn't mean I could get away.

Waller pulled me from the window.

"Get back on the table. This ain't the way to act just before a fight."

I got on to the table again.

"Think those Wops would shoot me, Henry, or is it bluff?"

"I know they would. They shot Boy O'Brien for pulling a double-cross a couple of years back. They bust Bennie Mason's hands when he got himself knocked out after Mr. Petelli had bet he'd go the distance. They threw acid in Tiger Freeman's face for winning in the seventh. Sure, they'd shoot you if that's what Mr. Petelli wants them to do."

I was still churning it over in my mind when Brant yelled through the door it was time to get down to the ring.

Henry helped me into the scarlet and blue dressing-gown Petelli had sent over for me to wear. It was a gaudy affair, with *Johnny Farrar* stitched in big white letters across the shoulders. At one time I would have been proud and happy to have worn it, but right now it made me feel bad.

As I reached the top of the ramp leading into the arena, they played the Kid in with a fanfare of trumpets. The crowd was giving him a big hand, and when he vaulted over the ropes into the ring, they howled their appreciation.

Brant joined me. He was sweating and worried.

"Okay, let's go," he said. "You first; the rest of us behind you."

The rest of us consisted of Brant, Waller, Pepi and Benno. I walked down the ramp towards the ring. It was a long walk, and the crowd stood up and yelled all the way. I wondered bleakly what kind of noise they'd be making on my return trip.

I reached the ring, ducked under the ropes and went to my corner. The Kid, in a yellow dressing-gown, was clowning in his corner, making out he was bow-legged, and then pretending to throw punches at his handlers. The crowd enjoyed it more than his handlers did.

I sat down, and Henry began putting on the tapes. The Kid's fat manager stood over me, watching, and breathing whisky and

31

cigar fumes in my face. It was because of his vile breath that I turned my head and looked at the crowd just below me, and it was then that I saw her.

VI

The announcer, a bald-headed little runt in a white suit a little too big for him, was bawling into a hand mike, but I didn't hear what he was saying. Even when he introduced me Waller had to prod me before I stood up to acknowledge the yells of the crowd.

I couldn't keep my eyes off the woman who was sitting just below my corner: near enough, if we both stretched out our arms, for us to touch fingers. Even as I waved to the crowd, I continued to stare at her, and she was worth staring at.

I've seen a good many beautiful women in my time, on the movies and off, but never one like this. Her hair was jet black and glossy, parted in the centre, a thin white line as exact as if it had been drawn with a sharp-edged tool and a ruler in marble. Her eyes were big and black and glittering. Her skin was like alabaster, and her mouth wide and scarlet. She was lean and lovely and hungry-looking.

Unlike the other women sitting at the ringside, she wasn't wearing an evening gown. She had on an apple-green linen suit, a white silk blouse and no hat. Her shoulders were broad, and to judge from her long, slim legs, she would be above the average height when she stood up. Under that smart, cool and provocative outfit was a shape that drove the fight, Petelli and the rest of the set-up clean out of my mind.

She was looking up at me, her eyes wide and excited, and we exchanged glances. The look she gave me turned my mouth dry and sent my pulse racing. Even a Trappist monk would have known what that look was saying, and I wasn't a Trappist monk.

"What's the matter with you?" Waller mumbled as he laced my gloves. "You look like someone's already socked you."

"Could have," I said, and smiled at her, and she smiled back: an intimate, we-could-have-fun-together kind of smile that hit me where I lived.

I turned to see who she was with: an expensive-looking item in a fawn seersucker suit. He was handsome enough with his dark, wavy hair, his olive complexion and his regular features, but his good looks were marred by his thin, hard mouth and the viciously angry expression in his eyes as he returned my curious stare.

"Get out there," Waller said, and shoved me to my feet. "The ref's waiting. What's the matter with you?"

And the referee was waiting, and the Kid was waiting too. I joined them in the middle of the ring.

"It's all right, chummy," the Kid sneered. "You don't have to hug your corner that long. I ain't going to hit you just yet."

"All right, boys," the referee said sharply, "let's cut out the funny stuff and get down to business. Now, listen to me . . ."

He started on the old routine I had heard so often before. While he was talking, I asked myself why she had looked at me like that. I don't claim to know much about women, but I knew that smile was an open invitation.

"Okay, boys," the referee said when he was through with the routine stuff, "back to your corners, and come out fighting."

"And, chummy, you'll know you've been in a fight when you leave feet first," the Kid said, slapping me on the back.

And so would he, I thought, as I returned to my corner.

Waller took off my dressing-gown and I turned to get a last look at her.

She leaned forward, her eyes sparkling.

"Knock that smug smile off his face, handsome," she called. "It's time someone did."

Her escort put his hand on her arm, scowling, but she shook it off impatiently.

"And good luck . . ."

"Thanks," I said.

Outraged, Waller got between her and me.

"Keep your mind on this fight," he said as the bell went.

The Kid came out fast, his chin tucked down into his left shoulder, a cocky grin on his face. He led with a left that was a foot short, weaved away and tossed over a right. That was short too. I moved around him looking for an opening. I wanted to land one hard jolt that would slow him down. I could see he was a lot faster on his feet than I was.

He caught me with a left to the face: not a hard punch. I countered with a left and right to the body. His left jumped into my face again, and he tried a right cross, but I ducked under it and socked him in the body. He got in close and began hammering away at my ribs, but I tied him up, and the referee had to pull us apart. I got in a good left jab to his face as we broke, and he didn't like it. He moved away fast, snorting, then came in again, throwing rights and lefts. I smothered everything he handed out, stepped in and nailed him with a block-buster that sent him down on his hands and knees.

The crowd went mad. A knock-down in the first two minutes

of the fight was something they hadn't expected, and they rose to their feet, screaming for me to go in and smash the Kid.

I had gone to a neutral corner while the referee began his count. I was a little worried. I hadn't meant to hit him that hard. He remained on hands and knees, looking up at the referee's arm, a glazed stare in his eyes. But he got up at the count of seven and immediately started back-pedalling. I went after him, hitting him with rights and lefts, but pulling my punches, not wanting to get him into more trouble, but putting up a show to please the crowd. They were pleased all right. Every now and then I landed with an open glove, and the slap it made sounded as if I were killing him.

He finally got his head clear and began to fight back. He was snarling and scared. I could tell how scared he was by the way he threw punches that were yards short. All he was thinking about now was to keep clear of my right. He had had one dose of it and he didn't want another.

The round ended with us leaning on each other and slamming at each other's ribs. At close quarters he was good, and he got in a couple of digs that hurt.

The bell went and I returned to my corner. While Waller was working over me, I looked in her direction.

She was staring up at me, not smiling, her eyes angry, her mouth set. I knew what was the matter with her. She hadn't been fooled by those open-glove slaps even if they had fooled the crowd. Waller shoved a sponge of cold water in my face. He was smart enough to see who was distracting my attention, and he moved around so his body blocked her from my sight.

Brant came up as Waller was drying my face.

"What are you playing at?" he demanded in a breathless whisper. His face was white and strained. "Why did you hit him like that?"

"Why not? He's in here for a fight, isn't he?"

"Petelli says . . ."

"Oh, the hell with Petelli!"

The bell went for the second round, and I moved out of my corner. The Kid came out cautiously, an apprehensive expression on his face. He kept pushing his left out, trying to keep me away, but I had the longer reach. I poked one in his face, stepped in and hooked him high up on the head. He fought back, catching me with a right and left that had a lot of steam in them, and for a few seconds we mixed it, socking each other about the body while the crowd roared its approval. The Kid was the first to break off.

I caught him with a hook as he moved away and opened a cut under his right eye. He was swearing at me now, and I went after him, jabbing at his face with lefts and rights. He kept covering up, trying to protect his damaged eye. I got in close and socked him in the body. It must have dawned on him he wasn't going to get an easy win, and in a frenzy of rage and desperation he suddenly cut loose.

He caught me with a right swing that had all his weight behind it. It was a stunning punch, and it dazed me. As I groped my way into a clinch, trying to get my head clear, he butted me in the face. I reeled back, covering up, and as he rushed, I slammed a left in his face, but he knew he had hurt me, and kept coming, throwing punches from every angle. I rode most of them, smothered the rest. It was a hectic minute, but I kept my head, knowing he was certain to give me an opening, and he did. He slung a wild right that left him as wide open as the ocean, and I stepped in and hung one on his jaw. He went down as if he had been cut off at the knees.

Before the referee could start a count, the bell went. The Kid's handlers rushed into the ring and dragged him to his corner.

I went slowly back to my stool and sat down. Pepi was waiting for me.

"Next round, you fixer," he snarled in my ear. "That's orders."

"Get away from me!" I said, and greatly daring, Waller shoved him off the apron of the ring and began to sponge my face. Waller was breathing heavily and grinned excitedly at me as he worked over me.

"You're doing fine," he said. "Watch his right. He can still punch."

I looked across the ring. They were working like madmen on the Kid, flapping towels at him, holding smelling-salts under his nose and massaging the back of his neck.

"Well, I guess this is it," I said. "Last round coming up."

"Yeah," Waller said. "Anyway, he's been in a fight. You ain't cheated anyone."

I looked over my shoulder at her. She was smiling again, and waved to me.

The bell went, and I moved out. The Kid started to back-pedal. He had a gash down the side of his nose, a cut under his right eye, and there were great red patches on his ribs where I had socked him.

I trapped him in a corner and nailed him bang on his damaged

35

nose. Blood spurted from his face as if I'd slammed a rotten tomato against a wall. The crowd screamed itself hoarse as he wilted and fell into a clinch. I had to hold him up or he would have gone down. I wrestled him around, trying to make it look good until he got a grip on himself.

"Okay, play-boy," I said in his ear. "Throw your best punch."

I broke and stepped back. He shoved out a left that wouldn't have dented a rice pudding. I ducked under it and came in, wide open. Somehow he managed to screw up enough strength to let go with an upper-cut. I went down on one knee. I wasn't hurt, but if I were going to take a dive I had to prepare the way for it.

I bet the yell that went up from the crowd could have been heard as far south as Miami.

The referee stood over me and began his count. I looked over at the Kid. The relief on his face was comic. He leaned against the ropes, blood dripping from his cuts, his knees buckling.

I shook my head as if I were dazed, and at six I got up. The Kid's face was a study. He had been sure I was going to stay down. Instead of coming in, he began to back away, and that got a jeering laugh from the crowd. His seconds yelled for him to go in and finish me, and with pitiful reluctance he changed direction and came at me. I made out I was wobbly, but I slipped the left he threw at me and landed another jab on his gashed face. At least he was going to earn his victory. Gasping with pain and fury, he lashed out as I dropped my guard. He caught me on the side of the jaw. Down I went.

I had walked right into it, intending to catch it, and I caught it.

For the first three seconds I was out, then I opened my eyes and found myself flat on my face, looking right down at her. She was standing up, her eyes like twin explosions, and as our eyes met, she screamed furiously, "Get up and fight! Get up, you quitter!"

She was so close she could have touched me. Half the ringside customers were on their feet, yelling at me, but I had ears only for her voice.

"Get up, Johnny!" she screamed at me. "You can't quit now!"

The anger, contempt and disappointment on her face electrified me. It was all I needed. It flashed through my mind I had never intended to obey Petelli's orders anyway, and that scornful, screaming voice and the black, furious eyes clinched it.

I heard the referee call ". . . seven . . . eight . . ."

I got up somehow, beating his down-sweeping arm by a split second, and as the Kid rushed in, I grabbed his arms and hung on like grim death. I knew by the desperate way he struggled to get free he realized I was going to double-cross Petelli, and he was going to lose the fight unless he could nail me before I had shaken off the effects of his punch.

I hung on in spite of all he did, and in spite of the referee trying to tear us apart. I only needed four or five seconds to get my head clear, and when I did decide it was safe to break, I stabbed my left into the Kid's cut-up face before he could get set to throw a finishing punch.

Panting and wild he came at me, but I weaved away, back-pedalled, and left him floundering. He was as wild as a rogue elephant now, and kept rushing at me while I dodged and retreated until I was good and ready to take him. Then as he came in for the fourth time I stopped in my tracks and brought over the right hook. It smashed against his jaw and down he went in a flurry of blood, rolled over and stiffened out.

It was a waste of time to count him out, but the referee went through the motions. When he reached ten, the Kid was still lying on his back as motionless as a corpse.

White and scared looking, the referee moved over to me and lifted my glove as if it was loaded with dynamite.

"Farrar's the winner!"

I looked at her. She was standing up, flushed and excited, and she blew me a kiss. Then the ring became crammed with press-men and photographers, and I lost sight of her.

Petelli appeared out of the crowd. He was smiling, but his eyes were hot and intent.

"Okay, Farrar," he said. "Well, you know what to expect."

He moved away to speak to the Kid's manager, and Waller, his face grey and his eyes rolling, came over to me and dropped my dressing-gown across my shoulders.

As I climbed out of the ring I caught sight of Pepi, a tight little grin on his face, waiting at the top of the ramp.

VII

I felt safe enough so long as the dressing-room was crowded with pressmen and fans who had come to shake hands with me and to tell me what a fine fighter I was, but when they began to drift away I knew trouble was creeping up on me.

Waller had returned to the dressing-room with me. He was scared all right, and as soon as he had finished rubbing me down, he began to cast nervous and longing glances at the door. Tom

Roche had been in, but I got rid of him quickly. I didn't want him mixed up in any trouble.

There were now only a couple of pressmen and three fans left, and they were arguing in a corner about who had the heaviest punch among the old heavyweights, and they weren't paying any attention to me.

"Okay, Henry," I said, as I fixed my tie. "Don't wait. Thanks for all you've done."

"There ain't anything I can do for you," Waller said. "You'd better get out fast. Don't let them catch you alone." He wiped his shiny face with the back of his hand. "You shouldn't have done it."

"Shouldn't have done – what?"

A creepy sensation ran up my spine as I turned. There she was in her apple-green linen suit, her big black eyes looking into mine, a cigarette between her white-gloved fingers. "What shouldn't you have done, Johnny?"

Waller edged away and slid out of the room, leaving me staring at her like a paralysed deaf mute. The little group in the corner stopped talking and eyed her hungrily.

One of the pressmen said, "Let's go, boys: this is the one time a fighter really likes to lose his friends."

They all laughed as if he had cracked the best joke in the world, but they went. The little room seemed suddenly vast and empty as the last of them drifted through the doorway.

"Hello," I said, and reached for my coat. "Did you win any money?"

She smiled. Her teeth were small and even and sharply white against her scarlet lips.

"A thousand, but you gave me a heart attack when you went down. I had to lay out four and I thought I was going to lose it."

"Sorry about that," I said. "I wasn't concentrating. There was a girl at the ringside who took my mind right off my business."

"Oh!" She looked at me from under her eyelashes. "How did she do that?"

"She happened to be the most beautiful woman I have ever seen."

"You should tell her that. Girls like being told things like that."

"I am telling her."

"I see." She continued to smile, but her eyes hardened. "That's very flattering, but I don't believe it. It looked like a dive to me."

My face reddened.

"What do you know about dives?"

"All the signs were on the wall. The funny little men whispering in your ear, the way you left yourself open. I go to all the fights. It happens every now and then. What made you change your mind?"

"The girl," I said, "and the thought of all the little mugs who were betting on me."

"This girl seems to have had quite an influence on you," she said, studying me, then she went on, "I think you're handsome, Johnny."

I leaned against the wall, aware I was wasting precious time. I shouldn't be talking to this girl. I should be getting out of here before the crowd left. That was my only chance of giving Pepi and Benno the slip. But not even Petelli himself could have got me out of this room at this moment.

"Who are you?" I asked. "Why did you come up here?"

Her face was serious now, but there was still that look in her eyes that kept sending tingles up my spine.

"Never mind who I am. Call me Della if you must call me something," she said. "I'm here because you're in trouble, and I guess it's partly my fault. You are in trouble, aren't you?"

"Yeah, but it's nothing you can do anything about."

"How bad is the trouble?"

"Two Wops are laying for me. If they catch up with me, it's probably curtains."

"You double-crossed Petelli?"

That startled me.

"You know him?"

"That little thug! I know of him, but I wouldn't know him if he were the last man on earth. We're wasting time. I'll get you out of here." She went to the window and looked out. "You can reach the car-park by climbing down that pipe."

I joined her at the window. There weren't many cars left in the park by now.

"There's my car: the first one on the right in the second row. If you can reach it without being seen, you'll be safe."

"Wait a minute," I said, looking at the low-slung Bentley coupé she was pointing at. "I can't drag you into this. These Wops are dangerous."

"Don't be a fool. They won't know a thing about it."

"Let's be sensible about this . . ."

"Oh, don't argue! I'm going down to the car now. Lock the

door after me. As soon as you see me down there, come on after me. I'll drive over to you. Get in the front seat and leave the rest to me."

Glancing at the Bentley again, I spotted the expensive-looking item in the seersucker suit. He was standing by the car, looking to right and left.

"Your friend won't like this," I said. "He's waiting for you now."

She laughed, a hard, humourless little sound that made me stare at her.

"He's not a friend: he's my husband," she said, and moved quickly to the door. "I won't be five minutes. Don't let anyone in." She was gone before I could stop her.

I crossed the room and shot the bolt. Now I was alone the room seemed horribly empty. I returned to the window. Her husband was pacing up and down beside the car. As I watched him he took out a cigarette-case and lit a cigarette. By the way he threw the match on the ground I could see he was exasperated.

A faint sound behind me made me turn quickly, my eyes going to the door. I saw the door handle begin to turn. Someone the other side of the door pushed gently against the panels. The bolt held, and the handle slowly reversed.

Well, they were out there now. I guessed they thought it was safe to call on me now the stadium was nearly cleared. Over the loud-speaker system dance music was blaring: loud enough to drown the sound of a shot.

I tiptoed across the room and examined the bolt. It wasn't too strong. I heard someone whispering outside. I couldn't hear what was said, but the sound made the hair on the nape of my neck bristle.

I caught hold of the rubbing-table and pulled it across to the door and wedged one end under the handle. I was thinking fast now: a little scared, but not in a panic. They knew the lay-out of the stadium a lot better than I did. They'd know the climb down from my window wasn't difficult, and as soon as they found they couldn't break in they'd guess it would be by the window I'd try to escape, and Pepi would be there to pick me off.

It wouldn't take him three or four minutes to get down the concrete steps, around to the side door and out to the parking-lot. He was probably on his way now. I had to get going at once.

As I swung my legs over the window-sill someone drove his shoulder against the door. The table held the door solid. I didn't look back, but climbed out of the window on to the ledge.

In my hurry to get to the drain-pipe I took a false step and my foot shot off into space. I managed to dig my fingers into the chinks of the uneven concrete wall, and hold myself steady. It was a pretty nasty moment. If I hadn't had strong fingers I would have fallen. Somehow I managed to regain my balance. I slowly drew up my foot and found the ledge again. With my heart hammering I kept on, reached the drain-pipe and began to climb down. Ten feet from the ground I let go and dropped.

I heard a car start up. I heard, too, the sound of running feet. For a moment I was tempted to bolt towards the car, but decided it would be safer to remain in the shadow of the wall rather than go out into the brightly lit car-park.

The Bentley swung towards me. She hadn't turned on the car lights. Beyond, and away to the left, I spotted Pepi. He was about a hundred yards from me, standing still, looking towards the window of the dressing-room as if waiting for me to appear, and I realized he didn't know I was already down. Then I heard a loud crash and knew the door of the dressing-room had been forced open.

The Bentley slowed down as it reached me, and the door swung open.

"Get in – quick!" Della cried, keeping the car on the move.

I scrambled in beside her and she shot the car forward. I managed to get the door shut as the car raced down the broad drive-in.

As she leaned forward to snap on the lights, she said, "Did they spot you?"

"I'm not sure."

I swung around in my seat to look through the rear window. The dark, curly haired man who she said was her husband was sitting at the back. It was too dark to see his face. I couldn't see any following car's headlights.

"Doesn't look like it," I said. "Anyway, they're not coming after us."

"You must be crazy to get us mixed up in this, Della!" the man at the back exploded. "Stop the car and let this fella out!"

She laughed.

"Oh, shut up, Paul. They were going to shoot him. I couldn't let them do that after he'd won me a grand."

"You little fool! You're always getting into trouble."

Again she laughed.

"I'm loving every minute of this."

He gave a grunt of disgust and slumped down in his seat.

"Well, let's get out of here. As soon as we're away from the stadium, stop and let him out."

"Don't take any notice of him," she said to me. "We're going to Lincoln Beach. Want to come?"

"Yes," I said.

We were approaching the main gates of the stadium now, and it suddenly occurred to me that Petelli might have got word down there to stop us. I told Della.

"Squat on the floor. You may be right."

There were a number of cars ahead of us now, moving slowly through the big gates, and she had to slow to a crawl.

"There're two guards looking into each car as it passes," she whispered to me. "I'm going to stop and let the other cars get on ahead."

"There's a car behind us and coming fast," Paul said, a rasp in his voice.

"You'd better let me out," I said, but she put her hand on my shoulder and pushed me lower.

"Be quiet!"

She swung around to look through the rear window. From where I crouched I had a good view of one long, shapely leg and a small foot in a white buckskin shoe. I could also see the glare of headlights coming through the rear window showing how close the other car was. A horn blared as she slowed down.

"Better not stop," Paul said. "Keep in the centre of the road so they can't pass, but keep moving."

The car continued to crawl forward.

"It's clearing ahead," she told me. "We're coming up to the gates."

I looked up. The car was moving a little faster now. Through the window I caught a glimpse of a man in a peak cap looking right at me.

"Hey! You! Just a minute . . ." he said excitedly, and wrenched open the door.

I grabbed the inside handle, slammed the door shut as Della trod down on the accelerator. The Bentley surged forward as the guard yelled again. I was sitting up now. Ahead of us was a car, blocking the way out. She swung the wheel and we bumped up on to the grass verge, missing the other car's fenders by inches, then we shot out on to the highway.

"Now . . ." she said, and increased speed.

"They're right on our tail," Paul cried furiously. "Goddamn it! I told you not to fool with this!"

Her reply was to push the accelerator to the boards. The needle of the speedometer began to flicker up to ninety. It hesitated, then crept up to ninety-two . . . three and hovered at ninety-four.

The glare of the following headlights receded.

"Losing them now," she cried, her eyes fixed on the pool of light that rushed before us from the Bentley's headlamps. "They can't catch us now."

"Watch the road or you'll have us over!" Paul shouted, and sat forward to look over her shoulder through the windshield. "The road curves ahead. You'll have to slow down before long."

"Don't pester me!" she snapped. "I know this road as well as you do!"

I looked behind. The pursuing car wasn't all that far in the rear: not more than two hundred yards, and as Della was forced to reduce speed as the road began to curve around the palmetto thickets that lay on either side, the big Cadillac began to creep up on us.

Della held the car in the middle of the road. The speedometer showed seventy-six now: too fast on a road like this.

"Watch out! Car ahead!" I exclaimed as I spotted the distant glare of approaching headlights.

Della dipped her lights and her foot eased off the accelerator.

The approaching car was coming like a bat out of hell. It flashed into view. I heard a high, squealing sound of tyres biting into tarmac behind us, and looking round saw the Cadillac was stopping. I felt the Bentley swerve to the right. I swung round. The car coming towards us sat right in the middle of the road, and its huge blinding lights hit us as it roared down on us.

Della pulled more to the right. The offside wheels banged and bumped along the grass verge. I saw her struggling frantically with the wheel, trying to keep the car straight.

The driver of the approaching car just didn't seem to see us. I heard Paul yell.

The car was on us now. It side-swiped us as it went past. Della screamed. There came a crunching, ripping noise. The car that had hit us slewed across the road, then crashed into the thickets. I grabbed hold of the dashboard as I felt the Bentley lift. The windshield suddenly turned into a spider's web of cracks and lines. There was a grinding noise of splintering wood, then a hell of a jolt, and a scorching white light burst before my eyes. Above the grinding, tearing sounds, I heard Della scream again, then the white light snuffed out and darkness came down on me.

PART TWO

FOG PATCH

I

THE smell of iodoform and ether told me I was in hospital. I made an effort and rolled back eyelids that weighed a ton. A tall, thin guy in a white coat was standing over me. Behind him I could see a fat nurse. There was a bored, harassed expression on her face.

"How do you feel?" the thin guy asked, leaning over me. "Do you feel better?"

He seemed so anxious I hadn't the heart to tell him I felt like hell. I screwed up a grin and closed my eyes.

Lights flickered behind my eyelids. I felt myself swimming off into misty darkness. I let myself go. Why bother? I thought, you can only die once.

The darkness crept down on me. Time stood still. I slipped off the edge of the world into mists, fog and silence.

It seemed to me I was down in the darkness for a very long time, but after a while lights began to flicker again and I became aware of the bed in which I was lying and the tightness of the sheets. A little later I became aware of the screens. There were tall white screens around the bed, and they worried me. I seemed to remember they only put screens around a bed when the patient was going to croak.

I also became aware that a thick-set man was sitting beside me. His hat rested on the back of his head, and he chewed a toothpick, a bored, tired expression on his fleshy, unshaven face. He had copper written all over him.

After a while he noticed my eyes were open, and he shifted forward to peer at me.

"I wouldn't win a dime with a double-headed coin," he said in disgust. "Talk about luck! So you have to come to the surface just when I'm signing off."

A nurse appeared from behind the screen. She also peered at me: not the fat nurse. This one was blonde and pretty.

"Hello," I said, and my voice sounded miles away.

44

"You mustn't talk," she said severely. "Just lie still and try to sleep."

"Sleep – hell!" the copper said. "He's gotta talk. Keep out of this, nurse. He wants to talk, don't you, pal?"

"Hello, copper," I said, and closed my eyes.

When I opened them again the thin guy in white was standing over me.

"How am I doing, doc?" I asked.

"You're doing fine," he told me. "You're a miracle."

I blinked him into focus. He was young and eager and interested. I liked him.

"Where am I?" I asked, and tried to lift my head, but it was too heavy.

"You've had an accident. Just take it easy. You're coming along fine."

The copper appeared from behind him.

"Can I talk to him?" he asked, an exasperated note in his voice. "Just one or two questions. That can't hurt him."

"Make it short," the doctor said. "He has a bad concussion."

He stood aside and the copper took his place. He had a notebook in his hand and an inch of blunt pencil in his thick fingers.

"What's your name, pal?" he asked. "Don't bear down on it. We just want to get things straightened out."

"John Farrar," I told him.

"Address?"

"I haven't one."

"You gotta sleep somewhere, haven't you?"

"I was hitch-hiking."

He blew out his fat cheeks and looked up at the ceiling as if he were praying.

"Well, okay, you were hitch-hiking. Got a father or a mother or a wife or someone?"

"No."

He turned and looked at the doctor.

"Now do you believe I never have any luck? Of all the guys who get snarled up in a car smash I have to pick me an orphan."

"You'd better cut this short," the doctor said, his fingers on my pulse. "He's not fit to talk yet."

"Wait a minute; wait a minute," the copper said, licking his pencil. "I've got to get this straightened out." He turned to me again. "Okay, pal. So there's no one to claim you. Well, how about the dame you was with? Who was she?"

A picture of her floated into my mind with her jet-black hair, her hungry look and the shape she had on her.

"I don't know. 'Call me Della if you must call me something.' That's what she said. She didn't tell me her other name."

The copper groaned.

"How is she?" I went on. "Is she badly hurt?"

"She's all right," the doctor said. "Don't worry about her."

"And her husband?" I asked.

"What husband?" the copper said, staring at me.

"The guy who was sitting at the back of the car. She said his name was Paul. Is he all right?"

"You don't have to worry about him, either," the doctor said.

The copper passed his hand over his face and shook his head. He seemed to be the one who was worrying.

"How did it happen? Maybe you can tell me that," he said, but there was no hope in his voice.

I couldn't be bothered to explain about Petelli. That would have taken too long. I wanted to close my eyes and forget about the car smash.

"Another car was coming towards us," I said. "He was coming fast. He didn't seem to see us. She tried to get out of his way, but he caught us. What happened to him?"

The copper drew in a deep breath.

"I'll say it this time," he said, with heavy sarcasm. "You don't have to worry about him. Now look, pal, let's get all this down on the mat and work at it. If you were hitch-hiking how come you were driving this Buick?"

It was my turn to stare at him now.

"It was a Bentley, and she was driving. I was sitting at her side, and her husband, Paul, was at the back."

"Well, smother my old father in a feather bed!" the copper exclaimed. He took off his hat and wiped his forehead with the back of his hand. Then he put his hat on again and pulled aggressively at the brim. "*You* were driving! *She* was at the back! And there was no goddamn husband." He leaned forward and wagged his finger at me as he bawled, "And the sonofabitch of a car was a Buick!"

I got excited.

"You've got it wrong!" I said, clutching hold of the sheet. "I tell you she was driving. The car was a black Bentley coupé. This other car hit us. Ask the driver. He'll tell you."

The copper waved his note-book in my face.

"There was no other car! What's the matter with you? What have you got to lie about?"

"That's enough," the doctor said, his voice sharp. "He's not in a fit state to be shouted at. You must leave him alone, sergeant."

"I'm not lying!" I said, and tried to sit up. That finished me. A light exploded inside my head, and I took a nose-dive into darkness.

It was daylight when I opened my eyes again. The screen at the foot of the bed had been removed, but the screens on either side were still there. I could see another bed facing me. From the sounds going on around me I guessed I was in a ward.

I looked to see if the copper was there, but he wasn't. I lay still, aware I was feeling a lot better, that my head didn't ache, although it was still sore, and when I moved my arms I could do so without effort.

After a while I got around to thinking about what that copper had said. It began to worry me. No other car, no husband, it was a Buick and not a Bentley, and I was driving. What did he mean? Maybe I had dreamed the copper. Maybe he was part of the mists and the fog and the darkness. He must be unless he was confusing me with someone else.

Then the doctor came around from behind the screen. He grinned cheerfully at me.

"You don't have to tell me you're better," he said. "I can see that for myself."

"I'm fine," I said. "How long have I been here?"

He glanced at my papers at the foot of the bed.

"You were admitted at eleven-thirty on the night of September 6th. Today is September 12th. So you've been here six days."

"September?"

"That's right."

"You mean July, don't you? It can't be September. We hit that car on July 29th: the night I fought the Miami Kid."

"I don't know about that. You were admitted on September 6th."

"That can't be right. I couldn't have remained unconscious for more than a month before I was found."

The doctor smiled.

"Of course you couldn't. As a matter of fact you were found almost at once. A speed-cop heard the crash, although he didn't see it happen. He arrived on the scene five minutes after the smash. You were brought here an hour later."

I licked my lips. My mouth had suddenly gone dry.

47

"You wouldn't be fooling about the date, doc?"

He shook his head.

"No. I wouldn't be fooling about the date." He sat on the edge of the bed. "Now, you mustn't worry about this. It'll work out all right. At the moment you're showing typical signs of concussion. You've had a severe head injury. You're lucky to be alive. For some time you must expect to be confused. Dates, details of who was in the car and who wasn't, even your past may not make sense, but they will sort themselves out in a little while. At the moment you are convinced the car crash happened on July 29th. You'll find it impossible to believe it happened on September 6th, but don't let that worry you. In a week or so your memory will function normally again. And another thing, don't let the police rattle you. I've explained the position to them, and they understand. They want you to help them if you can, but they know now that if you make mistakes you're not doing it intentionally. All you have to do is to take it easy and rest all you can. It's just a matter of time."

He was a nice guy, and he was doing his best for me, and I was grateful, but that didn't stop me worrying. I knew I had fought the Kid on July 29th, and the crash had happened on the same night. Nothing he could say would alter that fact.

"I don't want to argue about it, doc," I said, "but do me a favour, will you?"

"Certainly. What is it?"

"Della – the girl I was with. She's here, too, isn't she? Ask her. She'll tell you it was July 29th. Ask her husband. He'll tell you the same thing."

The cheerful, bedside manner slipped a little.

"Now, here is a case in point," he said. "This business about a husband. You must expect it, you know. Only she and you were found in the car. There was no husband."

My heart began to pound.

"Well, all right, there was no husband," I said, trying to control the shake in my voice. "Then ask her. She'll tell you. You're not going to say she wasn't there, are you? Go and ask her!"

He ran his hand over his sleek, dark hair. The smile had gone for good.

"A couple of days ago you weren't well enough to be told," he said gently. "I can tell you now. She broke her back. She was dead when they found you."

II

In the afternoon Police Lieutenant Bill Riskin came to see me. If the nurse hadn't told me he was a police lieutenant I wouldn't have believed it. He was a little guy, around fifty, with a sad, wrinkled face and bright little eyes that peered at me through a pair of horn spectacles. He carried his hat in his hand, and he walked on tiptoe, and when he spoke, his voice was soft and gentle.

By this time I was as jumpy as a nervous horse. I was ready to go into a flat spin at the drop of a hat. Maybe that's why they picked Riskin. If they had unleashed that fat sergeant on me again I'd have flipped my lid.

He pulled up a chair beside me and crossed his short legs. I saw he was wearing boots and white socks, and his ankles were as thin as match-sticks.

"Well, boy, how's the head?" he asked.

I said the head was fine. I was clutching on to the sheet, and sweating, suspicious of him, suspicious of everyone. At the back of my mind I was beginning to wonder if they weren't going to tell me I was crazy.

"Doc said you were upset," he went on. "You've got nothing to be upset about. You're not the first fella who had a crack on his head and has got confused. You want to take it easy, and let us boys do the worrying. All we want to do is to get this straightened out. The girl died. If someone hit you, they didn't stop, and that makes it a hit-and-run job. It's our business to find the fella and teach him not to do it again. We'll find him more quickly if you can help us. You want us to find him, don't you?"

That sounded reasonable enough, but he wasn't kidding me. I'd have seen that guy's car turn over and smash into a tree before I had blacked out. If they had found me five minutes after the crash, as the doctor had said, they would have found him, too.

I said I wanted them to find him.

Riskin nodded and peered at me.

"Is it right you were hitch-hiking?"

"Yeah."

"And the girl let you drive the car?"

I didn't say anything. I couldn't understand why they were so anxious for me to admit driving the car, unless they wanted to pin Della's death on me. I began to get the jumps again.

He repeated his question in his mild voice, and even gave me an encouraging smile.

"I was not driving!" I exclaimed, raising my voice. "She was driving. I was sitting at her side, and her husband was sitting at the back! How many more times do I have to tell you guys?"

I expected him to start yelling at me, but he didn't. He just nodded his head and looked a little sadder.

"I'm sorry, boy. You want to take it easy. You don't want to get worked up. I guess there's been a misunderstanding about who was driving."

"There damn well has!" I said. "That sergeant of yours . . ."

"Never mind about the sergeant. He's been taught to bawl people out. It's the system. I never could cotton on to it myself," and he grinned at me.

I was still a little suspicious of him, but in spite of that, I was beginning to like him.

"Where did she pick you up, boy?" he went on. "You were walking along some road and she overtook you and you showed her your thumb. Is that what happened?"

"No; you've got it all wrong. Look, will you let me tell you what did happen: right from the start?"

"That's just what I want you to do," he said, and took out a note-book. "Mind if I make a few notes? I'm not as young as I could be, and my memory ain't what it was," and he winked to show me he was kidding.

I gave him the whole works. I told him about Pittsburgh, how I wanted to get into the big money, how I'd hitch-hiked to Pelotta, how I had busted MacCready's jaw and double-crossed Petelli. I went on to tell him how Della had offered to help me, how Pepi and Benno had chased us, and how the other car had crashed into us.

It took time, and I had scarcely a whisper left in me by the time I was through, but I was so glad to get it all off my chest that I didn't care how I felt.

Riskin never said a word all the time I talked. He made notes, scratched his ear from time to time, but he didn't interrupt.

"That's a very comprehensive story," he said when he was sure I hadn't anything more to tell him. "Now you take it easy, boy. You've nothing to worry about. Maybe you'd better take a nap. You look tired: like me. I'm always tired, but the Chief never gives me any time for naps." He stood up. "Well, so long. I'll be in again in a day or two. If there's anything else you remember, just let me know."

"There isn't anything else to remember," I said. "You've got the lot."

"That's fine. Well, you take a nap. So long for now."

I watched him tiptoe out of the ward. Up to now I hadn't had any use for a cop, but that little guy was different. I decided he was the nicest cop of them all.

Two days went by. I was making progress. The doctor was pretty pleased with me.

"You keep on like this," he told me, "and we'll have you up in a couple of days. You have a constitution of an elephant, and a head like granite."

I grinned at him, but I wasn't all that easy. I was wondering what Riskin was up to, and if he were going to show up.

"I'm looking forward to seeing the town," I said. "I've heard enough about Lincoln Beach, but I've never had a chance of looking it over."

He looked surprised.

"This isn't Lincoln Beach. What gave you that idea? This is Miami."

"Miami?" I stared at him. "But they have a hospital at Lincoln Beach, haven't they?"

"Of course. It's a wonderful hospital." He smiled. "Almost as good as this one."

"Then why didn't they take me there? What was the idea of driving me over two hundred miles to Miami?"

"It wasn't two hundred miles," he said patiently. "It was more like seventy. As you were nearer to Miami than Lincoln Beach, they brought you here."

I began to get excited again.

"But I hadn't even reached Lincoln Beach before the crash," I said. "We were only a few miles outside Pelotta, on our way to Lincoln Beach, when that car hit us!"

"Don't bother your brains about it," he said, getting his bed-side smile hitched to his face. "It'll straighten out in a few days."

And when he left me, I lay there, feeling cold, wondering if the bang on the head had affected my brain, wondering if I were going crazy. I began to long for Riskin to come and see me. Every time anyone came into the ward, I raised my head and looked eagerly to see if it were him. I got so my heart pounded every time that door opened.

The next morning they moved me out of the ward.

"What's the idea?" I asked the nurses as they pushed the bed along a corridor. "Where are you taking me?"

"Doctor thought you'd like to have a room to yourself," the fat nurse said. "He wants you to rest more than you're doing."

That wasn't the reason, I told myself. Maybe they thought I was nuts and wouldn't be safe with the others. I began to get excited.

"I don't want to be alone!" I said. "Take me back! I'm fine as I am. I don't want a room to myself!"

The doctor appeared from nowhere.

"There's nothing to get excited about," he said. "You'll like this room. It's got a wonderful view."

I thought if I made too much commotion they'd put me in a strait-jacket: that's the kind of state I had worked myself into.

It was a nice room, and the view was swell, but I hated it. I had a feeling I had been put in there for a purpose, and I wanted to know what that purpose was.

In the evening, around six, when I was lying there alone, looking out of the window at the ocean and the pleasure boats and people surf-riding, the door pushed open and Riskin came in.

"Hello, boy," he said, easing the door shut, "how are you coming?"

"Why have they put me in here?" I said, trying to sit up. "What's the idea?"

He tiptoed across the room to the bed.

"Hey, hey, what's biting you? Don't you know a room like this costs dough?"

"Then what's the idea?"

He reached for a chair and sat down.

"I don't think that doc likes his other patients to see me coming in here," he said. "Maybe it's that. He's a nice guy, that doc. Maybe it occurred to him it might be embarrassing for you to have policemen asking questions with everyone in the ward trying to listen in. That might be an idea, too."

I looked at him for a long moment, then I drew in a deep breath, and ran my fingers over my face, feeling it was damp and hot.

"That angle didn't strike me. Know what? I was beginning to think I was going nuts, and that's why they had taken me out of the ward."

He produced a packet of cigarettes.

"Like a smoke, boy?" he said. "You don't want to get those ideas into your head." He struck a match and lit the cigarette for me. Then he lit one for himself. "I bet if the nurse catches us she'll raise blue murder," he went on. "Still, that's what nurses are for, aren't they?"

I grinned at him. I was feeling much, much better.

"I wish you had come before. I was getting worried."

"I've been busy." He examined the end of his cigarette, then his pale, sharp eyes looked right into mine. "I've got a little shock for you. Think you can take it?"

I drew on the cigarette, aware my heart was beginning to pound.

"I guess so. What is it?"

"That car wasn't a Bentley; it was a Buick convertible: a black job, with red-leather upholstery, disc wheels and built-in head and fog lamps. You were found in the driving seat. She was found wedged down in the back seat. They had to cut the front seats away to get her out. There was no third person found. There was no other car, either. I've been over the ground myself. I've seen all the photographs. I've seen the Buick. I've talked to the cop who found you."

I lay still and stared at him. I wanted to tell him he was lying, but the words wouldn't come. I felt the blood leave my face. The cigarette slipped out of my fingers and dropped on to the floor.

He bent and picked it up.

"Take it easy, boy," he said. "I warned you it'd be a shock. There's nothing to worry about. You don't have to look so scared."

"You're lying!" I said in a voice I didn't know was my own.

"Here, take your cigarette," he said. "Relax. Let's go over this thing together and see if we can make some sense of it."

I wouldn't take the cigarette. I was feeling sick. I had a sudden urge to jump out of bed and run before they could put me in a padded cell. I didn't believe he was lying: and yet I had to believe it.

"You told me this car hit you on the night of July 29th," he went on mildly. "The smash you were in took place on the night of September 6th. I've seen the cop's note-book. The hospital records say the same thing. Well, now, what do you make of that?"

"I don't make anything of it. All I know is we hit that car after my fight with the Miami Kid, and that was on July 29th. I'm telling you the truth!"

"You *think* you are. I'm sure of that, but it didn't happen that way. I told you I've been busy. I have. I think I've got the key to this business. I've talked it over with the doc. He thinks I'm on the right track. Maybe it's going to be difficult for you to accept the explanation, but let me put it to you. The doc says it may take weeks for you to get your memory back. You've had a brain injury, and until things settle down you are likely to get all kinds

53

of odd ideas into your head. You mustn't worry about them. The doc says so, and he knows what he's talking about. Now will you try to accept what I'm going to tell you? Get your mind in a receptive mood if you can. It'll make things easier for us both. Think you can?"

I licked my dry lips.

"Go ahead and tell me."

"There was a car smash on the night of July 29th, a few miles outside Pelotta. Two cars going in opposite directions and travelling at high speed nudged each other and both turned over. One of them was a black Bentley which caught fire. The driver of this car was a guy named Johnny Farrar, a boxer. He was killed."

That really got me going. I struggled up.

"Are you crazy?" I shouted. "I'm Farrar! I'm Johnny Farrar! What are you trying to do? Send me nuts or something?"

He patted my arm.

"Take it easy, boy. You and me have got to work this out together. Give me a chance, will you? You'll see where I'm heading if you'll let me tell you without getting excited."

I dropped back on the pillow. I was sweating and scared and shaking.

"The accident was fully reported in the local papers," he went on. "They gave every detail. You can see the report in a moment. It's obvious to me you must have read about that smash in the paper. It made an impression on your mind. Five weeks later you get into a smash yourself. You get concussion. You have a brain injury. Unconsciously you have identified yourself with Farrar. When you recovered consciousness you are sure you are Farrar. You're sure it was you who had the smash on July 29th. Do you get the idea? It'll take a few weeks for you to get over this delusion, but you will. The doc says so, and he ought to know. All you've got to do is to take it easy and rest. It'll come back the way it happened if you don't worry about it. But what you've got to get out of your mind is you're Farrar. You aren't. You weren't in that smash with the other car on July 29th. You're not a boxer, and you never fought the Miami Kid. Get that through your head and you're three-quarters home."

"Do you think for one moment I believe a yarn like that?" I said through clenched teeth. "I know I'm Farrar! I did fight the Kid! I've got friends who can prove it! There is a guy in Pelotta who knows me. Bring him here and let him identify me. His name is Tom Roche. He owns a café."

"That's right," Riskin said. "I've talked to him. His name was

54

in the paper. He and his wife, Alice, and a guy named Solly Brant, identified the body. Because you read about them, you're imagining they are your friends."

I clutched hold of his arm.

"Identified what body?"

"Farrar's body. Here, take a look at this. You'll find it all there, just as I told you."

He took a newspaper out of his pocket and gave it to me. It was all there, just as he had told me, but there was one thing he had missed out. It said in the paper that I had stolen the Bentley, and the owner hadn't come forward to claim it.

I threw the paper on the floor. I felt I was suffocating.

"I've tried to trace the Bentley," he went on, "but the licence plates are phoney. I have traced the Buick."

"You have! Who does it belong to?" I asked in a strangled voice.

"To you, boy. Your name is John Ricca, and your address is 3945, Apartment 4, Franklin Boulevard, Lincoln Beach."

"You're lying!"

"I wish you'd take it easy," he said. "I told you it'd take a little time for you to accept what I'm telling you. You've been identified."

It only needed that.

"Who identified me?"

"Your cousin. That's why you're in this private room. As soon as he found out who you were, he arranged for you to have the very best treatment."

"I haven't a cousin, and my name's not Ricca!" I cried, pounding the sheet with my fist. "I don't know what you're talking about!"

"He's your cousin all right. He took a look at you last night when you were asleep. He identified you right away. The car's registration clinches it."

"I don't believe a word of it!" I was shouting at him. "I haven't a cousin, I tell you! Do you hear me! I'm Farrar!"

He scratched his ear while he looked at me. There was that exasperated but kindly expression on his face people get when they are talking to lunatics.

"Well, look, boy, try to take it easy. Maybe you'd better see him. Maybe you'll know him when you see him."

My heart skipped a beat, then began to race.

"Him? Who do you mean? What are you talking about?"

"Your cousin, Ricca. He's waiting outside."

III

He came into the room as silently as a ghost: a short, fat man with a pot belly and short, thick legs. His face was round and fat, and small, purple veins made an unsightly network over his skin. He had snake's eyes, flat and glittering and as lifeless as glass. He was going bald, and had taken pains to spread his thinning black hair over the bald patches without much success. His thick, red lips were set in a meaningless, perpetual smile.

One thing I was certain of: I'd never seen him before in my life.

Everything about him shrieked of money: his clothes, his linen, his personal jewellery were the best money could buy. He had a diamond ring on his little finger: the stone was as big as a pigeon's egg.

He came silently across the room: his feet making no sound on the parquet floor. In his right hand he carried a large bunch of blood-red carnations, carefully wrapped in tissue paper.

He came to the foot of the bed and stood looking at me. Riskin stepped aside: a benign expression on his wrinkled face.

"Hello, Johnny," the fat man said. He had a soft, fruity voice as if it came from a throat well cushioned with fat.

I didn't say anything. I couldn't. It was as if I had been pitch-forked into a horrible nightmare.

"He looks fine, doesn't he?" the fat man went on, smiling at Riskin. "Jeepers, Johnny, you gave me a scare. I've been looking all over for you. How do you feel?"

"I don't know you," I said, and my voice was husky. "Get out of here!"

"Take it easy, boy," Riskin said mildly. "Give him a chance to talk to you. You want to get well, don't you? We've got to get this mind of yours working again."

"I tell you I don't know him!"

The fat man put the carnations down on the bedside table.

"You've taken a pretty bad knock, Johnny," he said. "The doc thinks I can help you. I want to help you. You know that."

I was scared of him. In spite of his smile there was something about his eyes that warned me he was as dangerous as a rattlesnake.

"I don't want to talk to you."

He puffed breath at me, and his diamond flashed in the sunlight coming through the open window.

"Come on, Johnny, let's try to get on top of this thing," he said. "There's Ginny to think of. You haven't forgotten Ginny? You can imagine how she is feeling. She wants to see you, Johnny."

Was there no end to this? I found myself clutching hold of the sheet again.

"I don't know what you're talking about! I don't want you in here. Get out!"

"You don't remember Ginny – the girl you're going to marry?" He looked over at Riskin, raising his fat shoulders. "I can't believe that. Would you like to see her? Is that what you'd like?"

I just lay there, staring at him while a cold wind blew through my mind.

"You two get together," Riskin said. "I gotta go. Take it easy, boy. It's going to work out all right, only you've got to be receptive."

I wanted to tell him to stay. I wanted to tell him to take this fat horror out of here, but no words came. He went off, scratching his ear and shaking his head.

There was a long pause after he had gone. The fat man puffed gently, his smile remained fixed, and his snake's eyes watched me.

"You get out, too," I said.

Instead, he reached for a chair and sat down.

"Know what they call that guy on the Force?" he asked. "They call him Foxy Riskin. He's made a hit with you, hasn't he, with his 'boy' this and his 'boy' that? You think he's trying to help you, don't you? Well, he isn't. All he wants to do is to get your confidence, and when he's got that, when he's softened you up and got your guard down, he's going to slap a murder rap on you, and he's going to make it stick."

I didn't know whether I was coming or going. I turned hot, then cold.

"If it wasn't for me," the fat man went on, resting his pudgy hands on his fat knees and staring at me, "you'd be in jail now. All he wants is the motive, and I could tell him that, but I've kept my mouth shut because you and I are going to make a deal."

"I won't listen to you," I said. "Get out of here!"

"They don't know who she is. I could tell them, and once they know, you're sunk," the fat man went on. "It doesn't suit me for them to find out, but if it has to come out, I'll handle it as I handle most things."

"I don't know what you're talking about. You're not my

cousin! I've never seen you before in my life!"

His smile widened.

"Of course I'm not your cousin, but do you want me to tell Riskin that? Do you want three murder raps pinned on you? Isn't one enough?"

I got hold of myself. I had to, or I'd have blown my top.

"You're mixing me up with someone else," I said, trying to keep my voice steady. "I'm John Farrar. I'm not Ricca, and I'm not your cousin. Now will you please get out!"

"I know you're Farrar. You're the guy who killed Wertham and Reisner. Sure, I know you, and you killed her, too. If it hadn't been for the gun they might have thought it was an accident, but they found the gun. It had her prints on it."

"You know I'm Farrar?" I said, leaning forward to stare at him. "Then all this talk about me being Ricca is a lie?"

"He thinks you're Ricca," the fat man said, "and so long as he thinks so I can swing it. Once he finds out you're Farrar, you're done for."

I put my head in my hands. I felt I was going crazy.

"Suppose we skip the comedy," the fat man went on, and his smile oozed off his face like a fish sliding off a fishmonger's slab. "You play with me and I'll play with you. I'll show you how to out-fox Riskin. With me behind you, you can beat this rap." He thrust his head forward: he looked like a tortoise sitting there, his hands on his knees, his head forward, his eyes hooded. "Where've you hidden the money?"

I didn't say anything. I didn't look at him. I went on holding my head in my hands. But I was getting my second wind. I was getting the hang of this set-up.

"Now, look," he said, "you're in a corner, and there's no way out for you unless you play along with me. I can fix it. I'll get Hame to handle it. He'll talk to Riskin. Tell me where the money is, and there'll be no blow-back. You can walk out of here as free as the air. What do you say?"

"I don't know what you're talking about," I said, and was surprised how steady my voice was now.

He studied me.

"Use your head, Farrar. You can't expect to get away with all that money. I tell you what I'll do. I'll stake you. I'll give you five grand, and I'll fix Riskin. That's fair, isn't it?"

"If you think Riskin can pin anything on me, go ahead and let him do it. You're mixing me up with someone else. I don't know anything about any money."

58

"Don't get excited," he said, his fat fingers drumming on his knees. "You don't trust me, do you? But ask yourself: why should I bother about you? You can walk out of here and do what you damn well like. Why should I care? She was the one who cared. I don't. Give me the dough and I'll see you right. Now come on. Where is it?"

"I don't know," I said. "And if I did know I wouldn't tell you. Now get out!"

His fat face turned into a mask of snarling fury. He looked like a demon.

"You fool!" he exclaimed, and his voice shook. "Do you think I'm taken in by this loss of memory stunt of yours? Where have you hidden it? If you don't tell me you'll wish you'd never been born. Where is it?"

"Get out!"

He got control of himself. The meaningless smile came back as he stood up.

"Okay, if that's the way you want to play it," he said. "Suit yourself. I'll talk to Riskin. In a couple of hours from now you'll be in jail. Maybe you think you can talk yourself out of one murder rap, but I'm damned sure you won't talk yourself out of three."

He walked silently to the door.

"Want to change your mind?" he asked, pausing to look back at me.

"Get out!" I said.

He went out quietly the way he had come in: like a ghost without a house to haunt.

IV

Before I could even start to think what all this meant a nurse came in.

"Did you enjoy your visitor?" she asked, smiling at me. "Imagine him being your cousin. You're not a bit alike."

"Cousins don't have to be," I said, surprised I could say anything.

"I guess that's right. Did he leave these?" She picked up the carnations. "Aren't they wonderful!"

"You have them. I don't care about flowers. I'll be glad if you'll take them away."

"Well, if you really mean that. Why, thanks. I think they're wonderful." She picked them up and sniffed at them. "Your cousin must have a lot of money. That diamond he was wearing and his car!"

"Yeah, he doesn't starve."

"I'm beginning to suspect you're someone very important."

"Who me? I'm nobody. What gave you that idea?"

"Well, those two policemen outside. They told me they were guarding you. I guess you must be important."

I kept a dead pan expression, but it was an effort.

"My cousin imagines someone's going to kidnap me. He's nuts, but there it is. I didn't know about the cops. How long have they been here?"

"Oh, they've just arrived."

I was beginning to get the shakes again.

"Tell me, nurse, what happened to my clothes?"

"They're in that closet; over there. Did you want something?"

"No, it's okay. I just wondered. The doc said something about me leaving at the end of the week. I just wondered what had happened to them."

"Well, they're right in that closet. Is there anything I can get you?"

"I guess not, thanks. I think I'll take a nap. Those two guys made me feel tired."

"Thanks for the flowers. They really are something."

"You're welcome."

I watched her leave the room, then as soon as I was sure she had gone, I sat up.

I had to get out of here. I had to go somewhere away from Riskin and Ricca and work this thing out for myself. The way I figured it there could be only two explanations: this was either a case of mistaken identity or one of them or even both of them were trying to frame me.

It was now twenty minutes past six. The nurse brought me supper at seven-fifteen sharp. That gave me fifty minutes to dress and get out of the hospital before I was missed.

I lowered my feet to the floor and stood up. I felt weak in the legs and wobbly, but not anything like so wobbly as I thought I was going to feel. I went over to the closet and opened the door. I was expecting to find the white tropical suit Brant had given me, but instead there was a dark-blue flannel suit on a hanger, a white silk shirt, a pair of black leather shoes, and a wide-brimmed hat on a shelf.

I stared at the clothes, knowing they weren't mine. But that wasn't going to stop me. If my clothes weren't to hand I'd take someone else's.

I pulled on the pair of blue and white check socks I found stuck in the shoes. I put the shoes on: they fitted me as if they were made for me. The shirt was a fit, too, and so was the suit.

It took me over ten minutes to get dressed, and I was feeling pretty bad by the time I was through. I had to sit on the bed until my heart stopped racing. I was panting like a worn-out horse.

I nearly forgot the hat, but that was important. I had to have something to hide the bandages around my head. I got it on. It was tight, and it made my head ache, but I had to wear it.

Then I crept over to the door, eased it open and glanced into the passage.

At the far end standing at the head of the stairs, were two cops; their backs to me. They stood with their hands behind them, and every now and then they flexed their knees the way cops do on the movies.

I looked to my right, but the corridor ended in big double windows. My only way out was down the stairs, and I wouldn't get far with those cops waiting there to stop me.

I closed the door and sneaked over to the window. Apart from being on the sixth floor, the ground below was packed with patients sun bathing. If I tried going out that way I'd be spotted in seconds.

While I was trying to figure a way out, I heard voices in the corridor. Creeping over to the door I opened it a crack and peered out, ready to make a dive for the bed.

There was a nurse and a guy in a white coat out there. They were manoeuvring a wheeled trolley into the room opposite mine.

I waited, my eyes on the clock on the overmantel. It was now ten minutes to seven. Time was running out. I had only twenty minutes before the nurse arrived with my supper. If I were going to get out I'd have to do something fast.

I was still at the door, trying to make up my mind what to do when the nurse and the attendant reappeared.

"I'll take her down after I've seen the doc," he said. "I've forgotten the mortician's certificate."

"One of these days you'll forget your head, not that it would be a great loss," the nurse said tartly, and turned away.

The attendant made a pass at her, but she anticipated it and whisked her rear out of reach.

"And if you don't keep your paws . . ."

"I know. I know," the attendant said wearily. "You'll tell the matron. Why don't you relax sometime?"

The nurse walked off down the corridor, and the attendant followed her. The two cops obligingly stood aside to let them go down the stairs.

I stood hesitating, then I eased open the door. The cops were leaning over the banisters; probably watching the nurse out of sight. Their backs were to me.

The attendant had given me the clue, and I sneaked across the corridor, turned the handle of the door opposite, eased it open and stepped inside. I was ready to jump out of my skin, and very nearly did when I saw a body under a sheet on the trolley.

I took hold of the corner of the sheet and lifted it. I was shaking now from head to foot. The dead woman looked as if she were asleep. What I was about to do horrified me, but I knew if I didn't go through with it I wasn't going to get away. I looked frantically around the room for a place to hide her, but there was nowhere. Close by was another door. I opened it an inch and peered into a luxuriously fitted bathroom.

I ran back to the trolley and wheeled it into the bathroom. Then I stripped off the sheet and keeping my eyes averted I lifted the body and staggered with it to the bath. It was as much as I could do to lower it into the bath, but I did it somehow. Then I pulled the shower curtains and shoved the trolley back into the bedroom.

By that time I was all in. I flopped down on the bed. I thought I was going to pass out. I was shaking like a leaf, and there was an awful swirling going on inside my head. I fought against it. It went away after a moment or so. I got a grip on myself. I didn't dare waste a moment. I got on the trolley and covered myself with the sheet. Then I took off my hat and lay down, pulling the sheet over my head.

I lay there, waiting. My head was beginning to ache now, and every now and then a shiver ran through me. I began to think I would be spotted before they even got me out of the room. I was in two minds whether to get up and hide in the bathroom when I heard the door open.

I turned to stone, holding my breath, trying to control the hammering of my heart. The trolley began to move. The guy pushing it was whistling under his breath. He sounded as if he hadn't a care in the world.

That short ride down the corridor was the worst experience I've ever been through. Even lying in a fox-hole with the scream of falling bombs in my ears was nothing to this.

"What have you got there, chum?" a voice asked.

I felt my blood congeal. I knew by the voice it could only be one of the cops.

"This is just up your street," the attendant said. "It's a corpse."

"Aw, hell. Don't you cure 'em in this hospital?"

"Not often. I guess the head doc draws a commission from the undertaker. He certainly keeps him busy."

"What is this? A man or woman?"

"A woman. She died of peritonitis. I guess the doc left his glove in her or something. I've never known a guy as absent-minded as he is."

The cop laughed and the trolley began to move again. It bumped over a step, and then I heard the faint swish of closing doors. A moment later I felt a downward movement and guessed we were in an elevator.

The attendant continued to whistle under his breath. The elevator bumped to a gentle standstill, the doors swished open and the trolley began to move again.

"Hi, Joe," a girl's voice said.

"Hi, sugar, how's it coming?"

The trolley stopped.

"Who's that?"

"Mrs. Ennismore. Room 44," the attendant said. "You're looking cute this evening."

"That's opposite Ricca's room, isn't it?"

"Yeah. There're two cops up there, keeping an eye on him."

"There are? I bet the matron had a fit, didn't she?"

"Riskin handled her. That guy's smart. I wouldn't want him after me. He's got Ricca fooled. Ricca imagines he's getting away with this loss of memory stuff, but he isn't. I heard Foxy tell Doc Summers he'll be good and ready to slap a murder charge on him tomorrow. I'd like to see his face when they march in and pinch him."

"Who did he murder?"

"Some dame. He must have been nuts. He nearly killed him-self as well. Listen, sugar, how about going for a ride with me in the elevator? It might break down between floors if we're lucky."

"If you're lucky, you mean."

63

"Lemme get rid of this stiff and let's try it." The trolley began to move again. "You wait right here, sugar. This is going to be something to put in your diary."

The foot of the trolley bumped against swing-doors. The attendant gave it a hard push and sent it forward to cannon against a wall.

I heard him say, "The guy who invented elevators was a public benefactor. Hop in, and I'll show you for why."

Then there was silence. I lay there for a moment or so until I heard the elevator doors swish to, then I pulled off the sheet and sat up.

The room was windowless, and in darkness, but the light from the passage, coming through the crack in the swing-doors, was enough for me to get a vague idea of the set-up. There were a number of trolleys covered with sheets standing against the walls. An overpowering smell of formaldehyde filled the air, and it was cold.

I slid off the trolley, again nearly forgetting my hat. I put it on. As my eyes became used to the semi-darkness, I spotted a door across the far end of the room. Faint daylight came from under it.

I went over to it, turned the handle and opened it a couple of inches. I looked into a narrow alley. Two big white motor ambulances were parked out there. The light was beginning to fade now, but it was still too light to be safe.

I opened the door and looked up the alley. Iron gates stood open at the far end. Beyond them I could see a main street. There was no one guarding the gates.

I started off down the alley towards the street. I had no idea where I was going or what I was going to do. I hadn't any money. There was nothing in my pockets, not even a handkerchief. But I didn't care. At least I was getting away from Riskin, the hospital and Ricca. That would do to get on with.

v

A big yellow moon threw amber light over the sea. There was a car parked on the sand, its lights out. The man and the girl, on either side of the car, began to undress. I was near enough to hear their voices, but not what they were saying.

This part of the beach was lonely and deserted but for these two and the car. I had lain hidden in the mangroves for the past three hours, then suddenly the car had arrived. It came just when I was giving up hope.

I watched the two of them run down to the sea and splash in. As soon as they were swimming I moved out of my hiding-place and headed for the car. I found his coat. My fingers closed around a wallet in his inside pocket. I hauled it out, and went around to the back of the car where they couldn't see me if they looked this way. The wallet was stuffed with money. I could scarcely believe my luck. I took a hundred and fifty dollars in small bills. That still left him enough to buy her a slap-up supper. I slid the wallet into the pocket and tossed the coat into the car, then I ran back to the darkness of the mangroves.

During the three hours I had remained hidden I had made a plan. Riskin would expect me to clear out of Miami as fast as I could. I had told him I had a talent for hitch-hiking. He'd probably cover every truck and car going out of town, and watch every road. I had decided my safest bet was to remain in Miami, and hole up somewhere. I had to find myself a quiet hotel, spin them a yarn I was waiting for my baggage, and hope they'd give me a room.

There should be dozens of suitable hotels if I could only find them. I'd have to be careful. My description was bound to be out now, and every patrolman would be looking for me: Ricca would probably be looking for me too.

I started off towards the bright lights of the water-front. I moved slowly. I was tired. I had walked miles since I had left the hospital. My head ached too. While I had been hiding I had taken off the bandages. They had shaved my head, but from the feel of it the wound was healed.

At least my hat fitted me now, and didn't bother me.

Ahead I could see the water-front and the harbour, the shops and cafés and saloons.

As I walked along the congested sidewalk I kept my eyes open for a patrolman, but I needn't have bothered. No patrolman could have spotted me in that teeming crowd.

A few minutes' walking brought me to an hotel. It seemed the kind of place I was looking for. It was dingy and quiet, and looking through the double swing-doors I saw the lounge was deserted.

I pushed open the doors and walked in.

Ahead of me was the reception desk. A little guy in a black alpaca coat was propping himself up against the desk. He was bald and wrinkled, and his deep-set eyes were bored.

"I'd like a room," I said.

"Ten bucks deposit," he said briefly. "For how long?"

"A couple of days, if I like it, maybe a week."

He scratched the top of his head with one finger.

"Don't see your baggage."

"It's at the station."

"We like baggage, mister. We could collect it for you."

I fished out two tens and dropped them on the desk.

"I'll get it in the morning. Let's have a room."

He reached for a key from the rack behind him, shoved the register at me and a pen.

I wrote John Crosby on the line he indicated with a dirty finger. My slight hesitation didn't fool him.

"Any relation to Bing?" he asked with a small sneer.

"Why, yes," I said. "I'm his sister. Where do I find the room?"

He gave me a cold, hostile look, stuck his thumb into a bell-push and turned his back on me.

After a while a middle-aged bell-hop materialized and took the key. He was a rat-faced guy with close-set eyes and a thin, hard mouth. His blue uniform and pill-box hat shone like a nickel plate.

"Second floor," he said. "No baggage?"

"No baggage," I said.

I tramped up the stairs after him. Eventually we came to a door which he unlocked and pushed open. He reached inside and turned on the light.

"The bathroom's at the end of the corridor. Don't use the shower. It don't work."

I went past him into a box of a room with a bed, a table, a chest of drawers and a strip of worn carpet.

"Just like Buckingham Palace," I said.

"A little more roomy, if anything."

He put the key on the chest of drawers and looked me over expectantly. I gave him a dollar. He nearly dropped in his tracks.

"Anything you want, mister?" he said eagerly. "How about a little company? I have a list of telephone numbers as long as my arm."

"Dust," I said.

"If you change your mind, call the desk and ask for me. My name's Maddux."

"Beat it!"

When he had gone I sat on the bed and took off my hat. I was so tired I could scarcely keep my eyes open. The bed felt as if it had been stuffed with golf-balls, but that didn't worry me. I could have slept right then on a bed of nails.

I sat there, yawning and turning the hat around in my hand, my mind empty. As far back as I could remember I had kept a ten-dollar bill behind the sweat-band of any hat I happened to own. I'd stick it there and forget about it. Then when I was broke I had something to fall back on. I wondered idly if the owner of this hat had the same idea. I turned down the sweat-band and looked inside.

My fingers hooked out a thin ribbon of paper, and as I unfolded it I realized I wasn't surprised to find it there. It was almost as if I had known it would be there before I looked for it.

I smoothed it out. It was a left-luggage receipt, and written in pencil across the top were the words:

> *John Farrar,*
> *Seaboard Air-Line Railway,*
> *Greater Miami.*

Under the heading, *Description of Articles,* was written *One suitcase.*

I was fully awake now, the longing for sleep washed right out of my mind. Then this hat, and obviously the clothes, did belong to me! I looked for the date on the receipt. There it was: September 6th! The time the suitcase was handed in was also there: 6.5 p.m.

For some minutes I sat staring down at the threadbare carpet. I felt like a sceptic in a haunted house who suddenly sees a horrifying apparition. There could be no doubt now. I must have lost my memory for forty-five days, and during that time, if I was to believe Ricca, I had murdered two men and a woman.

Ricca might be lying. If I were to remain sane I'd have to find out what had happened during those forty-five days. It started with the smash, five miles outside Pelotta. I would go to the scene of the accident and with any luck I might be able to trace my movements from there. I had been thrown out of the Bentley and had injured my head. From that moment until I had recovered consciousness in the hospital I had been going around with a blacked-out mind.

I flicked the receipt with my finger-nail. Maybe this suitcase contained the key to those missing forty-five days. According to the receipt the suitcase belonged to me, and I must have checked it in. I had no idea where the Seaboard Air-Line Railway was, but I had to get the suitcase tonight. I wouldn't sleep or rest until I had it.

I reached for the telephone.

"Send Maddux up here," I said to the reception clerk. "I want a packet of cigarettes. Tell him to hurry."

As he began to grumble, I hung up.

A couple of minutes later Maddux came in, panting, as if he had run up the two flights of stairs, his ratty face bright with expectation.

"Changed your mind?" he asked, closing the door and leaning against it. "What do you fancy . . .?"

I held out my hand.

"Cigarettes?"

He gave me a packet.

"There's a little blonde . . ."

"Forget it," I said, lit a cigarette, then took out two ten-dollar bills. I rustled them between my fingers.

"How would you like to earn these?"

His eyes bugged out and his mouth fell open.

"Try me," he said.

I handed him the left-luggage receipt.

"Get that case and bring it back here."

"What – now?"

"If you want to make twenty bucks."

He looked at the receipt.

"I thought your name was Crosby," he said, and gave me a quick, suspicious look.

I didn't say anything. I folded the two bills and slid them into my pocket.

"I didn't say anything," he said hurriedly. "That wasn't me talking."

"Get that case and make it snappy."

He went off as if fired from a gun.

While I waited I went over my meagre stock of information.

On the night of September 6th I had been driving a Buick convertible, registered in the name of John Ricca, along a road seventy-five miles from Miami. With me was a girl: whether it had been Della or not I couldn't say. Ricca knew who she was, but Riskin didn't. There had been a smash. Apparently I had lost control of the car, for there was no other car involved. The girl had been killed, and I had been found unconscious five minutes later by a speed-cop. There was some talk about a gun.

It had her fingerprints on it, and for some reason or other Riskin seemed to think the smash had been deliberate, making it murder.

I wiped my face with the back of my hand. I had to find out who the girl was and why she had a gun. I had to find out why I had lost control of the car.

Riskin had said I had an apartment on Franklin Boulevard, Lincoln Beach. I remembered Della had said she and her husband were going to Lincoln Beach, and did I want to go with them. It seemed in those forty-five missing days I had not only lived in Lincoln Beach, but I had even set up a home there.

To judge by the suit I was wearing, and the fact I had owned a Buick, I must have got hold of a lot of money. How had I done that in so short a time?

I switched my mind to the fat man, Ricca. He had given me a lot of obscure information. According to him I was engaged to a girl called Ginny. Where had I met her and where was she now?

I recalled what he had said. *You're the guy who killed Wertham and Reisner.* Who were they? *Where have you hidden the money?* he had asked. What money? *You can walk out of here and do what you damn well like. Why should I care? She was the one who cared.* Who was she? Why did she care?

I stretched out on the bed and smoked, staring up at the ceiling. There seemed no end to the questions, but how was I to find the answers? I realized I wasn't going to get far unless I had money to help me. At the moment I had only a little over a hundred dollars. I couldn't hope to make a thorough investigation without a substantial sum of money. I was suddenly up against a blank wall. Without money I was sunk. There could be no investigation. All I could do was to sneak out of Miami as soon as my hundred dollars ran out and get somewhere where I could lose myself.

I was still battering my brains out, trying to find a solution, when I heard Maddux coming pounding down the passage. I just had time to slap on my hat to cover my shaven head when he came in and dumped a big black pigskin suitcase on the bed.

"There you are, mister," he said. "Jeepers! That weighs a ton."

I was looking at the suitcase. As far as I knew I had never seen it before. There was a tie-on label hanging from the handle. It had my name on it, and it was written in my handwriting.

I tried the locks, but they didn't budge. They were good, strong locks, and they'd need a lot of breaking open.

"That's a nice-looking case," Maddux said, watching me closely.

"Yeah, but I've lost the key. Got a screw-driver handy?"

I saw his look of suspicion, but I ignored it.

"You don't want to bust the locks," he said. "I've got a hicky that'll open it."

"Get it," I said.

He went off as if he were jet-propelled.

I stood looking at the suitcase, fighting down a feeling of fear and excitement. Would this case contain the key to the missing forty-five days? Had I bought it or had I stolen it?

Maddux returned in six minutes. They seemed like six hours to me.

He bent over the case, screwed a bit of metal into the lock, twisted it and the lock flew up. He did the same to the other lock, then stood back.

"Easy, once you know how," he said.

I gave him the twenty I'd promised him.

"See you tomorrow," I said, anxious to get rid of him.

He looked longingly at the case, backed to the door, then hesitated.

"Well, if that's all, I guess I'll get downstairs."

"That's all."

The moment he closed the door I shot the bolt. Then I turned to the bed. I took hold of the lid of the case and threw it open.

I don't know what I expected to see, but certainly not what I did see. The case was crammed with money: thousands and thousands of dollars; more money than I had ever seen in my life.

For a long moment of time I stood staring. Then very carefully and with shaking hands I lifted the fat, neat packages on to the bed until the case was empty. There was nothing else in the case – just the money. A quarter of a million in hundred-dollar bills!

I understood then why Ricca had been so anxious to find the money. A quarter of a million! How did it get into the case? Where had it come from?

I suddenly felt horribly faint, and I put my hand on the bedrail to steady myself. My knees sagged, and I flopped down on the floor. But not for one moment did I take my eyes off that money.

A quarter of a million dollars!

A motive for murder! Had I really murdered two men and a woman for this? Was that what I had done?

If I hadn't been suspected of murder I wouldn't have touched that money. I would have taken the suitcase to Riskin and let him handle it, but what had I to lose? If I did hand over the suitcase to Riskin I might be handing him the motive he was hunting for to pin the murder rap on me. If I were caught with it, it wouldn't make much difference, if any. I was wanted for murder, nothing else mattered.

I wanted money to make an investigation. Well, I had a quarter of a million dollars and I was going to use it.

Once I had made up my mind to use it, everything became simple. I bought Maddux, and I bought the bald-headed reception clerk. Maddux cost me a hundred bucks. The clerk became co-operative for a mere fifty. Both of them found out who I was when they read the morning papers. The papers gave my name and an accurate description of me.

"This man is wanted for questioning concerning the murder of an unknown woman," said the account. "Anyone recognizing him from the description given above should communicate immediately with Lieutenant Bill Riskin of the Homicide Bureau."

But they didn't offer a reward, so the clerk and Maddux weren't interested. They were only interested in my welfare and my dollars.

I remained in the hotel bedroom for two weeks: time for my hair to grow over the scar and for me to raise a moustache. A moustache and a pair of horn spectacles changed my appearance considerably. Only a trained observer like Riskin could have spotted me. I was sure I had nothing to fear from the man in the street who might have read the police description.

I told Maddux I wanted a car and a gun. He got me a second-hand black Plymouth: just the car for the job I had on hand. He produced also a ·38 automatic and a ·22 in case I wanted something smaller, and a box of slugs to go with both guns. He made a big profit out of the purchases, but I didn't care. I had all the money in the world, and I was buying secrecy.

After sixteen days in the bedroom, I decided the heat had cooled off enough for me to leave. I drove away from the hotel on a moonless night a little after ten o'clock. On the bench seat beside me was the ·38. I had the ·22 in my hip pocket. I was ready for trouble. If anyone shot at me, I was going to shoot at them. I was in that kind of mood.

I drove along Bay Shore Drive, up the long, crowded Biscayne Boulevard towards the State Highway. I drove carefully, stopping at every red light, taking care no speed-cop could find an excuse to bawl me out. I saw a number of prowl cars and a number of speed-cops, but none of them took any notice of me.

After a six-hour drive I spotted the bright lights of Lincoln Beach. The town was laid out in a semi-circle, facing the sea and sheltered by rising ground. It seemed to be a blaze of lights even at three o'clock in the morning. I had no intention of driving through the town. My first call was to be the scene of the accident where the Bentley had crashed. I'd be coming back to Lincoln Beach later on.

I remembered where the car had hit us. There was a hill and palmetto thickets on either side. Fifty miles past Lincoln Beach I reduced speed. Somewhere here, I told myself. There was a hill ahead of me, and I could see the shadowy outlines of the palmetto thickets. I slowed to a crawl. By now it was close on five o'clock, and the sun was coming up reluctantly above the skyline. In another ten minutes it would be daylight.

I switched off the headlights and cruised to a standstill, drawing to the side of the road. I lit a cigarette, aware of the feeling of rising excitement, but I waited. I wanted plenty of light to do what I had come to do.

After a while I decided it was light enough, and I drove on. A mile farther up the road I came to the place. I knew it was the place by the uprooted tree, the torn grass and the skid marks that even sixty days hadn't yet blotted out.

I kept on driving until I was a quarter of a mile past the scene of the smash, then I ran the car off the road and into the shrubbery. I wasn't taking any risks. A parked car at the actual place of the smash might arouse the curiosity of any passing cop.

I walked back, my gun shoved down the waistband of my trousers, my eyes and ears alert for trouble. I saw no one and heard nothing.

After examining the ground for half an hour, I gave up. Apart from the skid marks, the churned-up grass and the uprooted tree, I found nothing. I knew the police had been here. If there had been anything to find they would have found it. I didn't expect to find anything. I hoped if I returned to the scene of the smash something there might jog my memory to life, but it didn't.

During those sixteen days at the hotel I had groped into the past, trying to push aside the blanket of fog that hid the happenings of those forty-five days. Every now and then I felt I was getting somewhere. I remembered a few things, but they were so disjointed they didn't make sense.

An enormous fat woman with blonde hair floated into my mind, and then before I could concentrate on her she turned into a sleek, ferocious lion that came rushing towards me with a coughing, snarling roar. That mind picture brought me out of an uneasy doze, sweating and scared. Had I been dreaming or had this fat woman and the lion actually played a part in those missing days?

Then later I had a very clear mind picture of myself on the verandah of a beach cabin. I was sitting in an armchair listening to the radio. I could hear the music distinctly, and although I never listened to classical music, I somehow knew this was a symphony concert, and it was by Beethoven. There was a blonde girl in a yellow swim-suit in the room. She kept coming on to the verandah, wanting me to turn off the radio, but I wouldn't let her. She said if the music stopped she would take off her swim-suit. Wouldn't I like that better than the music, and I said no. She got angry and slapped my face. This picture appeared again and again in my mind, but it didn't mean anything to me.

I sat down on the uprooted tree and lit a cigarette. I tried to concentrate while I absorbed the atmosphere of the thicket. I remembered the other car coming at us like a bat out of hell. I remembered Della's scream and the smash. I remembered grabbing hold of the dashboard as the Bentley began to turn over. I closed my eyes. There had been a blinding white light, and then darkness.

After a while I remembered a small wooden cabin, facing the sea. I could see it clearly in my mind. It had a tin roof, and the front window was cracked. There was a split panel in the front door.

This was new. This had happened after the smash! I was sure of that. Excited by this discovery, I jumped to my feet and looked around. There was a path through the palmettos, leading to the beach. I set off, walking quickly, aware that the path seemed vaguely familiar. I was pretty sure I had been this way before.

I came out of the thicket on to the sand dunes. The sea was in front of me. I stood looking to right and left. There was no sign of any cabin. I was turning to walk to the right when I changed my mind and walked instead to the left. I was like a blind man in a familiar room. All I had to do was to obey my instincts, and I knew I should arrive at the cabin.

I walked for ten minutes along the beach before I saw it. It

73

was exactly as I had pictured it in my mind, with its tin roof and cracked window-pane.

There was an elderly man in the doorway, smoking. He had on a pair of dirty dungarees and he was looking in my direction. There was a stiff alertness about him that told me I had startled him.

"Morning," I said as I drew near. "A lonely spot you've got here."

He stared at me, his lined, weather-beaten face uneasy.

"Where did you spring from, mister?"

"I've been driving all night. I wanted to stretch my legs. Could I buy a cup of coffee off you?"

"You can have a cup of coffee. I've just made some. I'll bring it to you."

I sat down on a wooden box and waited. I had an idea I had seen him before.

He came out with two pint mugs of steaming coffee. He kept staring at me while I drank.

"It's a funny thing," he said slowly, "but I've seen you somewhere before."

"You've seen my brother," I said, deciding this might be the best way to get the information out of him. "He had a car smash not far from here on July 29th. Remember?"

He hurriedly shifted his eyes.

"I don't know anything about a car smash."

I knew at once he was lying.

"My brother was hurt," I said, watching him. "He lost his memory. We don't know what happened. I'm trying to find out."

"I tell you I don't know anything about it," he said curtly. "If you've finished your coffee, I gotta get on."

I took out a roll of bills; peeled off a hundred in twenties and spread them out on my knee.

"I don't want to waste your time. I pay for information," I said.

"She said I wasn't to talk about it," he said, his eyes lighting up, "but as you're his brother . . ."

I gave him the money. My heart was beginning to pound, and my hand was unsteady.

"What happened?"

"She and your brother came here. She said he had been hit on the head and the car stolen, but I found out later she was lying. There had been a smash and the car caught fire. They found a body in it."

74

"That's right. What was this woman like?"

"Dark and pretty, but as hard as nails. She wore a green dress. From the look of her she had plenty of money."

Della!

"Go on," I said.

"Your brother made out he was pretty bad, but he wasn't. He was trying to fool me. She wanted me to call some fella, and she gave me a phone number. The phone's about half a mile down the road. I called this guy. He said he'd come over. When I got back to the cabin I looked through the window. Your brother was talking to the girl, but when I went in he made out he was still unconscious."

I didn't know what to make of all this.

"Do you remember the phone number?"

"Lincoln Beach 4444. It's an easy one to remember."

"Who was this fella you called?"

"Nick Reisner. That's what she said his name was."

I felt spider's legs run up my spine.

"What exactly did she say?"

He thought for a long moment, scratching his head, his eyebrows drawn down in a frown.

"She said Ricca had met with an accident, and this Reisner fella was to come and pick them up."

"Did he?"

"Yeah."

"Did you see him?"

He shook his head.

"No. I was asleep when he arrived."

I went on asking him questions, but there was nothing else of importance he could tell me. But I hadn't wasted my time. I had established that after the car crash Della and I had gone to the cabin. That meant her husband, Paul, and not me, as Riskin had thought, had been left in the burning car. Who Reisner was was something I had to find out. At least I had his telephone number. Why had Della called me Ricca? Had she been the girl who had died in the second car smash or was it someone else?

Before I could make sense of any of this, I had to get a bit more information. I thanked the old man for his help, and went back to where I had parked the car.

Around eight o'clock I drove into Lincoln Beach. At that hour in the morning the streets were almost deserted. I could tell at a glance this town was a millionaire's playground. The shops, buildings, the flowers growing along the sidewalks and the neatness all pointed to money. I found an hotel in one of the side streets.

Two bell-hops and the head porter who looked like an Admiral of the Fleet helped me out of the car and carried the black pig-skin case and two other cases into the reception lobby. They gave me a room big enough to garage three four-ton trucks, and a bathroom that was so luxurious I was scared to use it.

I lay on the bed and slept for three hours. After that all-night run I was dead beat. Around eleven-thirty I took the black pig-skin suitcase down to the car. I wasn't going to be parted from that for a moment. I locked it in the boot, then drove to Roosevelt Boulevard, the main shopping centre.

There were a lot of cars drifting up and down the broad street and quite a crowd of people on the sidewalks. Most of them were in beach dress; some of the girls were practically naked, but no one paid them any attention. I parked behind a big Packard and went into a drug store.

There was one thing I had to find out. I shut myself in a phone booth and dialled Lincoln Beach 4444. I listened to the burr-burr-burr of the ringing tone, and my heart skipped a beat when a girl's voice said, "Good morning. This is the Lincoln Beach Casino at your service."

"Connect me with Nick Reisner," I said, and my voice croaked.

"What was that again, please?"

"I said connect me with Nick Reisner."

"Mr. Reisner is no longer with us. Who is that calling?"

I ran a dry tongue over dryer lips.

"I'm a friend of his. I've just hit town. Where can I find him?"

"I'm sorry." She sounded embarrassed. "Mr. Reisner died."

"He did?" I tried to make my voice surprised. "I didn't know. When was that?"

"July 30th."

The day after he had come to the cabin and had taken Della and me away. I was getting the shakes again.

"What happened to him?"

"Will you hold it a moment, please?"

"Hey! Don't go off the line . . ."

There was a long pause. Sweat began to run down my face. Then there was a click, and a voice asked, "Who is calling?" A voice that came from a fat throat: Ricca's voice. I didn't say anything. I held the receiver against my ear, listening to his heavy breathing, aware of a cold chill creeping up my spine.

"Who is that?" he repeated. "Is it you, Johnny?"

I still said nothing. I wanted to put down the receiver, but that heavy breathing and that fat, oily voice hypnotized me.

Then suddenly another voice chipped in: a harsh, shouting voice.

"This is Police Captain Hame talking. Trace this call, miss!"

I hung up then and walked rapidly out of the store to my car. I had learned little, and I had risked much. It had been a bad move to have let them know I was in town.

I sat in the car, my hat pulled down over my eyes, my fingers on the gun butt, and waited. I didn't have to wait long. Their organization was pretty efficient. I was expecting cops, but it wasn't a police car I saw shooting along the boulevard. It was a big, black Cadillac. It pulled up outside the drug store, within fifty feet of me.

Two short, square-shouldered men got out, crossed the sidewalk and entered the drug store. The last two men I expected to see again on this earth: Pepi and Benno.

VII

I lit a cigarette with an unsteady hand. Where had these two sprung from? The obvious explanation was they had teamed up with Ricca. I remembered then that Waller, the Negro, had said they would keep after me until they had cornered me. I had completely forgotten them, but apparently they hadn't forgotten me.

I remained in the car, waiting. After a minute or so they came out of the drug store and paused on the sidewalk to look to right and left. Then they got into the Cadillac and drove away.

It seemed I was now up against stiff opposition. I had been ready to tackle Ricca on his own, but I wasn't too sure of my chances when it came to a combination of Ricca, Pepi and Benno. Those two lengthened the odds against me.

But no matter what happened to me, they were not going to get their hooks into that money. Now they knew I was in town I would be crazy to carry all that money around with me. I had to find a safe place to stash it.

I drove back to my hotel. The head porter sprang forward to open the car door.

"I'm not getting out," I said. "Is there a safe deposit around here?"

"First on your left, sir," he told me. "You can't miss it. The best there is."

He was right about not missing it. It was about twenty storeys high and occupied half the block. There were five uniformed guards on the sidewalk, armed to the teeth, and tough enough to scare any Chi hood out of his skin.

I pulled up and got out of the car.

One of the guards came over. The others watched me.

"I want to leave a suitcase," I said. "What do I do?"

"You have it with you, sir?"

I unlocked the boot and hauled out the case. He made to take it, but I waved him back.

"I'm not as weak as I look. Just tell me where to go."

"If you'll follow me, sir."

He took me into a vast reception lobby, surrounded by a wall of steel bars as thick as my wrist. On a low balcony surrounding the lobby, guards patrolled, automatic rifles cradled in their arms. There'd be no smash-and-grab raid in this place.

He led me to a pale young man who could have been a foreign prince, but obviously wasn't, as he stood up and bowed.

"Mr. Evesham will look after you, sir," the guard said, and went away.

"I want to deposit this suitcase," I said. "Can you fix it?"

Mr. Evesham, with another bow, said he would be happy to be of service.

"Do you wish to rent one of our strong rooms?"

I said I did.

"Will you come with me?"

We took the elevator to the fifth floor, walked along a corridor to a steel-mesh gate. A guard opened it and saluted.

"Let me have the key to room 46," Evesham said. He sounded like a prince when he was giving orders.

The guard produced a key, and a door was unlocked and opened. We entered a small room, steel lined, about the size of a prison cell, and furnished with two easy chairs, a table and a fitted grey carpet. Facing us was a wall safe.

"Good enough to sleep in," I said.

"Some of our clients like to consult their papers without taking them away," Evesham explained. "We try to make them as comfortable as possible." He turned to the safe. "The letters of the combination make up the word 'economic'. Will you remember that?"

I said I would remember it.

"Perhaps you would care to open the safe yourself? All you have to do . . ."

"Yeah, I know," I said. "I've handled a job like this before."

I spun the knob, pausing at each letter. When I had spelt out the complete word, there was a click and the door swung open.

"When you shut the door, the combination is automatically scrambled," Evesham went on. "And the safe is self locking."

"That's fine," I said.

"The key to this vault is kept with the guard. Our clients are not allowed to take keys off the premises. Have you any special instructions for us? Do you wish anyone to come here, or only yourself?"

"No one is to touch the safe unless I'm with them," I said. "Will your guard know me?"

He allowed himself a princely smile.

"When you opened the safe your photograph was automatically taken. It will be lodged in the guard-house and checked when you apply for the key."

"You certainly have thought this thing out."

"Perhaps you will come downstairs now and complete the formalities, sir?"

"I'd like to get the hang of the safe and check through the contents of my bag before I leave," I said. "Would it be all right if I joined you in a few minutes?"

"Certainly. You know where to find me. The guard will direct you to the elevator."

When he had gone I opened the suitcase and took from it ten one-hundred-dollar bills. That amount would hold me for a few days. As I tucked the roll into my hip pocket I felt the butt of the ·22. I had the ·38 in my coat pocket, and I didn't figure I'd need two guns, so I dropped the ·22 into the suitcase. Then I put the case into the safe and shut the door.

Twenty minutes later I was on my way to 3945, Apartment 4, Franklin Boulevard.

I hummed under my breath as I drove. For the first time since the suitcase had come into my possession I was relaxed and at ease. The money was safe. Neither Ricca nor Benno nor Pepi could possibly get their hands on it.

A mile or so along Franklin Boulevard I spotted the house: a big place set in its own grounds: a little run to seed, unpretentious and far from gaudy. I kept straight on.

At the next intersection I saw a filling-station. I swung the car into the circular drive-in and pulled up.

An attendant came over.

"Okay for me to leave this heap for a while?"

"As long as you like."

I walked back along the boulevard and paused at the double gates of 3945. There was a short drive leading directly to the house. No one appeared to be watching at the windows or hiding in the shrubbery. I knew I was taking a risk coming here, but if I could get into the apartment I was hoping I'd find something that would jog my memory to life again. There might be letters, a photograph or even a diary. I figured it was worth the risk.

I walked up the steps into the lobby. The stairs faced me. On the fourth floor I found Apartment 4.

I pulled out the ·38 and held it down by my side, then sank my thumb into the bell-push.

There was a long silence. I stood waiting, not expecting anyone to answer the door, but ready if they did. I rang again. I could hear the bell. Then I heard something else that brought me to a stiff, alert attention. I heard the sound of footsteps on the other side of the door.

I waited, the gun ready. The door opened.

A girl stood in the doorway: a girl with thick, short hair like burnished copper, whose big, startled eyes were as blue as the sky on a hot summer's day.

It was Ginny!

I stood there, transfixed, staring at her. The sight of her ripped away the blanket of fog that had hung over my mind. It was like a blind man suddenly being able to see.

"Oh, Johnny," she cried. "You've come back!"

Then everything seemed to happen at once. Terror jumped into her eyes. Her mouth opened to scream. I heard the swish of a descending cosh, and then a dazzling white light exploded inside my head. I groped wildly for her as I began to fall, but she was no longer there. I went on falling, down and down, out of the present into the past.

PART THREE

FLASH-BACK

I

A WOMAN screamed, but it wasn't Ginny.

I lifted a hand that felt as heavy as lead and groped into space, but found nothing. I tried to sit up, but the effort was too much for me.

The woman suddenly stopped screaming. The only sound I now heard was my own breathing. Each breath came very lightly as if it were going to be the last.

"Johnny!"

I knew that voice: a voice out of the past; Della's voice.

My mind groped to remember. I felt again the crushing punch the Kid had given me. I saw Della again, her black eyes twin explosions as she screamed: "Get up and fight, you quitter!"

Somehow I got my eyes open. The darkness bothered me. There should have been blazing lights coming down on me from the stadium batteries. I found myself thinking the Kid must have hit me with a hammer; that maybe he had blinded me. I struggled up in a sitting position.

"Johnny! Say something! Are you badly hurt?"

Della was bending over me. Beyond her I could see the out-lines of trees against the night sky. Then I remembered the car coming at us like a bat out of hell, heard again the grinding, crunching noise as it side-swiped us, and felt again the sensation of flying through space.

"I'm all right," I said. "Let me alone." I put my hand to my face. It felt wet and sticky. "What happened?"

"You must get up and help me," she said, her voice urgent. "I think he's dead."

"Dead? Who?"

"Paul! Come on, Johnny, don't just sit there. Help me!"

"Okay, okay; give me a minute."

My head began to pound and ache as I struggled to my knees. I waited a moment or so, then got to my feet. If she hadn't steadied me I would have fallen flat on my face.

"Pull yourself together!" she exclaimed, and the hard, impatient note in her voice startled me. "He's lying over there. He doesn't seem to be breathing."

I staggered over the sandy ground. Each step I took sent a stab of pain through my head, but I kept on until I reached him. He was lying on his side by the smashed Bentley, his head resting on his arm, one leg drawn up almost to his chin.

I knelt by his side. It was too dark to see much of him, but when I turned him and he flopped over on his back, his head remained on his arm. That told me his neck was broken. I touched his hand, felt his pulse, but it was a waste of time.

She dropped down on her knees beside me, her hand on my arm. I could feel her trembling.

"He's dead," I told her.

She didn't say anything, but her fingers closed on my arm, her nails digging into my flesh.

"Stay here," I said, getting to my feet. "I'll see if I can get someone to help us."

"Are you sure he's dead?" Her voice sounded hard and cold.

"He's dead all right. His neck's broken."

She stood up and moved away from me and leaned against a twisted palmetto tree. Her sleek black hair was dishevelled; there was a six-inch rip in her skirt, and one stocking was down to her ankle. The moonlight, coming through the tangle of overhead branches, fell on her face. There was a smear of blood down the side of her nose. Her eyes seemed to have sunk deep into her head, and she was staring sightlessly at me as if her mind were furiously preoccupied with some urgent decision.

"The other car's across the road, Johnny," she said. "See what's happened to the driver."

"And Pepi's car?"

"No sign of it. Maybe they thought we were killed. But go and find out what's happened to the other car."

Moving slowly, still dazed, I made my way on to the highway. Away from the palmetto thicket the moonlight lit up the white road brilliantly, but even in that light it took me several minutes before I found the car. It had crashed into the thicket on the other side of the road, and lay on its side: a big Packard, now fit only for the scrap-heap.

I peered through the shattered window. The driver still sat behind the wheel: a young fellow with a set, fixed grin on his face and horror in his wide, staring eyes. The steering-column had been driven into his body like a grotesque spear: from his neck to his waist he was pulp.

I stepped back. There was no one else in the car, and there was nothing I could do for him. I crossed the road again and went back to the thicket where she was waiting.

"Well?" she asked, her eyes searching my face.

"He's dead."

"Anyone else in the car?"

"No."

"You're sure he's dead?"

"Yes."

She gave a funny little strangled gulp.

"What a marvellously lucky break!"

I stared at her. It suddenly occurred to me that the smash, the death of her husband and the death of the other driver were utterly remote to her. She wasn't thinking of them at all. There was something else occupying her mind: something so urgent and important to her that even the shock of being thrown out of a car at over sixty miles an hour had made no impression on her.

"What's the matter with you?" I demanded.

"I want my handbag, Johnny."

"To hell with your handbag! Are you all right?"

"Yes." She moved unsteadily towards the smashed Bentley. "Help me find my handbag."

"There are more important things to do than look for your bag," I said sharply. "I've got to fetch the police."

"The police?" She paused, turned and stared at me. "What good will they do?"

"We've got to get them here," I said impatiently. "What's the matter with you?" My head was pounding, my nerves were flayed and I was shouting at her. "We've got two bodies on our hands! We've got to report this. . . ."

"I must have my bag, Johnny," she said with an obstinacy that infuriated me. "There's something very valuable in it. I must find it before we worry about the police."

"All right! All right! We'll find it!" I said, and went over to the Bentley and wrenched open the door.

"Let me look," she said, pushing me aside, and began groping about on the floor of the car.

I went around to the off-side, but the door was jammed and wouldn't open.

"I can't see a thing!" she exclaimed. "Haven't you a match?"

I struck a match and held the flame through the shattered

window. She found the bag wedged between the brake and clutch pedals.

"Okay, now you have it, you'd better sit down and take it easy," I said, stepping away from the car. "I'll hunt up a phone."

She came around the car to where I was standing.

"No, Johnny. We won't bother about the police. No one must know he's dead."

"They'll find him sooner or later. They'll identify the car ..." I stopped and stared at her. "What is all this? Why shouldn't they know he's dead?"

"I can't explain now; later, Johnny. Don't look so worried. It's all right. I'll tell you later."

"You're suffering from shock," I said sharply. "Sit down. I'm going for the police."

She dipped her hand into the bag and brought out a ·38 automatic.

"You'll stay where you are," she said softly, and pointed the gun at me.

II

The headlights of an approaching car lit up the sky as it climbed the long, sloping hill from Pelotta. A moment or so later the car swept into sight: headlamps blazing. It was going fast, and roared past us with a snarl and a rush of wind.

Neither she nor I moved. The moonlight fell directly on the glittering barrel of the automatic: the gun looked menacing and large in her hand.

"Don't do anything stupid," she said, and her voice was as hard and as cold as a chunk of ice.

"Have you gone crazy?" I said, not moving. "Put it down!"

"I believe this is the most important moment in my life," she said. "You and I are the only two who know Paul is dead. You don't realize yet how essential it is that no one else should know. Now listen, Johnny, you can either come in with me or I'm going to kill you. There's no other way I can be certain you'll keep your mouth shut."

I thought she had taken leave of her senses, but that didn't alter the fact that she meant what she was saying. I felt a little prickle run up my spine.

"There isn't time to tell you what it's all about," she went on. "But if you come in with me you'll make money: big money, Johnny. What's it to be?"

"What do you want me to do?" I said, and my voice was

husky as yours would have been if you had seen those glittering eyes and the hard, ruthless line of her mouth.

"Take his clothes off and put yours on him," she said. "They've got to think it was you who died in the car."

"Me? They know me in Pelotta. They'll identify me."

"No, they won't. You're going to put him back in the car and set fire to it."

"I can't do that! Now wait . . ."

"You'll do it or I'll have to get rid of you, Johnny. There's no other alternative."

The bang I had taken on my head when I was thrown out of the car made clear thinking impossible. If I hadn't been so punch-drunk I might have tried to get the gun from her. As it was, I knew I hadn't a chance to reach her before she fired, and she would fire, the look in her eyes told me that.

"Get going," she said softly. "We've wasted enough time already."

"But tell me why!"

"Later. Are you going to change clothes with him?" There was a fixed, awful little smile on her lips now, and her knuckle showed white as she took in the slack of the trigger. I was one heart-beat away from being shot. I knew it, and she could see I knew it.

"Yes."

She relaxed, and the smile went away.

"Hurry, Johnny."

With cold sweat on my face I walked over to where he was lying and began to strip him. Apart from his broken neck he wasn't hurt and hadn't bled. I changed into his clothes while she watched me, the gun covering me. Then I got my clothes on him. It was a gruesome job, but I did it. But when I came to put my shoes on his feet, I gave up.

"I can't do it."

"Throw them in the car," she said, and her voice was as unsteady as mine. "It's all right. They'll think they came off in the crash. Get him in and put him behind the steering-wheel."

I dragged him over to the car. He was no light weight, and it was all I could do to get him into the car. I propped him up against the driver's door. He fell forward across the wheel.

"Loosen the carburettor pipe," she said, "then tie your handkerchief over the leak and touch it off with a match."

"They could send us to jail for this," I said, breathing heavily.

"Get on with it! The tool case is clipped inside the hood. You want a spanner . . . hurry!"

I loosened the carburettor pipe, burning my hand against the cylinder head as I did so. I was working in a trance. My head kept expanding and contracting, and my legs felt as if they were made of rubber. I did exactly what she told me to do. I tied one end of my handkerchief around the leaking pipe.

"Now set fire to it."

I struck a match. A moment later a long tongue of flame shot out of the car's engine, and spread in a hot, glaring mass to the coachwork.

I jumped back just in time.

She came running towards me.

"Come on!" she said. "Before anyone comes."

I went with her because there was nothing else to do.

We moved fast, and in silence, until the glare of the burning car died away in the distance, and we came out on to the soft white sand of the beach.

"Wait, Johnny," she said, and stopped.

I turned to look at her. She still held the gun, but it was no longer pointing at me.

"There's not much time, but I have to talk to you," she said. "I wish I knew more about you. It's fantastic we should meet like this, and be in this position together. Do you realize that from now on you and I have got to trust each other, work with each other, and stay with each other as if we had known each other for years? What sort of nerve have you got? Just how ambitious are you? I wish I knew what kind of man you are."

"And do you realize they could send us to jail for what we've done?" I said. "Have you gone crazy . . .?"

"Don't worry about that. They won't find out. Do you want to get your hands on some money? Real money, Johnny? If you have the right kind of nerve we can help ourselves to half a million dollars: half for you and half for me."

I stiffened. A quarter of a million dollars! That was the kind of money I had always dreamed of making.

"You're lying," I said.

"Sit down. We haven't much time, but enough for me to explain the set-up to you. Go on, Johnny, sit down and listen."

I sat down. She sat a few yards from me, the gun in her lap, the moonlight on her face, and in spite of her dishevelled hair and the streak of blood down the side of her nose, she still looked lovely.

Speaking rapidly, she told me the dead man was Paul Wertham, a big-time gambler, the owner of three casinos.

"He's the head of an organization worth millions," she said. "The moment it's known he's dead, the vultures will move in and grab. He has a manager for each casino. They'd grab everything and leave me to whistle for my share. But so long as they think he's alive, it can be handled. That's the set-up. I can't handle it on my own. I can handle it with your help. The take is half a million, and you'll get half of it: two hundred and fifty thousand dollars. It's easy. All you want is nerve, and if you do what I tell you, we can't go wrong."

That was my cue to say no: when I should have walked away and taken the chance of getting a slug in the back; when I should have remembered what Tom Roche had said about big and sudden money leading to trouble.

But I didn't say no. I suddenly realized she was deadly serious. She actually meant half a million, and I started to think what that much money could buy.

"How can you keep his death quiet?" I asked. "How long do you think it'll be before they find out?"

Then she smiled and relaxed because she knew I was on the hook and all she had to do was to hit the line to sink the barb in too deep for me to jump off.

"We have only to keep it quiet for three or four days: not longer; and the money's ours. It's as easy as that."

"Go on; keep talking."

"Each casino has a large cash reserve in case there's a run on the bank. The casino at Lincoln Beach caters for millionaires. The reserve there is half a million in cash. Each casino is in charge of a manager. Jack Ricca runs the Los Angeles place. Nick Reisner takes care of Lincoln Beach, and Pete Levinsky, the Paris end." She was leaning forward, speaking fast and softly, and I didn't miss a word of what she was saying. "Paul was going to Paris when he was tipped that Reisner was dipping into the reserve to cover his own gambling losses. He had to act fast. The Paris trip was important so he arranged for Ricca to go to Lincoln Beach. He phoned Reisner and told him Ricca was on his way and was to have access to the books. But at the last moment Ricca went on a drinking jag. Every so often he gets the urge and hides himself away with a crate of whisky, and that's all anyone knows about him until he reappears again. Paul had to cancel his Paris trip. There was no time to tell Reisner he was coming in Ricca's place. He and I were on our way when we stopped at Pelotta to watch the fights." She reached out and put her hand on my knee. "*Reisner doesn't know Paul was coming in place of Ricca,*

87

and Reisner has never seen Ricca. You're going to be Ricca for just as long as it takes us to collect that reserve. That's the set-up. How do you like it?"

I sat looking at her.

"And my cut will be a quarter of a million?"

"Yes, Johnny, word of honour. There can be no blowback to this. I've as much right to it as Reisner has. I have more right to it. Every nickel of it belongs to Paul. If he had made a will he would have left it to me."

"Can we get away with it?"

"Yes. It just needs nerve."

This was the chance I had been waiting for. I knew it meant trouble, but money that big had to mean trouble. Well, the opportunity was there: right in my lap. I wasn't going to pass it up.

"Count me in," I said.

III

We had been walking maybe for ten minutes when we saw a light shining in the darkness. Another twenty yards brought us to a small wooden cabin, facing the sea.

"Are you all set, Johnny?" she asked, stopping. "You know what to do. You're suffering from concussion. Leave all the talking to me."

"I know what to do."

I flopped down on the sand and stretched out while she went on towards the cabin. While I waited I tried to keep my mind blank, but it couldn't be done. I kept thinking of the trouble that was piling up for me, but I wasn't going to side-step it. Come hail, come sunshine, I was going to have that money.

I heard voices. I heard her say, "He just passed out. I think it's concussion." The anxious, frightened note in her voice even fooled me.

A man said, "I'll get him in, miss. Just you take it easy."

Hands turned me over on my back. I let out a groan to tell him how bad I was, and looked through my eyelashes as he bent over me. I couldn't see much of him in the half darkness. He seemed short and powerfully built, and that was about all I could see.

He was powerful all right, for he got me to my feet as if I weighed a few pounds. I made an effort to keep upright, then slumped heavily on him.

"Take it easy," he said. "It ain't far. Lean on me as hard as you like."

I felt Della take my arm, and supported between the two of them I made a slow, staggering journey across the sand to the cabin.

They got me on to a bed. I lay still, my eyes closed. I heard him say, "He sure is knocked about. What do you want me to do, miss? Get a doctor?"

"How far is it to the nearest telephone?" she asked.

"About half a mile down the road."

He had moved away from me now, and I took a peep at him. He was elderly, with a tanned, lined face and stubbly white hair. I looked from him to her. She had dropped into a chair. Her face was tight and hard, and as white as a bone. She must have been tough to have withstood the shock of the crash and her husband's death and still be able to plan and act as she had done. But now she looked ready to flop, and the old guy seemed to think so too. He went hastily to a cupboard and brought out a bottle of whisky. He poured her a stiff drink, and she put it down as if it were water.

"Our car was stolen," she said huskily. "We were held up. My friend was hit on the head. It's important we should get to Lincoln Beach at once. I wonder if you would telephone to our friends and ask them to come and pick us up?"

"Why, sure. I'll do it right away. The name's Jud Harkness. I'll be glad to do anything I can for you."

"I can't say how grateful I am, Mr. Harkness," she said, and smiled at him. "We were on our way to Lincoln Beach when this hold-up happened. If you could phone . . ."

"Give me the number, miss, and I'll do it. Want me to call the cops?"

"I want to get him home first. I'll report the hold-up from Lincoln Beach. The number is Lincoln Beach 4444. Can you remember that?"

"Sure, that's an easy one."

"Ask for Nick Reisner. Tell him Ricca has met with an accident and for him to come out here as soon as he can. Will you do that?"

Harkness repeated the message.

"I can't thank you enough."

When he had left the cabin I sat up.

"What's the idea of the hold-up? That'll bring in the police."

She looked at me, a far-away expression in her eyes, as if she were thinking of other things besides what I was saying.

"The car might be traced to Paul. I don't think there's much chance of it because the plates are phoneys, but they might trace it. If they do, the car has to be stolen. You can see that, can't you?"

She was right, of course, but I didn't like it. Sooner or later the story would get back to Pelotta, and Tom and Alice Roche would hear I had not only clubbed the driver, but had stolen the car. Even if they had to think I was dead, I didn't like the idea of them thinking I'd turned thug.

"Listen, Johnny," she said, coming to sit on the bed by my side, "in a little while Reisner will be here. You've got to watch your step. He's no fool. Don't let him question you. I'll do the talking. So far as he's concerned you're suffering from concussion, and you're not fit to answer questions."

I nodded.

"The one thing he's going to find suspicious is why I'm with you," she went on. "He'll wonder why Paul let me come with you from Los Angeles. He'll probably phone the casino and try and contact Paul. All they'll be able to tell him is Paul's on his way to Paris, and Ricca on his way to Lincoln Beach, and that's what we want him to know. If Reisner gets too suspicious he may try to contact Levinsky in Paris. But Levinsky can't tell him anything until the boat Paul was supposed to be on docks. That gives us four days to swing the job, Johnny."

"You said it would be easy."

"It is easy. Don't let Reisner jump anything on you. Leave the talking to me."

She got up to look out of the window to see if there was any sign of Harkness. I looked at her slim, square-shouldered back, and a stab of desire went through me. There was something about her as she stood at the window that would have brought out the primitive in any man. Uneasily I shifted my eyes away from her and felt in my pockets for a cigarette. In the hip pocket I found a gold cigarette-case. It was then I remembered I was wearing Wertham's clothes, and that gave me the creeps. I lit a cigarette and pushed the case into my hip pocket again.

She came back to the bed.

"Better not smoke, Johnny," she said. "You're supposed to be pretty bad." She leaned forward and took the cigarette and put it between her lips. I looked up at her, my mouth going dry. I had to fight against the urge to grab her and pull her down beside me.

She must have realized the way I was feeling, for she stepped away from me, her face hardening.

"Get your mind on what I'm going to tell you," she said. "You've got to know something about Paul, how he lived, the things he liked. It's so easy to be tripped up on the small things."

I got a grip on myself. It wasn't easy, but I did it.

"Go ahead," I said huskily.

She told me where Wertham lived in Los Angeles, his telephone number, the kind of car he drove and a lot of details about his personal life. In a very short time she had given me a heap of facts that only a man who had lived with Wertham and worked with him could have known.

She went on to tell me about the casino, what it looked like, the kind of tables used, the number of croupiers employed, the amount of profit made in an evening, how much the various members of the staff were paid, how many crooked tables there were and how they operated. Then she switched to Jack Ricca, and gave me his background. He had joined Wertham's organization about a year ago. No one knew much about him. It was rumoured he used to run a night-club in New York, but he had neither admitted nor denied it. He was a man who said little about himself.

"Every so often he goes on a drinking jag," Della concluded, "and it's my bet he's in some sanatorium, tapering off."

"You mean Wertham employed a drunk like that?"

"He's sober ten months of the year. Paul said he has one of the sharpest brains in the business. Since Ricca took over the casino they've trebled the take."

"Well, you've told me about Wertham and Ricca," I said, looking at her, "how about telling me something about yourself?"

"Are you getting interested in me, Johnny?" she asked.

That was the wrong word, but I didn't tell her. Without any warning, and apparently because I had seen her at a different angle, she had suddenly touched off my blood: I was on fire for her.

"Call it that if you like," I said. "If we're going to work together, shouldn't I know something about you?"

She gave me a jeering little smile that told me I wasn't fooling her for a moment.

"I met Paul two years ago when I was trying to break into the movies. I was down to my last dollar when he showed up. As a man he meant nothing to me. He was selfish, arrogant and cruel, but he had money and he threw it around. He fell for me, and I played hard to get. He spent hundreds on me, took me everywhere, but I was angling for marriage. Finally he got so worked up he said he would marry me." Her full, scarlet lips parted in a bitter smile. "He had me for a sucker. The ceremony was phoney. He had a wife already, but I only found that out after eighteen months of living with him. He promised to divorce her, and he did. The divorce comes through next month, but it's a little late. All his personal money goes to his wife. I get nothing. I've lived pretty well these past two years, and I'm not going back to the old racket again. That's why I'm going ahead with this set-up, Johnny, and no one's going to stop me."

She was still talking when we heard the door latch click up. I only just had time to flop back on the bed and close my eyes before Jud Harkness came in.

"Did you get through?" Della asked him.

"Yeah, and he's coming right away," Harkness said.

There was a note in his voice I didn't like, and I peered at him from between my eyelashes. He was looking towards me.

"Hasn't he come around yet?" he asked.

"I think he's sleeping," Della said. "He seems to be breathing more evenly."

There was a long, uneasy silence, then Harkness said, "The party reckoned it'd take him an hour to get here. If it's all the same to you I'll turn in. I've got to make an early start in the morning."

"Why, of course. We won't disturb you. I'm very grateful for what you've done."

"That's okay. Sure there's nothing you want?"

"I have everything." She stood up. "Don't bother to get up when Mr. Reisner comes." She paused, then went on, "I'd like you to accept . . ."

"It ain't necessary." His voice sharpened.

"Oh, but you must." I watched her open her bag. She took out a hundred-dollar bill and put it on the table. "Can I rely on you to say nothing about this hold-up, Mr. Harkness? If anyone should ask you . . . It's a personal matter."

He hesitated, then picked up the bill.

"Well, thanks. I don't talk about what doesn't concern me."

He went into the far room and closed the door.

I lifted my head.

Della pointed to the uncurtained window.

"I think he was watching us," she whispered.

I thought so, too.

IV

From the little Della had told me about Nick Reisner, I had imagined him to be one of those brutal-looking characters you see after dark in Chicago's Loop who pack a gun and a set of brass knuckles and loll up against a wall, waiting for trouble.

But he wasn't like that at all.

He was tall and thin and stiffly upright. Although only around thirty-eight, his hair was chalk white and thick, taken straight back off a forehead any professor would have been proud to own. His nose was hooked and his nostrils flared back, giving him the look of a hawk. He got his menace from his thin, sadistic mouth and the cold, remote expression in his deep-set eyes.

He came into the cabin and paused just inside the doorway to stare at Della.

"Hello, Nick," she said, and smiled. "Explanations can wait. Let's get out of here."

The corners of his mouth lifted in a stiff little smile. His eyes went to me.

"Ricca?"

His voice was soft, unexpectedly effeminate, and I noticed the tuxedo he wore was exaggeratedly tailored, with wide lapels and a sharply cut waist, hinting at foppishness that his mouth and eyes contradicted.

"Yeah," I said, and got slowly off the bed.

"Look a little roughed up. Who did it?" he asked.

"Let's get out of here," I said.

"Sure."

He stood aside.

"Help him, Nick," Della said. "He's got concussion. We were held up, and the Bentley was stolen."

"Too bad," Reisner said, without moving. "My car's just outside. I came on my own."

I went past him out of the cabin, taking my time, knowing he was watching me, knowing, too, how hostile he was. Della followed, caught up with me and took my arm. The car was parked on the dirt track about twenty yards from the cabin: an Oldsmobile, as big as a battleship.

Della and I got in at the back. Reisner strolled after us and slid under the steering-wheel.

"I didn't expect you, Mrs. Wertham," he said as he trod on the starter. "Quite a surprise."

"Paul thought I'd cramp his style in Paris," she said, and laughed. "Besides, he wanted me along with Johnny."

"Johnny?" Reisner said, driving the car slowly up the dirt track towards the highway.

"I call him Johnny. I prefer it to Jack. Any objection?"

"Paul didn't say you were coming," Reisner said, ignoring the sharp note in her voice.

"He made up his mind at the last moment. Besides, we thought it would be a nice surprise for you."

"Yeah." He didn't seem to think much of that remark. "So you were held up? What happened?"

"I guess we asked for it. We gave a fellow a ride. When we reached a lonely stretch of road he hit Johnny over the head, made me stop, tossed us out and went off with the car."

"Told the cops yet?"

"No. I wanted to get Johnny to Lincoln Beach first."

"Like me to handle it? Hame will keep it out of the newspapers."

"I wish you would."

"What was this fella like to look at?"

"He was big, built on Johnny's lines. He looked as if he had been in a fight. He wore a white tropical suit. I didn't notice anything special about him."

"Why did you give him a ride?"

"He seemed in a hurry to get out of town. It wasn't as if he looked a tough. He said he was heading for Miami and his car had broken down, and could we take him as far as Lincoln Beach."

"What town?"

"Pelotta."

"Okay, I'll fix it. Paul won't like losing the Bentley."

"He certainly won't."

Reisner was driving fast now, and for some minutes none of us spoke, then he said, "You don't talk much, Ricca. Kind of a quiet character, huh?"

"You wouldn't talk either if you'd had a lump of iron bounced on your skull," I said.

"Yeah, I guess that's right. You look as if you'd been in a fight yourself."

"You don't think Johnny let this thug hit him and get away

94

with it, do you?" Della put in. "Although he was practically out on his feet, he made a fight of it."

"A strong as well as a silent character," Reisner said, and the sneer in his voice was unmistakable. "Not like you, Mrs. Wertham, to stand on the sidelines and cheer."

"What should I have done – joined in the brawl?" she said sarcastically.

"I was under the impression you always carried a gun. Not much use carrying it if you don't use it when you have to."

I saw her clench her fists. He had scored a point there.

"I wasn't carrying a gun."

"You weren't? About the first time, isn't it?" He glanced at her in the driving mirror. "Well, well, it always rains when you haven't an umbrella."

I was getting the idea he wasn't talking just to hear the sound of his own voice. He was suspicious, and although there was a bantering, don't-give-a-damn-if-you-answer-or-not tone in his voice, he was after information.

I touched Della's knee, and when she looked at me I cautiously pointed to her handbag, then to myself. She got it the first time. Keeping the bag below the level of the driving seat so Reisner couldn't see what was going on, she took out the gun and passed it to me. I slid it in my pocket. It wouldn't do to let him spot the outline of the gun in her bag as we got out of the car. Our story had to stick.

"How come you stopped at Pelotta?" Reisner asked suddenly.

Della and I exchanged glances. I didn't need any prompting. Now was the time to show him he couldn't go on asking any questions that came into his head.

"Look," I said curtly, "do you mind if we cut out the small talk? I've a head on me like a ten-day hangover. I'd just as soon catch up some sleep as answer your questions."

There was a moment's silence. Then he said, "Sure. Think nothing of it. I've always been a little gabby."

He increased speed, and the big car raced along the broad highway, skirted on one side by palmetto thickets and on the other side by the ocean. After a while we began to climb, and when we got to the top of a steep hill I could see in the distance the lights of a fair-sized town.

"Lincoln Beach," Della said.

I sat forward to stare out of the window. The town was laid out in a semicircle, facing the sea and sheltered by rising ground. We were moving too fast to see much of it, but what I could see told me it was quite a different proposition from any of the other coast towns I'd seen up to now. Even at two o'clock in the morning it was brilliantly floodlit. Blue, amber and red lights outlined the long promenade. Many of the white buildings were plastered with neon lights. From the hill road the town looked like something out of fairyland.

"Pretty nice," I said.

"That's the casino: the flood-lit building at the far end of the bay," she said, pointing. "Looks good, Nick."

"So would I if someone spent a million bucks on me," Reisner said indifferently.

It took us twenty minutes by the dashboard clock to negotiate the twisting hill road, to drive through the town and reach the casino.

The fifteen-foot high gates were guarded by two men in black uniforms, not unlike those Hitler's storm-troopers used to wear. They saluted, their faces expressionless as we drove through the gateway.

The mile-long, palm-lined drive was flood-lit with green lamps that created the extraordinary illusion of driving under water.

"I had these lamps fixed a couple of months ago," Reisner said. "There's scarcely a square foot of the place now that isn't lighted. Funny how the mugs go for lights. Business has been pretty good since I put this lot in."

His voice was soft and remote, as if he were talking to himself. He didn't seem to expect Della or me to make any comments, and when Della began to say how well it all looked, he interrupted her as if her remarks were of no interest to him to point out a big bed of giant dahlias that were flood-lit by daylight lamps.

"Every flower has its special lighting," he said. "Paul was crabbing about the cost, but it's worth it. We get mugs from miles around coming to gawp at the flowers: then, of course, they visit the bar and the restaurants and spend their dough."

The drive suddenly opened on to a vast stretch of lawn, and facing us was the brilliantly lit casino. It was the most impressive and ornate building I have ever seen, like something out of the *Arabian Nights*: a huge, white building of Moorish architecture, its six domed towers and bulbous minarets piercing the night sky.

Amber, white, green and red lights, controlled by automatic time switches, played alternately on the front of the building.

"You have nothing like this in Los Angeles, have you, Ricca?" Reisner said. "We spent ten grand lighting this joint."

He continued to drive along the broad carriage-way, past the casino and on through the pleasure gardens, past the flood-lit swimming-pool where a number of men and women were still swimming or lounging in hammocks in spite of the late hour through another double gate, also guarded by two stiff-necked men in uniform, past a pitch-and-putt course to a colony of beach cabins built in a semi-circle a hundred yards or so from the ocean, each screened from the other by palms and tropical flowering shrubs.

He pulled up outside one of the cabins.

"Here we are. Everything's ready for you, Mrs. Wertham," he said, twisting around in the driver's seat to look at Della. "Your usual cabin. Where do you want me to put Ricca?"

"He can have the cabin next to mine: the one Paul has," she said, and got out of the car.

"Want me to get the doc down to look at him?" Reisner asked, not moving from behind the wheel.

"I'm okay," I said, joining Della. "Nothing that a good sleep won't put right."

"Suit yourself," he returned, making no attempt to conceal his indifference.

"Don't wait, Nick," Della said. "We'll have a talk in the morning. Thanks for picking us up."

Reisner smiled. His eyes went from Della to me, and back to Della again.

"Well, so long. Call up at the office around noon. We'll have a drink and a get-together."

The big car moved off. Della and I stood watching its bright twin rear lights until they had disappeared, then she drew in a deep breath.

"Well, that's Reisner," she said. "What do you think of him?"

"Tricky."

"Yes. Well, come in. I could do with a drink."

She led me into the cabin and switched on the lights. The place consisted of one large room that served as a sitting-room by day and a bedroom by night, a bathroom and a kitchenette. No expense had been spared to make it luxurious and comfortable. It was unbelievably lavish with its press-button gadgets that operated the windows, the curtains and let down the wall-bed and opened the built-in cupboards. Everything in the place seemed to be worked by pressing buttons.

"Like it?" she asked, flopping on the bed. "Paul had a flair for this kind of thing. There are thirty other cabins on the estate, each with its own special *décor*, but I like this one best. Get me a drink, Johnny. You'll find whisky in that cabinet over there."

"I'll say I like it," I said as I mixed a whisky and soda. "And the casino! He must have spent millions on it."

"He did." She leaned back on her elbows and looked fixedly at me. The white silk blouse pulled hard across her breasts, and her thick, dark hair fell away from her face and neck, showing the white column of her throat. "All this could be mine if it wasn't for Reisner."

"Would you know what to do with it if you had it?" I said, not paying much attention to what I was saying. The sight of her like that had got me going again.

She took the whisky.

"Wouldn't you, Johnny?"

"I don't know." I went over to a panel in the wall on which were a number of ivory buttons. I pressed one of them marked curtains, and watched the dark-green plastic curtains swing smoothly across the big double windows. "Can you imagine Reisner parting with half a million? I can't."

"He will if we handle him right." She looked down and noticed the rip in her skirt. From where I was standing I could see, through the tear, the white line of her flesh above the top of her stocking. "I must look a wreck," she went on, got to her feet and stared at herself in the mirror that concealed the door to the bathroom.

I came up behind her and we stared at our reflections in the mirror.

Apart from her dishevelled hair, the little cut on the side of her nose, and her ripped skirt, she still looked good – too good for my present mood.

Our eyes met in the mirror. She looked fixedly at me, her dark, glittering eyes suddenly tense.

"Better go to your cabin now, Johnny."

"No."

My hands were shaking, and I was suddenly short of breath.

"It'll happen sooner or later if we're going to work together," she said, "but I don't want it to happen now. Please go, Johnny. Not now. It's not safe."

My hands closed over her shoulders. I felt a shiver run through her. I turned her, pulling her against me.

"You've had your say ever since we met," I said. "You've dictated the terms and I've jumped through the hoop. It's going to be different now. I'm having the say and you're jumping through the hoop."

Her arms came up and slid around my neck.

"I like you when you talk like that, Johnny."

v

I had finished a regal breakfast served by a Sphinx-faced Filipino, and had wandered out on to the verandah to smoke a cigarette in the sunshine when I saw Della coming from her cabin towards me.

The sight of her in a sky-blue, off-the-shoulder linen dress, a big picture hat and a pair of sun-glasses the size of doughnuts started my heart thumping. I ran down the steps to meet her.

"Hi, Johnny," she said, smiling up at me.

"You look good enough to eat."

"You don't look so bad yourself." Her blue eyes approved the white slacks and the sweat-shirt the Filipino had laid out for me. "And they fit, too."

"They sure do. Where did they come from?"

"I fixed it. I've been busy fixing all kinds of things this morning. We'll go down to the tailor's shop some time and get you properly fitted out. You have to dress the part here."

"I can't believe this is happening to me. I expect to wake up and find myself in a truck heading for Miami."

She laughed.

"It's happening all right. Come and look at the place before we talk to Nick."

We spent an hour wandering around the vast estate. There wasn't a trick Wertham had missed. There were acres of pleasure gardens, an aquarium and sunken lily ponds. Not far from the casino was an arcade of shops where you could buy anything from a diamond necklace to an aspirin tablet. An artificial waterway surrounding the estate, screened by oak trees, hung with spanish moss, offered a fine hiding-place for you and your girl if you wanted to go for a tour in an electrically driven canoe. There was even a zoo at the back of the casino where peacocks, flamingoes and ibis strutted on the vast stretches of lawn.

"Come and look at the lion pit," Della said. "This is Reisner's pet idea. He's crazy about lions. You'd be surprised how many people come here just to gape at them."

We stood side by side, our arms touching, and looked down into the deep pit, guarded by steel railings where six full-grown

99

lions sprawled lazily in the sunshine.

"I can gape at them, too," I said. "There's something about a lion . . ."

"Reisner feeds them himself. He gives up all his spare time to them." She turned away. "Well, we'd better get on. There's still a lot to see."

Farther along the broad carriage-way we passed an open-air restaurant with its glass dance-floor. A fat, middle-aged Italian in a faultlessly cut morning-coat and a white gardenia in his buttonhole hurried towards us.

"Johnny, this is Louis who looks after our three restaurants," Della said as he bent to kiss her hand. "How are you, Louis? I want you to meet Johnny Ricca."

The Italian gave me a quick, appraising stare, bowed and shook hands.

"I have heard about you, Mr. Ricca," he said. "Is all well in Los Angeles?"

"Certainly is," I said, "but we've got nothing to touch this."

He looked gratified.

"And Mr. Wertham? He is well?" he asked, turning to Della.

"He's fine. On his way to Paris, the lucky man."

"Paris?" Louis lifted his shoulders. "Well, they have nothing as good as this in Paris either. You will be lunching in the restaurant?"

"I guess so."

"I will have something very special for you and Mr. Ricca."

"Fine," I said.

"See you later, Louis," Della said, and moved on.

"You mean we eat in that place for all our meals?" I asked as soon as we were out of hearing.

"Or the other two restaurants. Why not? They're all Paul's, and until they find out he's dead, they're mine, too."

"Yeah," I said, feeling as if I'd suddenly walked into a brick wall. "I hadn't thought of that."

She gave me a sharp glance and lifted her shoulders. We walked towards the casino in silence. There were a few men and women on the wide verandah. They seemed to be catching up with the sleep they had missed the previous night. Some of the women were good enough to go into an Art magazine. I found myself gaping until Della said tartly, "Must you act like a half-wit?"

I grinned.

"Sorry, but this place gets me."

Then I noticed a convertible Buick, drawn up outside the main entrance of the casino.

"Some car," I said.

It was a glittering black job, with scarlet leather upholstery, disc wheels and built-in head and fog lamps.

"Like it?" she said. "It's Paul's. He always used it when he stayed here. It's yours, now, Johnny."

"Mine?" My voice croaked.

"Why, yes." She smiled, but her eyes were as hard as stone. "Yours, until they find out he's dead. I don't suppose they'll let you keep it then."

I felt suddenly creepy. That was the second time she had cracked that one in ten minutes. I didn't like it.

"What's the idea, Della?"

"No idea." She walked over to the car, opened the offside door and got in.

I leaned on the door, looking down at her.

"Are you trying to tell me something?"

"Get in, Johnny. They're watching you."

I looked up. A few of the rich sofa-pets were hanging over the verandah rail staring at us. I got in under the steering-wheel.

"We'll go and look at the town," she said. "Drive to the gates and I'll tell you from there."

I switched on, trod on the starter and drove the car down the broad carriage-way.

"You still haven't answered my question."

She turned her head: her face was expressionless, and the dark-green sun-glasses masked her eyes.

"I'm not trying to tell you anything. All this is yours and mine until they find out he's dead. That's a fact, isn't it, Johnny?"

"Yeah, I guess that's right, but there's still the half million. You make it sound as if that was nothing. It'll buy something, won't it?"

"Do you think it could buy the casino and all that goes with it?"

"I guess not, but it could buy this car and a lot of other things."

"Have you thought how long a quarter of a million would last you, Johnny?"

"I'd invest it. It'd pay off a respectable income. What are you getting at?"

"You wouldn't have a lot left to invest by the time you had bought a car, a house and a wardrobe. I know I wouldn't."

"What's on your mind?" I asked, sure now she was preparing the ground for something. "I thought all you wanted was the half million."

"Turn right at the gates and then follow the main road," she said, and leaned forward to wave to the guards who were opening the gates. "Nothing's on my mind – yet. I'm wondering how we'll feel in a year or so, knowing Reisner's the boss of Lincoln Beach, and you and I have only a lump sum that'll melt like snow in the sun, and not a chance of making any more."

"Now, wait a minute," I said. "We're talking about half a million. That's not going to melt all that fast. You're exaggerating, and besides, we haven't even got that yet."

"That's right, Johnny."

I couldn't figure out what she was getting at, but I didn't like her tone nor the hard look in her eyes.

"We're going to Bay Street," she said, opening her bag for a cigarette. "Ever heard of Bay Street?"

"No. What's special about it?"

"Paul built every brick of it. They call it the Kasbah of Florida. I don't know what the take is, but I do know Paul collects fifteen per cent, and it's free of tax."

"This husband of yours must have been quite a guy."

"He was. None of the others have the magic touch Paul had."

Eventually we arrived at Bay Street: a misnomer to call it a street. Actually it was no better than an alley, about a hundred yards long and scarcely wide enough to take two cars – but what an alley!

I had thought the honky-tonk district of Pittsburgh was an eye-opener, but it had nothing on Bay Street. Packed shoulder to shoulder, amid blatant signs that left nothing to the imagination, were burlesque bars, saloons, palaces of peel, gambling-dens, brothels, a couple of dubious looking hotels, restaurants and gin dives.

"Pull over to the parking-lot," Della said. "We'll walk."

"You mean Wertham owns this as well as the casino?" I asked, as I drove into the lot and cut the engine.

"He leases it to a syndicate with a controlling interest. He knew sooner or later the millionaires, their wives and girl friends would get tired of the luxury of the casino. So he created Bay Street where they could work off their repressions, and he could still make money out of them. Handled properly, vice pays dividends, and nowhere is it better handled than here."

We walked across the street to a large building plastered with neon lights and crude, life-size pictures of half-dressed show-girls.

"Liberty Inn," Della said. "It's run by Zoe Elsner. She's big people in Bay Street. You'd better come in and meet her. And, Johnny, remember you're big people, too. Ricca is well known by reputation here."

We went in and met Zoe Elsner: a gigantic, middle-aged, chemical blonde who must have weighed over two hundred pounds. She made a great fuss of Della and treated me with a deference that embarrassed me, insisting on serving champagne while we talked. The speciality of Liberty Inn, she told me with a leer, were muscle dancers and strippers.

"They're hand picked, Mr. Ricca. We change them every month, and they come from the four corners of the earth. You want to come in around midnight when we're really kicking the can around. It's something to see."

From the Liberty Inn we went across to the Pump Room, a plush and gold gambling saloon, where I was introduced to Jerry Itta, a hawk-faced man in shirt sleeves who ran the joint. He told me the poker game in session at the moment had been on for three days.

"We get ten per cent of the final hand," he said, chewing on his dead cigar. "And by the look of it, it'll be worth five grand."

Both Zoe Elsner and Itta seemed scared of Della, and they enquired after Wertham with bated breath. It was the same story wherever we went. Our visits were brief, our reception royal, and Wertham's power always obvious.

"Time we got back," Della said after we had met a dozen or so characters and looked over most of the sin-dives. "We have a date with Nick."

"There must be a fortune tied up in that alley," I said as I got into the car. "Don't the cops interfere with this set-up?"

"They would if they weren't taken care of," Della returned, and laughed. "Captain of Police Hame collects five hundred a week from Reisner. You'll meet him before long. He's all right so long as he gets his money, but if it stopped, he'd slam us shut overnight."

"How do you reckon this set-up will make out now Wertham's dead?" I asked, steering the Buick through the stream of traffic.

"I don't think Nick can handle it. Zoe and Itta have ideas, and would like to break away from us if they dared. That's why I wanted them to meet you."

"What's that got to do with it?"

She gave me a queer little smile.

"It may have plenty to do with it, Johnny."

VI

Reisner was sitting behind a big, flat-topped desk, a cigarette drooping from his thin lips. To his right, lounging in an arm-chair, was a short, thick-set man whose iron-grey hair was clipped short, and his square, brutal face burned red by the sun. He jumped to his feet when he saw Della, a wide grin lighting up his face.

"Why, Mrs. Wertham, this is a surprise and a pleasure," he said, taking her hand. "It must be almost a year since we last met. How are you? Still looking as beautiful as ever, I see."

Della gave him a bright, provocative smile, and allowed him to hold her hand a little longer than necessary.

"It's nice to see you again. I'd like you to meet Johnny Ricca who's in charge of the Los Angeles casino." Turning to me, she went on, "This is Captain of Police Jim Hame. He's a very good friend of ours."

Hame lost his smile as he shook hands with me. He tried to crack my knuckles, but my grip was a little stronger than his.

"Glad to know you, Ricca," he said curtly. It seemed he only kept his charm for the ladies. "I've been hearing about you."

I said I had been hearing about him, too. Reisner got to his feet and began to mix cocktails.

"Jim has bad news for you, Mrs. Wertham," he said as he gave Della a dry martini. "Tell her, Jim."

Hame settled himself in his armchair again. He took a highball from Reisner with a grunt of thanks.

"We've found your car," he said.

"You have?" Della's expression was a nice blend of surprise and admiration. "Why, that's quick work, Captain."

"It was easy," Hame said, and his cold, blue eyes brooded over her face. "A report came in last night, and when Nick phoned this morning it clinched it."

"Clinched – what?"

"There was a smash on the road out of Pelotta last night. Both drivers were killed. One of them was driving your car. It's completely burned out."

Her look of startled consternation was just right.

"Burned out? Paul will be furious!"

"Yeah, that was a swell car," Hame said, stroking his heavy jowl. "How come you give this fella a ride?"

While Della was going through the story again, Reisner came over to me.

"What'll you drink? Scotch?"

Without thinking I said, "I don't touch the stuff. I'll have a beer."

The black eyes surveyed me.

"I thought you lived on Scotch."

Then I remembered Ricca was a whisky-soak and my heart skipped a beat.

"I'm on the wagon now. I've taken up beer."

I don't know if he spotted my shifty look, but his face was expressionless as he opened a can of beer.

Hame was saying, "Dangerous to give a stranger a ride, Mrs. Wertham. You should know that."

"I had Johnny with me. It never crossed my mind."

I thought it was time I showed a little interest in the proceedings.

"Who was the guy, anyway?"

Both Reisner and Hame looked at me.

"There wasn't much left of him by the time we got him out of the car," Hame said, "but he's been identified. His name is Johnny Farrar: a third-rate fighter who was hitch-hiking his way to Miami. He stopped off at Pelotta and got himself a fight at the stadium. After the fight he disappeared. He must have taken a liking to the Bentley."

"You certainly have collected a lot of information fast," I said. "Nice work."

"Nothing to it, once you know how and have got the organization," Hame said, lifting his massive shoulders. "Farrar had a silver medallion in his pocket. A woman who runs a café in Pelotta gave it to him. She identified it, and a guy named Brant, who gave Farrar a suit of clothes, identified what was left of the suit."

"Well, I don't give a damn who he was," Della said. "It's the car I'm worrying about. Paul will be furious. He had the body specially built."

"Just one of those things," Reisner said. "I've contacted the insurance people. They've agreed to settle."

"Thank you, Nick."

"Just to keep the record straight," Hame said, looking at me, "can you give me a description of Farrar? I have one from Brant and this woman. I'd like to see if it checks with your man."

I hadn't thought of that angle. Did they suspect I was Farrar? For a moment I was flustered.

Della cut in smoothly before I could think what to say.

"Funnily enough he wasn't unlike Johnny to look at: same build, fair and tall. He wore a white linen suit, a green and brown tie and a cream silk shirt."

"That's the fella," Hame said. "Well, what do you know? Nick and I were a little foxed. The description of Farrar seemed oddly like Ricca. We couldn't figure it out."

"He was very like Johnny," Della said, completely unruffled. "But Johnny wouldn't have it. I pointed it out at the time, but I guess he thinks he's a lot better looking than he really is."

That got a laugh from Hame, but Reisner continued to stare thoughtfully at me.

Hame rose to his feet.

"Well, I guess that takes care of that," he said. "I'll be running along. We won't need either of you at the inquest. Our yarn to the coroner will be that Farrar stole your car from the parking-lot, and you didn't catch sight of him. Okay?"

"That's very sweet of you," Della said.

"Glad to save you any bother, Mrs. Wertham." Again she let him hold her hand longer than necessary. "Look me up when you're passing headquarters. Always glad to have a beautiful woman in the office." He nodded to me. "So long, Ricca."

When he had gone, I said, "Nice obliging cop."

"So he should be," Reisner said curtly. "We pay him enough." He moved to his desk and sat down. "Well, now we've got that straightened out, let's get down to business."

"Yes," Della said, "Paul wanted Johnny and me to check the books, Nick."

Reisner favoured her with a cold stare.

"You? First time you've had anything to do with the business, isn't it?"

There was a short pause while they looked at each other, then Della laughed.

"I have to make a start sometime. As Paul couldn't come himself, he asked me to represent him."

Reisner picked up a paper-knife and began to dig holes with it in his blotter. There was a vague little smile hovering around his thin lips.

"So you're his representative? That's interesting. Have you got it in writing?"

Della's eyes snapped.

"Writing? Are you trying to be funny, Nick?"

"No." Reisner leaned back in his chair. "Paul told me Ricca was to check the books. Okay, he can check them, but Paul didn't say anything about you taking a look, and you don't until I have Paul's authority."

"Paul told me she and I were to work together," I said, feeling it was time I took a hand in this. "He said she was to see everything."

Reisner dug more holes in the blotter.

"I'm not interested in what Paul said to you. He didn't say it to me."

"Now, look . . ." I began heatedly, but Della cut in.

"Keep out of this, Johnny. I can handle it." She stood up. "Paul thinks you've been dipping into the reserve," she went on to Reisner. "We're here to check it. A stall like this won't get you anywhere. If you don't want to get the heave, you'll give me the keys."

Reisner threw back his head and laughed. He seemed genuinely amused.

"Who's going to give me the heave?" he asked. "That's funny. When Paul walks in here and tells me to get out, I'll get out, and not before. If you and Ricca imagine you can push me around, you've got another think coming. You're both off your home ground, and you'll find out just how far off you are if you crowd me much more."

"Don't be a fool, Nick," Della said, her face white. "That's not the way to talk to me, and you know it!"

Reisner lifted his eyebrows mockingly.

"But it's you who're putting on the pressure. I'm merely obeying orders. Ricca can look at the books whenever he likes. If Paul wants you to stick your pretty nose into the business – and I doubt very much if he does – I want a written order from him. Sorry, Mrs. Wertham, but that's final!"

I thought she was going to hit him, but she didn't. She moved away from his desk, her fist clenched, her eyes dark explosions.

"We'll see about that," she said, then turning to me, went on, "Come on, Johnny, we'll have lunch."

She went out of the room without another look at Reisner. I got slowly to my feet.

Reisner put down the paper-knife and reached for a cigarette. "Women are funny animals," he said as he lit up, "and she's no exception. Well, any time you want to get down to business, you'll find me right here."

"You're playing this wrong," I said. "I heard Paul tell her to check the books."

"Too bad I didn't," Reisner said, and smiled. "Too damned bad." He slipped his hand into his pocket and took out a gold cigarette-case. "By the way, Ricca, you left this lying around in your cabin. Your servant brought it to me." He laid the case on the desk and poked at it with a long finger while his eyes searched my face.

I stared at the case, then my heart turned over. It was Wertham's case: the case I had found in his suit and had been fool enough to keep instead of throwing away.

"Why, thanks," I said, and my voice was husky. "Careless of me."

I reached forward to pick it up, but his hand covered it.

"Is it yours?"

"What do you mean?"

"I was under the impression it belongs to Paul. It has his initials on it,"

"What of it?"

"I'm curious to know why you have it. Did he give it to you?"

We stared at each other. I don't suppose I looked any more guilty than any sneak-thief caught in the act.

"He lent it to me. I liked the design. I was going to have it copied."

Even to me it sounded terrible.

Reisner's eyes bored into my face.

"You were? I see. You'd better take more care of it." He lifted his hand and sat back. "Not like Paul to lend his things. He's always been funny about that."

"Not with me." I picked up the case, feeling a trickle of sweat run down the back of my ear. "Well, I guess I'll get along."

"Oh, Ricca . . ."

I turned at the door, wondering what was coming.

"Who did you leave in charge in Los Angeles?"

Who was it Della had said? For a moment I was rattled, then I remembered.

"Hollenheimer. Why?"

"Curiosity," he said. He picked up the paper-knife again and began punching more holes in the blotter. "I'm a very curious man, Ricca."

"We'd better dust while we can," I said.

Della reached for a cigarette. She lit it and put the lighter down with exaggerated care. She was lying on the divan near the window. The sunblinds were drawn, and there was a subdued, restful light in the room. Out on the beach I could hear voices and laughter. There was quite a crowd lounging on the sands, but no one was bathing. It was too soon after lunch.

She had taken off her dress, and was wearing a blue silk wrap. There was a cold, brooding expression on her face, and she drew on the cigarette hungrily, blowing a long stream of tobacco smoke to the ceiling.

I stood in the middle of the room, my hands in my trouser pockets, my nerves jumpy, my eyes on her. Slowly she turned her head until she was looking at me.

"Scared, Johnny?" she asked, and her eyebrows lifted.

"It is not a matter of being scared," I said. "It's a matter of knowing when you're licked. We've played our best card, and he's trumped it. I don't know the first thing about checking his accounts, but that's neither here nor there. Even if I could read a balance sheet that still doesn't give us access to the reserve. I always thought this was a screwy idea. What made you think he would hand over his keys?"

She stared at her cigarette, flicked ash on the floor, and smiled secretively to herself.

"So you want to run away?"

"There's no alternative. Can't you see that? All he has to do is to put a call through to Hollenheimer and ask him for a description of Ricca: then up goes the balloon."

"There was always that risk. You don't think I hadn't taken that into consideration?"

I stared at her.

"Had you?"

"I thought it was more than likely he'd check with Hollenheimer. Nick's no fool."

I moved closer and stood at the foot of the divan.

"What's the answer, then? What do you suggest we do when he finds out I'm not Ricca? He's probably found out by now."

"Let's not worry about that," she said. "There are more important things to think about."

"Not for me there aren't. Suppose Reisner gives Hame the

story? Then it'll all come out, and we'll go to jail for what we did to Wertham."

"Poor Johnny," she said, and laughed. "How fussed you're getting. Can't you see Reisner will be as anxious as we are that no one should find out Paul's dead? When a kingdom loses its king, there's always a scramble to grab. Zoe, Itta, Hame and Ricca – especially Ricca – aren't going to stand aside and let Reisner take over, and he knows it. He'll be as anxious as we are that no one should know Paul is dead until he has got control of the casino. He won't tell Hame. He won't tell anyone. Now do you see why we haven't a lot to worry about?"

I sat on the foot of the divan. This was something I hadn't figured on.

"That guy's dangerous," I said. "Okay, suppose he keeps his mouth shut? What's he going to do about us?"

She lifted a long, slender leg and examined it critically.

"He'll probably put a bullet through our heads," she said calmly. "It would be the most sensible thing to do so far as he's concerned. He's good at arranging accidents. Does that scare you, Johnny?"

Did it? Maybe it did, but I wasn't going to admit it.

"That doesn't come into it."

"Are you sure? It would be easy. He could fix Hame. You'd be surprised what Hame does for money."

"But not murder. You don't kid me he'd cover up murder."

"I didn't say murder. I said an accident."

I got up and began to move restlessly about the room.

"What's on your mind, Della? All day you've been hinting at something. Let's have it."

"I haven't been hinting at anything. I've been showing you a kingdom you can inherit. Hasn't it sunk into your head yet the casino and the rake-off from Bay Street are yours for the taking? Yours and mine? Can't you see that?"

"No, I can't. What are you getting at?" Looking at the intent, set expression on her face I suddenly felt my mouth go dry.

"With me behind you, Johnny, you could run this place. Between us we could clean up a fortune. Do you really think I'm so cock-eyed as to imagine Reisner would let us walk off with the reserve?"

I was getting rattled now, and I came and stood over her.

"But that was the idea, wasn't it? That's why you brought me here!"

"That's what I told you," she said, and swung her legs off the divan and stood up. "I wanted you to see the set-up. It was a bait to bring you here. Well, you've seen it. Haven't you the itch to take it? And you can. You can take over right away – if you have the guts."

I lit a cigarette. My hands were unsteady: whether from excitement or fear I didn't know.

"So there's no half million?"

"Of course there is. That goes with the casino, but we can't walk off with it. Take over the casino and you take over the reserve."

"And Reisner? What's he supposed to do? Welcome me with open arms? Dust off his desk chair for me? A moment ago you said he was going to put a bullet in me."

"I said if you had the guts, Johnny. Reisner must meet with an accident."

Well, it was out now. At the back of my mind I had known this was coming. The way she had talked all the morning pointed to it, but I had refused to believe it. Now the cards were on the table, face up.

I stubbed out my cigarette, not looking at her.

"Get rid of Reisner," she went on as calmly as if she were discussing the weather, "and the casino and Bay Street automatically fall into our laps. By the time Ricca tries to move in it'll be too late. Once we get our hands on the reserve and books, he'll have to make a deal with us. We'll keep Lincoln Beach. He can have Los Angeles, and Levinsky can have Paris. Then we're set for life." She moved closer. I could smell the perfume in her hair. Her hands slid up to my shoulders while she looked into my eyes. "What are you going to do about it, Johnny?"

I knew right away what I was going to do about it. She had made one mistake, and she didn't know it. She was certain she had sunk her hook in too deep to come out, but she hadn't. All right, I was sold on the place. The idea of taking control of a set-up like this was something that got me by the throat, but not at that price.

"You talk about an accident," I said, "but it won't be an accident: it'll be murder."

She continued to look at me, her face as set and as cold as granite.

"It's your life or his, Johnny. As soon as he finds out you're not Ricca he's coming for you with a gun. You've got to get in first. That's not murder: it's self-defence."

I shook my head.

"Don't let's kid ourselves. It's murder."

She moved away from me and walked over to the window.

"This is what we tell Hame," she said, her back to me. "Reisner has been dipping into the reserve. We came down to check the books. He is caught, and he knows it. There's no out for him, so what does he do? He walks to the window of his office and keeps walking. They find him lying on the terrace with a broken neck."

"Do you think Hame would believe that? Reisner's not the suicide type."

"He would believe it. It would cost money, but he'd believe it. Use your head, Johnny. The casino is yours if you've got the nerve to take it. All you have to do is to give Reisner a push. That's not asking much, is it?"

"It's murder," I said. "And I'm not touching it. I don't care how much it pays off. It's murder."

She sat on the divan and held out her hand to me.

"Come and sit down," she said. "Don't look at me like that. You love me, don't you?"

I didn't move.

"We'll leave love out of it," I said. "Look, maybe I am only a third-rate fighter, but I hope I'm not a dope. You worked this out ten seconds after you found Wertham was dead, didn't you? You knew unless you could get rid of Reisner you were sunk. Someone had to kill him, and you picked on me. You thought all you had to do was to show me this place, give me a car and throw yourself in as a make-weight, and I'd take murder in my stride. Well, you're wrong. I can only hope you don't realize what it means to commit murder. It's a thing you live with for the rest of your life. Maybe you haven't thought of it like that. I hope you haven't. Even if we could fix Hame, we have still ourselves to live with, and every now and then the thought will drop into our minds we killed Reisner, and that thought will poison any happiness we can get out of this place. We'll never know if Hame will continue to keep his mouth shut. He'll have us on a spot for the rest of our days. He'll want more money and more power as he gets used to the idea. It won't be long before he'll want to run the casino himself. He might even do a deal with you. He might pin the murder on me and take my place. Oh, no, I'm not getting into a jam like that. I'm not all that crazy. Murder is out! I'm not doing it: not for you nor the casino nor for all the money in Lincoln Beach!"

She sat still, watching me while I talked, her face expression-less, her eyes hot and intent.

"You don't really believe that, Johnny," she said, and got up. "It's not true." She came over to me and put her hands on my arms, looking up at me. "I do love you. I didn't give myself to you for any other reason except I love you. I couldn't refuse you last night. I knew it was dangerous. I knew we were taking a risk that could ruin my plans, but I couldn't refuse you." Her arms went round my neck. "Oh, darling, I'm crazy about you. I've never felt like this before about any man. You must believe me! I know you're right about Nick. But what are we to do?" She was clinging to me now, her face pressed against mine. "If we don't get rid of him, he'll get rid of us. Can't you see that? We'll have nothing. We'll be lucky to get out of here with our lives. It's he or us, Johnny. You must see that!"

I started to say something, but her mouth covered mine, and I felt her breath against the back of my throat. We stood like that for a long moment of time; my heart was hammering, blood pounded in my head.

"Johnny . . ."

She pressed herself against me. Her eyes were closed. Only she and I mattered at this moment; the rest of it, Reisner, the casino, the money and murder were a bad dream after you had wakened up.

My fingers sank into the hard, firm flesh above her hips. She gave a soft little moan and her mouth opened against mine.

"All right, break it up," Reisner's soft voice said from the doorway. "There's a time and place for everything."

I felt her shudder and stiffen, and she tore herself away from me with a strangled scream. Her face had gone blue-white like the colour of ice. I turned.

Reisner was standing just inside the room. His mouth was fixed in a stiff little smile, and the ·45 automatic in his hand looked as big as a cannon.

"And don't make any silly moves," he went on, not raising his voice. He jerked the gun to an armchair near me. "Sit down, Farrar. And you, Mrs. Wertham, sit on the divan. If either of you make a move I'll drill you and think up a reason for it after."

Della collapsed on the divan. She looked as if she were going to faint. I sat in the armchair, a tightness in my throat that made breathing difficult.

"That's fine," he went on, came farther into the room and closed the door with his heel. "Well, you two certainly know how to pass the time." He moved to the centre of the room. The gun pointed to a spot just between us. "Played it pretty rough, didn't you?" he said. "Didn't it occur to either of you I'd come back last night to see what you were up to? Imagine my surprise when I found one of the cabins empty." He looked at me, his eyes glittering. "What have you done with Wertham?"

Neither of us said anything.

"Is he dead?" He hooked a chair towards him and sat down. "Did you kill him?"

"Are you crazy?" Della said. Her voice sounded as if she were speaking through locked teeth. "He's on his way to Paris."

"On his way to hell, you mean," Reisner said. "Did you really think you could get away with this wet idea? The moment I saw you I knew something was phoney. Paul wouldn't let you travel with Ricca or anyone else all the way from Los Angeles to Lincoln Beach without someone to keep an eye on you. You've quite a reputation for taking a tumble in the hay whenever there's an opportunity, and Paul knows that as well as I do."

"How dare you talk to me like that!" Della said furiously.

"There were three of you in the car: you, Wertham and Farrar. One of you died," Reisner went on, crossing his legs. "This guy isn't Ricca, so that makes him Farrar. It makes the dead man Wertham. The set-up's gone sour. You may as well admit it."

"Wait, Nick," Della said, leaning forward, her clenched fists pressed tight between her knees. "You, I and Johnny can do a deal. No one but we three know Paul's dead. Cut us in on half shares and we'll work our passage. You can do with help now Paul is dead. You know I've picked up a lot of his ideas. I could be useful to you, Nick."

Reisner seemed surprised. He glanced at me.

"Where does he come in? Why should I cut him in on anything?"

"Take a look at him," Della said. "Don't you think he'd scare Ricca? He's a gunman as well as a fighter. You'd need someone like him around once the news leaked out."

I sat still, listening, as surprised as Reisner seemed to be.

"And suppose I didn't want to share?" Reisner asked quietly. "What then?"

Della licked her lips. Her face was still white, but she had steadied herself. She was gambling with her last buck. You could tell that by looking at her. She was playing a king, and only an ace could beat it, and she wasn't sure if Reisner held the ace.

"Then we talk, Nick. We tell Hame, Ricca, Itta and Zoe, and let them move in. I don't think you're big enough to handle them all."

Reisner smiled.

"So he really is dead. Well, well, that's the best news I've heard in thirty-eight years. Paul dead, huh? And a damn good riddance. It's something I've been praying for."

Della's hand closed on a yellow and red cushion lying at her side. She gripped it, a fixed smile on her white face.

"When we hit that car, he was thrown out," she said. "He broke his neck."

"That's your story," Reisner returned, still smiling, "but suppose you two killed him? Has it crossed your minds I could slap a murder rap on you both and make it stick? Hame would frame you two for a grand. He's a little short of money."

I felt suddenly cold.

"That still wouldn't stop the news leaking out," Della said, but her face stiffened.

"That's right," Reisner said, "but maybe it can't be helped. Now look, this is the way I see it. I happen to overhear you two talking, and I get the idea you killed Paul. I walk in on you and Farrar pulls a gun. I beat him to the draw. I'm pretty quick with a rod, and Hame knows it. You pull a gun, too. So you both get shot. I then put a proposition up to Hame. He gets a slice from the casino if he takes care of me. He might even be persuaded to toss Itta and Zoe in the can until I get things organized. There'd be no difficulty in making a charge against them. Then by the time Ricca's got over his drinking jag – oh, yes, Hollenheimer told me about that – it'd be too late for him to start trouble. How do you like it?"

"You wouldn't want to cut Hame in," Della said, and shifted forward. "He'd take the lot in time. He's like that, and you know it."

Reisner gnawed at his lower lip, his eyes thoughtful.

"Maybe," he said, "but it's a way out of this mess."

"There's another way," Della said softly.

"What's that?"

She turned to look at me. The expression in her eyes set my heart pounding.

"We could kill you, Nick. That'd be the best way. We were talking about it when you came in."

Reisner continued to smile, but his eyes turned to ice.

"Yeah, I heard you. That's why I like my idea, and that's why it's going to be my idea."

"Not with the safety-catch on, Nick."

It was well done. Even I looked at the gun. Reisner's eyes shifted from us and looked down. Della threw the cushion she had been grasping in one swift, violent movement. It caught Reisner in the face. She flung herself off the bed and clamped her hands on his hand and the gun, wedging her finger against the trigger so he couldn't fire.

I jumped from my chair as Reisner, swearing softly, staggered to his feet, his fist raised to club Della as she hung with all her weight on his gun arm.

I hit him on the side of his face with a long, looping right that exploded on his cheek-bone with the impact of a steam-hammer. He wasn't built for a punch like that. I felt the bone splinter as he shot backwards, dragging her with him. He cannoned into the wall, bounced away and began to sag as I stepped up close and smashed a right to his jaw. He went down, his face coming squarely on a big glass bowl of floating dahlia heads that stood on a table. The bowl flew into fragments, and the table smashed like matchwood. Water and flowers scattered over Della and the carpet.

She screamed as the water hit her, but she didn't let go of the gun until I grabbed her wrist and pulled her to her feet.

We stood side by side, looking down at Reisner. He had rolled over on his back. A long splinter of glass from the broken bowl, like a tiny dagger, had gone deep into his right eye. His lips were drawn back from his teeth in a snarl of pain and fear, and his right cheek was a pulp of splintered bone, teeth and blood. He looked terrible.

Della drew closer to me. I could hear her breathing: quick, short gasps, rasping in a dry throat.

Neither of us moved. We just stared down at him.

He was dead.

PART FOUR

FADE-IN

I

It was like a movie-projector operating inside my head, throwing images of the past on to the white screen that was my mind. I saw again the room and Della in her blue wrap that hung open to show her long, slender legs and the beauty of her body. I saw myself with blood out of my face, my fists clenched, and a sick feeling deep inside me, knowing I had killed him, and that I'd carry the image of his battered face with me to the grave.

"He's dead, Johnny."

She gave a little sigh, then stepped back, gathering her wrap about her, turning to look at me.

I didn't say anything. I couldn't. This was murder. All right, I hadn't meant to kill him, but I had killed him, and he was there, dead on the floor, and that made it murder.

"He's bleeding!"

She ran into the bathroom and came back with a bath-towel and did something I couldn't have done. She caught hold of his long, chalk-white hair, lifted his head and slid the towel under it.

There was blood on her hands when she stood up, and I looked at the red stains in horror.

"Johnny!"

"I've killed him!"

"Pull yourself together!" Her voice was sharp. "No one knows but you and I. This is what I've been praying for."

I remembered Reisner had said the same thing when he had heard Wertham was dead. Some prayers to have! That made them a pair.

"But they'll find out," I said. "We've got to get out of here!"

She came up to me.

"Don't be a fool! Can't you see this is what we want? This is the set-up! He's dead, and we can take over. There's no one to stop us now!"

I stared at her. There was a ruthless look of triumph in her black, glittering eyes, and her scarlet lips were parted. There was

117

no fear in that hard, lovely face: only triumph, and a suppressed and violent excitement.

I grabbed hold of her arm and shook her.

"It's you who're the fool!" I shouted at her. "We've killed him – you and I! They'll come after us! They'll catch us and they'll fry us! Don't you think you're going to get away with this! You're not! Maybe we can hide the body for an hour or so, but they'll find him. . . ."

She put her hand over my mouth.

"Sit down, Johnny, and be quiet. It's going to be all right. Keep your nerve: that's all you have to do. I know how to handle this. It's going to be all right."

I sat down, my back to Reisner's body. All right, I admit it. I was in a bad way. I had killed a man, and it was like taking a punch in the belly.

"What are you going to do?" I managed to jerk out.

"Look at his face. Doesn't that tell you what to do?"

I couldn't look at his face.

"What are you getting at? You make me sick! Haven't you a spark of feeling? How can you look at his face?"

She came around the bed to stand in front of me.

"Perhaps I've more guts than you, Johnny. Aren't the stakes worth while? He was going to shoot us! You killed him in self-defence. Why should you care about him?"

"It's murder! It's something that's going to live with me! It's something that'll poison my whole goddamn life!"

"In a week you'll have forgotten he ever existed. But if you don't pull yourself together and help me, we'll both go to the chair. Can't you see that, you poor, frightened booby?"

Slowly I turned and looked at him. He was still a horrible sight, with the splinter of glass in his eye and his face smashed and bloody.

She bent over him and gently pulled out the glass. It was the most gruesome thing I'd ever watched. I couldn't look away, and the horror of it brought me out into an ice-cold sweat.

She squatted back on her heels, the splinter of glass between her finger and thumb, and looked at the battered dead face, her brows drawn down in a frown of concentration.

"He could have been mauled by an animal," she said softly. "And that's what they are going to think." She glanced up. "Don't you see the way out, Johnny? All we have to do is to drop him into the lion's pit. It's as simple as that. He feeds them. He even goes into their cages. Sooner or later there was bound to be an accident. Everyone knows the risks he took. Hame knows, and that's important. They won't think anything of it if we don't make mistakes. It's fool-proof."

I could only sit and stare at her.

"You mean you've just thought that up?"

"Why not? You have only to look at him to see it's the way out."

Spider's legs ran up my spine. She was incredible. The moment she was in a jam, her brain devised a way out. Wertham hadn't been cold before she had thought up how she could use me to gain control of the casino. Reisner hadn't stopped bleeding before she had a fool-proof idea to explain away his death. And it was fool-proof if we could only get him to the pit without anyone seeing us. She just wasn't human.

"It's all right, isn't it, Johnny?"

She looked up at me, her black eyes glittering, her fingers blood-stained, and she was like a lovely, gruesome ghoul.

"Yes, it's all right if no one sees us." Already I was beginning to breathe more freely, and my heart eased off its violent hammering. "We can't do it until after dark."

"No. Stand up and let me look you over. Show me your hands." Her examination was searching and thorough, but finally she satisfied herself I had no blood on my clothes. "You're all right. Now, listen: go out into the grounds and be seen. Go and play a round of golf. If you can get someone to play with you, so much the better. Don't come back until midnight. If anyone asks you where Reisner is, tell them he's with me, and we're not to be disturbed."

"Golf? Do you think I could play golf with this on my mind?" I was almost yelling at her. "Are you crazy? Haven't you a spark of feeling?"

"It's you who are crazy. If you can't play golf, have a swim or walk around or go to the bar! Do anything you damn well please, but get out of here and let them see you! You've got to keep them away from here. That's your job. You've got to make them think he and I are too busy to be disturbed. Get a grip on yourself. Play this wrong, and we're sunk!"

I drew in a deep breath.

"And what are you going to do?"

The awful little smile I had seen when she was a split second away from shooting me flickered across her mouth.

"I'm staying here – with him. I'm making sure no one gets in and finds him. That's what I'm going to do."

"You've got nine hours of it."

"That won't kill me. I've things to think about. You don't think I'm scared to be alone with him, do you? He's dead. I'm not squeamish, even if you are. I've got my life to plan."

I longed to get away from that ghastly room, from her, from him. I wouldn't have stayed with that battered body for nine hours for all the money in the world.

I moved to the door.

"And, Johnny . . ."

I paused.

"What is it?" Out of the corner of my eye I could see his white and brown shoes and his gaudy yellow socks. I hurriedly looked away.

"We have to trust each other, Johnny," she said, as still as a statue. "Don't lose your nerve and run away. You might be tempted, but don't do it. If you did I couldn't cover this up. I must have your help. So don't run away."

"I'm not going to run away."

"You might be tempted. A nine-hours' start is tempting, but if you did bolt I'd have to tell Hame it was you who killed him, and Hame would believe it."

"I'm not going to run away," I said, and my voice was a croak.

She came to me and put her arms around my neck, and I felt a shudder run through me at her touch.

"You still love me, don't you, Johnny? It's going to be all right. It's going to work out the way we planned. We're set up for life now."

All I could think of was that her fingers, stained with his blood, were touching the back of my neck. I wanted to shove her away from me, but I didn't because I knew she was as dangerous as a rattlesnake, and there was nothing to stop her going to Hame and pinning the murder on me. So I kissed her, and the touch of her hot, yielding lips made me feel sick, and the sight of him lying there with his head wrapped in the towel made me feel even sicker.

"I'll be waiting for you," she said, her face against mine. "Keep your nerve, Johnny. It's going to be all right."

Then I was outside, with the hot afternoon sun on my face and nine hours of hell in front of me. I had a frantic urge to run and keep running until I'd put miles between me and that cabin where she was keeping watch over his dead body, but I knew I wasn't going to run away because she had me in a trap from which, as far as I could see, there was no way out.

II

The bar-room with its sun awnings and lavish fitments, its mahogany, horseshoe-shaped bar, and its pink-tinted mirrors was empty when I walked stiff-legged across its expanse of parquet flooring. The square-shaped clock above the rows of bottles told me it was twenty-five minutes past three: not the hour to start drinking, but that wasn't going to stop me. If I didn't get a drink inside me quick I'd flip my lid.

The barman appeared from behind a jazz-patterned curtain and looked at me with polite enquiry. He was a tall, thin bird with a high, bald dome, shaggy eyebrows and a long, beaky nose. His white coat was as clean as soap and water could make it, and as stiff with starch as a bishop watching a muscle dance.

"Yes, Mr. Ricca?"

I wasn't expecting to be recognized, and I flinched.

"Scotch," I said. My voice sounded like a gramophone record with a crack in it. "Set up the bottle."

"Yes, Mr. Ricca."

He reached up to a shelf and took down a bottle still wrapped in tissue paper. His long, bony fingers ripped off the paper, and he put the bottle in front of me.

"Four Roses, sir," he said, "or would you prefer Lord Calvert?"

I picked up the bottle and poured myself a slug. My hand was shaking and I slopped the stuff on the polished counter. I felt him watching me.

"Get the hell out of here," I said.

"Yes, Mr. Ricca."

He went away behind the jazz-patterned curtain.

I knew I shouldn't have snarled at him, but I wanted that drink so badly I couldn't control myself, and I knew I couldn't have carried the glass to my mouth with him there to watch the unsteady journey.

And it was unsteady. I slopped most of it, but I got the rest down. I poured myself another slug. I hoisted that one without spilling a drop, and the tight horror that was coiled up inside me began to loosen up.

I lit a cigarette, and dragged down smoke, staring at the face of the clock just above my head. Eight and a half hours! What in hell was I going to do with myself all that time?

I poured another slug. The back of my throat was burning, but

I didn't care. It had to be Scotch or I'd dive off the deep end. I kept thinking of the black Buick out there below the terrace, and how easy it would be to get in it and get out of here. In that car I'd be miles away with an eight-hour start.

I drank the Scotch and dragged down more smoke. I was feeling steadier now; not so scared. My nerves weren't jumping; maybe fluttering, but not jumping any more, and the Scotch was hot, comforting and good. I reached for the bottle again when from behind the curtain a telephone bell began to ring. The shrill sound made me jump, and I nearly knocked the bottle on to the floor.

I heard the barman say, "He's not in the bar, miss. No, I haven't seen him since lunch-time. He looked in around one o'clock, but I haven't seen him since."

I stubbed out my cigarette. The muscles in my face had stiffened until they hurt.

"Yeah, if I see him," the barman went on, "I'll tell him."

He hung up.

They were looking for Reisner already! I had to do something. She had said my job was to keep them away from the cabin. If they began looking for him . . .

"Hey! You!"

The barman pushed aside the curtain and came out. His eyes went to the bottle. I could see him counting the number of slugs I had had.

"Yes, Mr. Ricca?"

"Who was that on the phone?"

"Miss Doering, Mr. Reisner's secretary. She has an urgent call for him. Would you know where he is, sir?"

I knew where he was all right. Just to hear his name brought up a picture of him, lying on his back, his face smashed in and his right eye cut in half.

I wanted to pour another slug, but I was scared he'd see my hand shaking. Without looking at him I said as casually as I could, "He's with Mrs. Wertham, but they're busy. They're more than busy, they're not to be disturbed."

I felt, rather than saw, him stiffen. He had got beyond the bees and flowers stuff. He knew what I meant.

"Better tell Miss Doering," I went on. "Nothing is as important as what they are doing right now."

"Yes, Mr. Ricca."

The shocked, cold tone in his voice told me I'd driven it a shade too far into the ground. He went back behind the curtain.

I nearly knocked the bottle over again in my haste to fill my glass.

I heard him say, "Mr. Ricca is in the bar. He says Mr. Reisner is with Mrs. Wertham, and they are not to be disturbed. That's right. It doesn't matter how important it is."

I wiped the sweat off my face and hands with my handkerchief. Well, I'd played it: a little rough, perhaps, but I'd played it.

The Scotch was hitting me now. I felt a little drunk. Regretfully I put the cork back in the bottle. I couldn't risk getting plastered. She had said I was to go out and show myself. That's what I had to do.

I walked out of the bar and on to the terrace. It was hot out there. Below stood the Buick. All I had to do . . . I dragged my eyes away from it and walked along the terrace, down the steps, not thinking where I was going, but aware of the need to get away from the car and the temptation to bolt.

A sudden noise brought me to a standstill: a deep-chested, guttural sound that seemed to shake the ground, and which ended in a coughing grunt.

For a moment that sound had me going, then I realized it was the roar of a lion. I was heading towards the zoo, and that transfixed me. The vision of throwing Reisner's dead body into the pit floated into my mind, and I felt my knees give under me.

I looked back over my shoulder. The Buick still stood there in the sunshine. What was I waiting for? I had to get out of here. I had seven hours and fifty minutes start. In that car I could be four hundred miles away before they even began to look for me.

All right, I was plastered, and I was scared. The roar of the lion, reminding me what I had to do at midnight, stampeded me. I turned and walked to the car, got in, trod on the starter and slipped the gear stick into second. I took a quick look over my shoulder. No one shouted at me. No one tried to stop me. The car moved away smoothly, gathering speed as I changed in top. I drove along the wide carriage-way, thinking in another minute or so I'd be out on the highway where I could tread on the gas and go.

Ahead of me I could see the massive gates. They were closed, and the two uniformed guards were standing in front of them, their hands on their hips. I touched the horn button, slowed down, waiting for them to open up, but they didn't. They just stood, watching me, their faces expressionless under the hard peaks of their black caps.

I pulled up.

"What do you expect me to do – drive through those goddamn things?"

I didn't recognize my voice. It sounded as harsh as a file on rusty iron.

One of the guards sauntered up to me: a tough-looking bird with close-set eyes and a nose that spread over his face, as if someone had given him the heel some time in his life.

"Sorry, Mr. Ricca," he said. "But I gotta message for you."

I looked at him, my hands gripping the steering-wheel until the muscles in my arms ached.

"What is it?"

"Mrs. Wertham said if you come this way we were to turn you back. She and Mr. Reisner want to see you."

I knew I could take him. He was leaning forward, wide open for a hook to the jaw. My eyes shifted to his companion. He was standing away to my left, his hand on the butt of a gun he carried in a holster at his hip. He looked ready to go into action.

"That's okay," I said, trying to smile. "I've seen them. Get those gates open. I'm in a hurry."

The guard's cold, green eyes sneered at me.

"Then I guess they want to see you again. The call's just come through. Sorry, but orders is orders."

"Okay," I said, knowing I was licked. "I'll see what they want." I slid the gear stick into reverse.

They stood watching me as I made a U-turn. They were still watching me as I drove back to the casino.

I parked the Buick below the terrace and got out. I was trembling, and blood hammered against my temples. I might have guessed I wasn't going to out-smart her quite so easily. She thought of everything: even with Reisner bleeding on her rug, she still had time to take care of me.

I walked down towards the beach. A car sneaked up beside me, and a girl's voice said, "I'm going your way. Let's go together."

I stopped and looked at her: a cute blonde with bed in her eyes and a pert little face that knew all the answers, and the questions, too. She was in a yellow, strapless swimsuit that gripped her curves and set off a figure that'd make a mountain goat lose its foothold. On her fair, fluffy head was a big picture hat of plain straw, with a rose pinned to the under-brim. She was the kind of girl I wouldn't have tangled with sober, but the kind I wanted the way I was feeling now.

I opened the off-side door of the car and got in beside her.

She drove on towards the beach, her small hands patting the

steering-wheel in time to the swing that was coming over the car radio, and she kept looking at me out of the corners of her eyes.

"As soon as I saw you I knew I had to know you," she said. "I like big men, and you're the strongest, biggest man I've ever seen."

I couldn't think of anything adequate to say to that one, so I let it ride.

"What are you going to do – swim?" she asked, giving me a cute little smile that was supposed to have me on my hands and knees begging for favours.

"That's the idea. Do you swim in that outfit?"

"Don't you like it?"

"It likes you – I can see that."

She giggled.

"We can always go somewhere where I needn't wear it. Shall we?"

"It's your car," I said.

She spun the wheel at the next intersection and increased the speed.

"I know a place. We'll go there."

I sat staring through the windshield, asking myself if this was what I wanted. I didn't know. I didn't think so, but it had dropped out of the sky into my lap, and it might blunt the edges of what lay ahead of me.

"You're Johnny Ricca, aren't you?" she said as she drove the car along a narrow road lined on either side by royal palms.

"How did you know that?"

"Everyone is talking about you. You're the big-time gambler from Los Angeles. Someone said you were a gangster. I love gangsters."

"Well, that's good news. And who are you?"

"I'm Georgia Harris Brown. Everyone knows me. My father is Gallway Harris Brown, the steel millionaire."

"Does he love gangsters too?"

She laughed.

"I never thought to ask him."

She swung the car off the road and bumped over grass, over sand and pulled up on a lonely stretch of beach, screened by blue palmettos and palm trees.

"Nice, isn't it?" she said, taking off her hat and tossing it on the back seat. She slid out of the car on to the sand. "Well, I'm going to have a swim. Coming?"

As I got out of the car I suddenly decided I wasn't going ahead with this. I shouldn't be here. I should be where I could be seen: where anyone looking for Reisner could ask me if I had seen him. I must have been crazy to have come with this blonde in the first place. If I couldn't get away from the casino, the least I could do was to try to safeguard my own neck, and I wasn't doing that by remaining in this out-of-the-way spot with this blonde who was one jump lower than an animal.

"I guess not," I said. "I've just remembered I've work to do. You wouldn't like to drive me back?"

The cute little smile went away as if wiped off by a sponge.

"I don't get it," she said, and her voice went shrill.

"Never mind: I'll walk," I said. "You go ahead and have your swim."

I knew she'd take a swing at me, and she did. I gave her the satisfaction of landing on me. It would have been easy enough to have slipped inside her flying hand, but I didn't want her to feel all that frustrated. For her size she carried a good slap. It made my cheek burn.

"So long," I said, and walked away. I didn't look back, and she didn't yell after me.

Instead of keeping to the road I moved through the palmetto thicket, heading back the way I had come, but not paying much attention to where I was going. After a while I realized I had been walking for some time and I was still not within sight of the casino.

I paused to look around me. Over to my right I could see the blue, almost motionless ocean through the trees. To my left was a forest of mangroves. I had no idea now if I were walking away from the casino or towards it, and knowing I should get back there, I got worried.

This stretch of beach was as lonely and as deserted as a pauper's funeral, and I was in two minds to turn back and make a fresh start when I heard a girl singing. She was singing *Temptation*, a song that had always given me a creepy sensation whenever I'd heard it.

She wasn't tearing into it as most singers do, but singing it in an absent-minded kind of way, as if her mind were only half concentrating on the song.

I moved forward cautiously, wanting to catch a glimpse of her before she saw me. From the sound of her voice she'd be around the next clump of mangroves.

My shoes made no sound in the soft sand. I got behind a shrub and peered over it.

She was sitting on a camp-stool, an artist's easel in front of her, and she was painting in water-colours. I couldn't see the painting, for she was facing me, and I wouldn't have bothered much if I could have seen it. I looked at her: she was the only picture I wanted to look at.

She wore a blue and white bolero jacket that left her midriff bare, a pair of white shorts, and blue plastic and cork sandals. She was bare-headed, and her thick, short hair looked like burnished copper in the strong sunlight. She was as different from the blonde cutie as a Ming vase is from a vase you win at a shooting-gallery, and lovely without being sensational. Her eyes were big and blue and serious; her mouth, with just the right amount of lipstick, wide and generous, and her figure neat, compact and curved where it should be curved.

I stood looking at her. The Scotch was still giving me a false sense of security. I seemed to have stepped out of the darkness into the sunlight, and to have turned my back on something that was as unreal as a bad dream. Just to look at this girl, singing to herself, unaware of me, made Della and Reisner, and the immediate horrible future, go out of my mind the way dirty water leaves a sink when you pull out the plug.

III

I stood for maybe a minute, listening to her song, and watching her sun-browned hand and the paint-brush at work, wondering who she was and how she came to be in such an out-of-the-way place. Then suddenly she must have felt me watching her, for she looked up and saw me. She gave a little start and dropped her brush.

I came out from behind the shrub.

"I'm sorry. I didn't mean to startle you. I heard you singing and wondered who it was."

Not a very brilliant approach, but it was, at the moment, the best I could do. For the first time since I had left the cabin my voice didn't sound like the croak of a frog.

She bent to pick up the brush.

"I've missed my way, and I think I'm lost," I went on. "I'm trying to find the casino."

"Oh." The explanation seemed to reassure her. "It's easy to do that. I suppose you came through the mangroves."

"That's right." I moved to one side so I could see her painting. The sea, sand and palms and the blue of the sky made a vivid and attractive picture. "That's good," I said. "It's absolutely life-like."

That seemed to amuse her, for she laughed.

"It's supposed to be."

"Maybe, but a lot of people couldn't do it."

I fumbled in my hip pocket for a packet of cigarettes, flicked out two and offered them.

"No, thank you. I don't smoke."

I lit up.

"Just how far away am I from the casino?"

"About three miles. You're walking away from it."

She began to clean the brush that had dropped into the sand.

"You mean I'm off the casino's beach?"

"Yes; you're on my beach."

"I'm sorry. I didn't mean to trespass."

"I didn't mean it that way," she said, smiling. "It's all right. Are you staying at the casino?"

It flashed into my mind that I didn't want her to know me as Johnny Ricca, gambler and gangster. It didn't matter to me that the blonde, Georgia Harris Brown, should think so, but this girl was different.

"I'm only staying a few days. Some place, isn't it?" Then I asked her, "Do you live around here?"

"I have a beach cabin close by. I'm collecting background material for display work."

"What was that again?"

I dropped on the sand, away from her, watching to see if she disapproved, but her expression didn't change.

"I work for Keston's in Miami. It's a big store. You may have heard of it," she explained. "I provide sketches and colour schemes for window dressing and special displays."

"Sounds interesting."

"Oh, it is." Her face lit up. "Last year I went to the West Indies and did a series of paintings. We turned one of the departments into a West Indian village. It was a terrific success."

"Must be a nice job," I said. "I hope you don't mind me holding up your work. I'll get along if you do."

She shook her head.

"It's all right. I've just finished." She began putting away her brushes. "I've been working since ten. I guess I've earned some lunch."

"A little late for lunch, isn't it?"

"Not when you live alone."

She studied the painting, and I watched her. I decided she was the prettiest and nicest girl I'd ever met.

"I think that'll do," she said, and stood up. "The easiest way back to the casino is for you to walk along the beach."

"I'm Johnny Farrar," I said, not moving. "I suppose I couldn't carry your stuff back for you? There seems a lot of it."

"Sounds as if you're inviting yourself to lunch," she said, smiling. "I'm Virginia Laverick. If you haven't anything better to do . . ."

I jumped to my feet.

"I haven't a thing. I guess I'm sick of my own company, and meeting you . . ."

I picked up the easel and her other stuff when she had packed it, and went with her across the hot sand.

"I can't ask you in," she said suddenly, "I live alone."

"That's okay," I said, only too glad to be walking at her side. "But I'm harmless, or maybe you don't think so."

She laughed.

"Big men usually are," she said.

After a short walk we came to a bungalow, screened by flowering shrubs, with a green-painted roof and gay flowers in the window-boxes and a wide verandah on which were lounging chairs, a radio set and a refectory table.

"Sit down," she said, waving to one of the chairs. "Make yourself at home. I'll get you a drink – Scotch?"

"Fine," I said.

"I won't be a minute."

But she was a lot longer than that, and I was pacing up and down the verandah, my nerves on the jump again, by the time she reappeared. I saw why she had been so long. She had changed out of the sun-suit which she had probably decided wasn't suitable to be wearing when entertaining a strange man in an empty bungalow, and she was now in a white linen dress, shoes and stockings. I gave her full marks for good sense.

She carried a tray on which were bottles, glasses and plates of sandwiches. She set down the tray on the table, smiling at me.

"Go ahead and fix yourself a drink," she said. "If you feel like eating, there's plenty."

I poured myself a big slug of Scotch, splashed ice water in it, while she flopped into an armchair and started on the sandwiches.

"You look as if you've been in a fight," she said.

"Yeah, I know." I felt my nose, embarrassed. It was still a little sore and swollen. "I got into an argument with a guy. It looks worse than it feels." I took a mouthful of Scotch. It hit the spot all right.

She was drinking orange juice, and I was aware she watched me just a little uneasily.

"It's nice of you to take pity on me," I said. "I was feeling pretty low. You know how it is. I've been around on my own, and got sick of my own company."

"I thought there were lots of attractive girls staying at the casino."

"Maybe there are, but they don't happen to be my style."

She smiled.

"What is your style?"

I never believe in pulling punches, in or out of the ring. I let her have it.

"Well, you are, I guess," I said, and added hastily, "and don't think that's your cue to yell for help. You asked me, and I've told you, and another thing while we're on the subject, I'm not the type who makes a girl yell for help."

She looked steadily at me.

"I didn't think you were or I wouldn't have asked you here."

That took care of that. Anyway, it cleared the air. She started talking about her work. From what she told me it seemed to be well paid, and she seemed to do more or less what she liked, and go where she liked.

I was happy enough to sit there in the sunshine and listen. The Scotch was taking care of my nerves, and she was taking care of my thoughts. For the first time since that car crash I relaxed.

After a while she said, "But I'm talking too much about myself. What do you do?"

I was expecting that one, and had the answer ready.

"Insurance," I said. "I'm a leg man for the Pittsburgh General Insurance."

"Do you like it?"

"It's all right. Like you, I get around."

"It must pay well if you can stay at the casino."

I had to get that straightened out at once.

"I promised myself I'd live like a millionaire for a couple of days, and I've saved for years to pull it off. Well, this is it, but I'll be moving into the town on Tuesday."

"Do you like being a millionaire?"

"There's nothing like it."

"That's the last thing I'd want to be."

"Well, I guess I've never had enough money," I said, surprised at her emphatic tone. "It's my greatest ambition to get my hands on a roll and spend it. The casino is a kind of dress rehearsal."

"You mean really big money?" She was looking at me with interest.

"You bet I mean big money."

"Well, how will you get it?"

That stopped me. I suddenly realized I was talking too much.

"I haven't an idea. It's all a pipe-dream, of course. Maybe someone will die and leave me a fortune." I didn't get the joke over, and I noticed she looked curiously at me.

I was floundering around to change the subject when she remembered they were giving a recording of Beethoven's Fifth Symphony on the radio.

"Toscanini is conducting," she said. "Could you bear it?"

"Go ahead."

I had never heard Beethoven's Fifth Symphony; for that matter I had never heard any symphony, and I had only the vaguest idea what it was all about. But when the music came pouring out into the sunlit silence, its richness and its surging onrush had me gripping my chair. And when it was finally over, Virginia leaned forward and shut off the radio and looked at me enquiringly.

"Well?"

"I've never heard anything like that before," I said. "I've steered clear of that kind of music. I thought it was only for highbrows."

"Does that mean you liked it?"

"I don't know about that. It did something to me, if that's anything. All that sound, the movement, the way that fella built it up – well, I guess it was something."

"Like some more?"

"Is there any?"

"I have records inside. The Ninth's even better. The choral'll make your hair stand on end."

"Then I'd like to hear it."

She stood up.

"Come and help me load up. I've one of these record-changing gadgets."

I followed her into the big lounge: a comfortable, well-furnished room, full of books and water-colours I guessed were hers.

Against the wall was a massive radiogram, and by it a cabinet full of records.

"Is this place yours?" I asked, looking round.

"Oh, yes, but I don't come here often. I don't get the chance. When I'm not here I rent it to a girl friend who writes novels. She's in New York right now, but she'll be back in a couple of weeks."

"And where will you be?"

"Anywhere. I might be in China, for all I know."

That was a disturbing thought.

"But you're here for a couple of weeks?"

"Possibly three."

She loaded the record holder, putting on Beethoven's Ninth and the Eroica.

She sat on the settee away from the radiogram and I sat in an armchair near the open casement windows where I could see the beach.

She was right about the choral in the Ninth. It did make my hair stand on end. When the Eroica came to an end she loaded the record holder with a symphony by Mendelssohn and another by Schubert, saying she wanted me to hear the differences in their technique.

It was getting on for seven o'clock by the time we were through playing records, and that still gave me five more hours before midnight.

"You wouldn't care to go some place for dinner?" I asked. "Nowhere very grand. I don't want to go back and change. But maybe you've a date, or something."

I waited for her to turn me down, but she didn't.

"Have you been to Raul's yet?"

"No. Where's that?"

"Oh, it's part of your education to go to Raul's. It's on the water-front. Let's go. It's fun."

We went to Raul's in her Lincoln convertible. It was a small Greek restaurant full of lighted fish tanks set in the walls, plush seats and gilt-framed mirrors.

Raul himself, a fat, cheerful Greek, waited on us. He said he knew just what we'd like. He didn't consult us, and started us with bean soup, then turtle steaks and young asparagus shoots and baked guava duff to follow.

While we ate, we talked. Don't ask me what we talked about. All I can remember was she was the easiest person in the world to talk to, and there wasn't one moment's silence during the whole meal.

We went on the verandah, overlooking the water-front, and

had coffee and brandy, and talked some more. By the time we had finished the coffee I was calling her Ginny and she was calling me Johnny. It seemed like we had known each other for years.

Later we walked along the water-front and watched the fishing-boats going out for a night's fishing. She told me she had gone out in one of them the last time she was in Lincoln Beach.

"You must go, Johnny," she said. "Out beyond the bar the water is phosphorous. It's like sailing through a sea of fire. And the fish are phosphorous, too, and when they pull in the nets, it's marvellous. Let's go, Johnny, one night. It'll be fun, and you'll love it."

"Why, sure," I said. "We will. Maybe you can . . ." I broke off as a street clock not far away started to chime, and I stood still, counting the chimes, and each stroke was like a bang under the heart with a mail-clad fist.

Ten . . . eleven . . . twelve.

"What's the matter, Johnny?" she asked, looking at me.

"Nothing. I've got to get back. I've just remembered a very important date . . ." That was as far as I could get. It came to me like a punch in the face that for the past eight hours I'd been living in a pipe-dream.

"I'll drive you back. We won't be ten minutes."

We got into the car. My mouth had dried up and the back of my throat ached, and my heart was going like a steam-hammer.

She must have guessed something was wrong, but she didn't ask questions. She drove fast. We reached the casino gates in seven minutes. I knew that because I kept my eyes glued to the clock on the dashboard.

I got out of the car. My knees were shaking. Reisner, Della and the lion pit were now as real as the warm wind against my cold, sweating face.

"So long, and thanks," I said, and my voice croaked. I wanted to say something else, make a date, let her know how wonderful I thought she was, but the words wouldn't come.

"Are you in trouble, Johnny?" she asked anxiously.

"No. It's all right. I'll look out for you."

I left her sitting in the car, wide-eyed and startled, and I walked towards the gates of the casino.

The guards opened them. The one with the green eyes gaped at me, and caught his breath sharply, but I walked on past him and headed up the long, green-lit carriage-way.

IV

I pushed open the door of the cabin and walked in. The radio was playing muted swing, and every light in the room was on.

Della was lying on the divan, a cigarette between her lips, her face as expressionless as a china mask, and as hard. She still had on the blue wrap, and her hands were clasped behind her head.

My eyes flickered from her to where he had been lying, but he wasn't there, and I felt my heart contract.

"Where is he?"

"In there." She pointed to the bathroom. "Where have you been?"

"Killing time. Did anyone . . . ?"

"I told you to keep them away from here, didn't I?" There was suppressed fury in her voice.

"I did."

"They phoned three times, and Louis came rapping on the door. Do you call that keeping them away?"

"I told them you weren't to be disturbed."

"That was at half-past three. When you left here. What happened after that? At six o'clock they really began to look for him. That's when you should have been around. Where were you?"

I was more scared of her than I was of the dead body in the bathroom. I knew instinctively she must never find out about Ginny.

"I got lost. I went down to the beach." The words ran out of my mouth in a blurred stream. "I took the wrong turning. I got snarled up in a forest."

She studied me, and I couldn't meet her eyes.

"You tried to run away, Johnny."

I didn't say anything. There was nothing to say.

"You're lucky I told the guards to stop you. You'd be under arrest by now."

"I wasn't trying to get away," I said. "I was going for a ride. I went instead for a hell of a long walk, but I came back."

She stared at me for a moment or so, then shrugged.

"Well, they're still looking for him. I had to tell them he left me at six. I said I thought he was going for a swim."

"Who's looking for him?"

"That fat fool Louis and Miss Doering." She stubbed out her cigarette. "I've done my share in this. You'd better do yours.

You know what to do. Be careful. They're still out there searching the beach."

I went over to the liquor cabinet and poured myself a shot of Scotch.

"What do I do?"

"You take him down to the lion's pit and you throw him in."

I drank the Scotch. It was like drinking water.

"And what do you do while I'm doing it?"

Her lips moved into a frozen smile.

"I stay here. What do you think I'm going to do?"

"You'd better come with me. If I ran into anyone . . ."

"I'm staying here, Johnny. You haven't been much help up to now. Go ahead and make yourself useful. You killed him, lover. I didn't."

The thought of tackling this job alone scared the daylights out of me.

"Now, wait a minute. You're in this, too. You got his gun. If they're out there looking for him . . ." I stopped, the words freezing in my mouth. A sharp rap had sounded on the door.

I looked at her and she looked at me. Very slowly I put down the half-finished Scotch. I was as stiff as a statue.

The rap came again.

"Are you there, Mrs. Wertham? This is Hame."

His voice sounded sharp and impatient.

I was so scared I couldn't move or even think. I stood there while she slid off the divan.

"One moment, Captain," she called, her voice steady and calm, but I could see by her eyes she was nearly as shaken as I was. "Go in there," she breathed, pointing to the bathroom. "Don't make a sound."

I opened the door, slid into darkness and closed the door, holding on to the handle so the catch wouldn't make a noise.

There was a five-second pause, then Hame said, "Sorry to disturb you, Mrs. Wertham. You've heard Reisner's missing?"

"Come in," she said. "Hasn't he turned up yet?"

"No." His heavy footfalls creaked across the carpet. "Miss Doering is worried about him. She phoned me so I thought I'd call up."

"But there's nothing to worry about, surely?" Her voice sounded mildly amused. "I expect he's over at Bay Street."

"He hasn't left the grounds."

"Do sit down. Won't you have a drink?"

I stood with my head pressed against the door panels, my heart pounding, and listened.

"I guess not." His voice was curt. "I'm on duty."

"Nick'll be very flattered when he hears you came up here because his secretary was lonely without him," Della said, and laughed.

"This may be serious. He was with you all the afternoon, I understand?"

"Why, yes. He left at six. He said he was going for a swim."

"No one saw him on the beach." There was a pause, then he asked, "Were you two talking business?"

Again there was a pause. I could imagine her looking at him: he wasn't likely to rattle her.

"Perhaps, after all, Captain, I'd better take you into my confidence," she said. "Please sit down."

Once again there was a lengthy pause, and I guessed there was a clash of wills going on. Then a chair creaked, and I knew she had got her way.

"And a drink, Captain. I don't like drinking alone."

"Looks like you were managing all right before I showed up," Hame said. "There's a glass of Scotch on the cabinet."

"No wonder you have such a reputation for being a clever police officer," she said, and laughed.

"I guess I don't miss much."

He sounded mollified.

I heard her splash soda into a glass.

Then he said, "Well, here's how." He grunted. "That's pretty good Scotch. What's this you were saying about taking me into your confidence?"

"Perhaps you have wondered why Ricca and I are here," she said. "Paul sent us. Nick's been dipping into the reserve to cover his gambling losses. Ricca had orders from Paul to heave him out. Well, he's gone."

I had to hand it to her. She was ready for any emergency. Her voice, now cool and matter-of-fact, was very convincing.

"You don't say." Hame sounded startled. "Much missing?"

"We don't know for certain – something like ten thousand. We haven't had time for a thorough check. He didn't deny it. He could have been difficult, but as he handed over the keys and didn't make trouble, I promised him twelve hours start. I didn't anticipate that fool of a girl would bring you into it."

"So that's it. Well I'll be double damned." There was a pause, then Hame said reluctantly, "Want me to do anything about him?"

"No. He knows too much. He might talk."

"I was thinking of that. Where's he gone?"

"I have no idea. He must have gone by way of the beach. That's why the guards didn't see him."

"Must have. Funny thing, he hasn't packed. I checked his room."

I held my breath while I waited for her to talk herself out of that one.

"He keeps a lot of stuff with Zoe. He knew this wouldn't last and was ready to skip."

There was no hesitation in her voice.

"He was no fool," Hame said, his voice ponderous. "It'll be odd not to have him around."

"It won't make any difference to you. Ricca and I will be taking charge."

"Did Wertham say it wouldn't make any difference?"

"He said more than that," Della said coolly. "He left instructions about you. He said we should do a little more for you."

"Is that right? What did he mean by that?"

There was a pause, then she said, "We think you're doing a good job for us, Captain. Paul had already spoken to Nick about you, but Nick said you were getting enough. Paul wanted to show his appreciation, but Nick blocked him off. Well, Nick's gone now. We thought another two-fifty a week might be useful. Paul said it should be back-dated six months. I'd planned to pay it into your account tomorrow as a little surprise."

"That's pretty nice of you," Hame said, suddenly jovial. "I guess I could use it. I got expenses same as anyone. Sounds as if we're going to get along together all right. Where's Ricca?"

Again I held my breath.

"I have an idea he's enjoying himself at Zoe's place. I don't know, but that's my guess. Come up and see him tomorrow. There'll be things to talk about."

"I will, Mrs. Wertham." The chair creaked as he stood up. "Guess I won't keep you any longer. Had I better have a word with Miss Doering? They're still searching for Reisner."

"Perhaps you'd better. Don't tell her what's happened. We don't want it talked about. You might say you've heard he's in town. We'll straighten things out tomorrow."

"I'll do that. Well, good night. I'm looking forward to working with you two. I'm looking forward to it very much."

"And so are we, Captain."

I listened to him tramp across the room.

"I'll be dropping in on my bank tomorrow afternoon."

"We'll be there before that, Captain." I could imagine the smile she gave him. "Good night."

The door shut.

We waited: she out there, and I in the darkness with Reisner's dead body somewhere behind me. We heard a car start up and drive away.

She pushed open the bathroom door.

"Well, I handled him, Johnny."

"Yes." I moved out of the darkness.

There was that cold, triumphant gleam in her eyes I had seen before.

"Better get going," she said. "We're practically in the clear now. They'll think he went to say good-bye to the lions and got too close. Get going, Johnny."

I looked over my shoulder into the dark bathroom. I didn't want to do it, but I could think of no other way out. The thought of carrying him through the darkness brought me out in goose-pimples.

"My car's outside," she said, speaking softly. "Put him in it and follow the carriage-way around to the back of the casino. You know where the pit is. It shouldn't take more than five minutes. Hurry, Johnny."

"Maybe you'd better handle the car . . ."

"I'm staying right here. This is where you earn your share of the money, Johnny. Make a mistake and it's all yours. You killed him; you fix it. Get going!"

I went into the bathroom and turned on the light. He was lying on his back, his head still wrapped in the towel. I kept my eyes averted as I took hold of him. His muscles were wooden, and he was heavy. I got him across my shoulder and stood up. Sweat ran down my face, and I had trouble with my breathing. As I came out of the bathroom with him, she turned off the lights and opened the door.

As I passed her she jerked at the towel, pulling it away. I didn't stop. The car was where she had said it would be. It was an open convertible, and I dropped him in the back seat without any trouble. She came up with a blanket and spread it over him.

"Good luck, Johnny," she said. "Come straight back. I want to talk to you."

I got in the car, trod on the starter and drove away without looking at her. The clock on the dashboard showed twenty to one. In the distance I could see the bright lights around the swimming-pool. People were out there, bathing. The casino was lit up like a Christmas tree. I could see men and women, in evening dress, on the verandah, caught glimpses of them through the windows of the gambling rooms, and heard their hard, strident voices, raised in excitement.

I drove slowly, with only the parking lights on, and followed the carriage-way past the casino. There were too many lights, and it was like driving with a searchlight focused on me. But beyond the casino it was dark. I kept the car moving. I could smell the lions now. One of them gave a sudden grunting cough. I slowed down. Ahead of me I could just make out the white posts supporting the iron railings around the pit. I stopped the car and turned off the lights.

For a minute or so I sat motionless, my eyes searching the darkness, my ears straining for any sound. I saw nothing. I heard only the restless movement in the pit: the soft pad, pad, pad of one of the lions as it paced up and down. I got out of the car, crossed the grass verge to the railings and looked down. It was too dark to see anything: the smell of the lion came up to me; the padding suddenly stopped. I looked to right and left. No one was likely to be here. There was nothing to see. The zoo was the only place on the estate Reisner hadn't flood-lit.

Drawing in a deep breath I returned to the car. I pulled the blanket off him and carefully folded it, putting it on the seat next to the driving seat. Again I looked to right and left, then I caught hold of him and heaved him out of the car. His stiff, claw-like hand brushed across my face as I got him over my shoulder, and I nearly dropped him. I was panting, and my heart was jumping about in my chest like a flea on a hot stove. I staggered with him across the close-cut grass. The lion below must have smelt him. It gave a sudden choked roar.

I leaned my heaving chest against the railings and bent forward. Reisner's body began to slide slowly off my shoulder. I shoved it into the darkness. It went easily enough. I continued to lean against the railings, my eyes closed, my hands gripping the iron spikes. I heard his body thud on to the concrete below. It was a thirty-foot drop. There was a rushing sound as the lion bounded forward.

I pushed myself away from the railings, gulping in warm air, turned and moved unsteadily back to the car. Well, it was done. The horrible sounds coming out of the dark pit told me I was safe. By the time they found him no one would know I had killed him.

I crossed the grass, trying to shut out the snarling, flurrying rush of the other lions as they came out of their cave. The roaring, snarling and growling filled the silent night with a hideous pandemonium.

I began to sweat as I got hurriedly into the car. I hadn't reckoned on this awful noise. I had to get away quick. My foot went down on the starter. Nothing happened. I could see the brightly lit verandah of the casino, not a hundred yards away. Men and women, sitting under the lights, were getting up and coming to the verandah rail, looking in the direction of the pit.

Again I trod on the starter, still nothing happened. Sweat was running off my face. I had to control a crazy impulse to get out of the car and run. I had to get it started! Then it flashed through my mind I hadn't turned on the ignition. As my shaking hand reached for the key I saw three or four men running down the terrace steps. I touched the starter again and the engine fired. Keeping in bottom gear I let the car move silently forward. I was shaking like a leaf. I got around the bend as the first of the men came pounding across the lawn. Shifting through the gears, I kept the car moving. They couldn't hear the engine above the hideous uproar that was coming from the pit.

I increased speed. A couple of minutes later I saw the lights of Della's cabin. I pulled up, got out and walked up the path. She stood in the doorway waiting. Even as far away as we were now from the zoo, we could hear the choked roars and screams of the lions.

I pushed past her, went into the cabin and slopped myself a big whisky.

She came in and shut the door. Her face was pale, and her eyes wide and shadowy.

"Did they see you?"

I shook my head.

"Better pull yourself together," she said impatiently. "Hame may be back."

"Easy for you to talk!" I snarled at her. "You didn't have to do it."

"I had to sit with him for nine hours. I've done my share."

I finished the Scotch and poured another.

"Go into the bathroom and smarten yourself up. If Hame sees you like this, he'll know you did it."

I went into the bathroom. She had cleaned up the mess in

there. I caught sight of my face in the mirror. I looked like hell: my face was running with sweat, my hair hung over my eyes and my skin was the colour of a fish's belly.

I ran cold water into the basin and stuck my face in it. I rubbed my skin hard with a towel until it got back a little colour. I fixed my hair. I was still trembling.

She stood in the doorway, watching me.

Then suddenly she said softly, "Who was she, Johnny?"

I didn't think I had heard aright.

"What was that?"

"Who was she?"

I went on combing my hair, but my insides turned cold.

"Who was who? What are you talking about?" Somehow I managed to keep my voice steady and my face expressionless.

"The girl who brought you back. The guards told me. Who was she?"

"How the hell do I know?" I said, and turned to face her. "I'd lost my way. I told you. I was late. I wanted to get back quick. She passed and I thumbed a ride. I didn't ask her who she was. What does it matter, anyway?"

She stared at me, and I stared right back.

"I only wondered," she said. "You're good at thumbing rides, aren't you?" She moved into the sitting-room, and I followed her. "From now on, Johnny, our future lies together. Even if we didn't happen to love each other, we know too much about each other ever to part. You do understand that, don't you?" She didn't wait for an answer, but went right on, "I think we'd better have an understanding together. There must be no other girls. I mean that. I'd never share you with anyone. I told Paul the same thing. I just won't tolerate cheating. If the idea that you can play around with other women ever enters your head, I'll get rid of you, and there's only one way to do that. I'll turn you over to Hame."

I started to say something when the telephone bell rang. She walked swiftly across the room, picked up the receiver and said, "Hello?"

I stood and watched her. She listened to the excited voice for what seemed a long time, then she said, "I can hear the noise now. How awful. He was always a fool, going into their cages. Paul warned him time and again. Yes, Ricca's here. He's just got back. No, we'll keep clear of it. Will you handle it? We don't want to get mixed up with the newspaper men. That's fine.

I'll see you tomorrow. Thank you so much, Captain." She listened, laughed, and said, "Good-bye, now," and hung up.

She looked at me.

"It's all right. It's working out just the way I said it would. Hame is making himself useful. We keep out of it." She came over to me. "Pour me a drink, darling. We must celebrate."

I gave her a whisky.

"Well, here's to us. We're set now. We're rich. Life's just beginning for us. Can you believe it, Johnny?"

I didn't say anything. I couldn't.

She drank the whisky, her eyes on my face, then she moved across the room, smiling, and pushed home the bolt on the door.

"No one will disturb us, darling. They're all too busy. Let's celebrate properly. Show me how much you love me, Johnny."

I hated her as I had never hated anyone before. She had me where she wanted me. A word from her and they'd send me to the chair. I was fixed unless I did exactly what she told me.

No other girls.

I thought of Ginny.

"We have all the money in the world," Della went on. "This is the biggest moment in my life. The biggest moment in your life, too. Can you believe it?"

"I can believe it all right," I said.

She slid her arms around my neck. I stood looking down into the black, hard, triumphant eyes.

"What's it feel like to be a millionaire?"

I said it felt fine.

"Kiss me, Johnny."

I kissed her. I even caught hold of her, crushing her to me. I even carried her over to the divan.

Up to now she had been a lot smarter than I. If I was to save my neck I had to be the one to be smarter, and I had to be patient, too.

I knelt over her and grinned down at her. It would have been easy to have put my hands on her white throat and throttled her, but that wouldn't have been smart. If I were going to beat this rap I'd have to out-fox her. Killing her wouldn't help me. It would only make things worse. With her help I had covered up one murder. I knew I wouldn't get away with another.

No, I had to out-fox her somehow. I wouldn't do it in five minutes, but I was going to do it.

The next four weeks were spent consolidating our position as Della called it. What she really meant was she was consolidating her position. I had little to say in the matter.

Although she didn't refer to it again, I knew she didn't believe for one moment that I had lost myself when I had been away from the casino during those nine hours she kept guard over Reisner's body. Nor did she believe that the girl I had said had given me a lift was a complete stranger to me. Instead of being her partner, I found myself acting as her assistant, and having to pretend I was satisfied with the position.

Trust her to be one jump ahead of me all the time. When I had left her alone with Reisner's body, she had gone through his pockets, and had got his keys and the combination of the safe. But she didn't tell me what the combination was, nor did I set eyes on the keys.

The agreement between us had been that we should share the reserve: a quarter of a million for her, and a quarter for me, but I didn't get it.

"We're in business now, Johnny," she said, when I rather hesitantly suggested it was time my share was paid over. "We need the reserve. Being in control of a money-maker like the casino is fifty times better than a lump sum of money."

I didn't see it that way. With a quarter of a million I could have skipped out of the country and taken Ginny with me, but with the hundred bucks Della paid me each week, all found, including clothes, I wasn't going to get far, and she knew it.

"You're not used to money, Johnny," she went on, lying on the divan, her wrap open, showing me her legs. "I have plans for you. You're going to get your share, but not just yet. I'm keeping it for you; investing it. I know the markets, you don't. I'll have a fortune for you in a little while. Be patient."

Neither of us believed this nonsense, but there was nothing I could do about it.

"Besides, if you want anything, you know you have only to ask me for it," she continued, smiling at me. "I want you to be happy, darling. You are happy, aren't you?"

And I'd twist up my face into a grin, and say I was happy, and hate her with my mind, brain, soul and guts, and tell myself my time would come. It was just a matter of waiting for the right opportunity.

But she didn't have it entirely her own way. She found to her surprise that no one at the casino wanted a woman boss, and when I say no one, I mean not only the staff, but the millionaires and their wives, kids, girl friends and hangers-on.

She started off by sitting in Reisner's office, ready to do business with the visitors, ready to tell the staff what to do and what not to do. She got a big bang out of sitting behind that desk, throwing her weight about and giving orders, but it didn't last long.

The first visitor she had was Gallway Harris Brown, the steel millionaire. He came bursting into the office like a runaway train: a short, fat, purple-faced bird with battle in his eyes and cuss words queueing up behind his lips.

I happened to be in the office at the time, admiring the view, while she was lording it at the desk.

She smiled at him as he came pounding in, but he took as much notice of her as he would the invisible woman. He burned a trail across the carpet towards me.

"Hey! You, Ricca?" He had a voice like a sea captain. It pretty near shattered the windows.

I said I was Ricca.

"I've no hot water in my cabin this morning. What kind of dump are you running?"

Still smiling, but her eyes snapping, Della came over.

"Perhaps I can help you . . ." she began.

That's as far as she got. He jumped around and glared at her, cutting her off with a wave of his hand.

"Listen, young woman, when I make a complaint I deal with men, understand? This guy's Ricca, isn't he? Well, then, you keep out of it. I'm going to swear at him."

There was nothing for her to do but to take three graceful steps to the rear and try to look ornamental. She was smart enough not to argue with a thousand dollar profit a week. But in spite of her smile, she looked as if she been bitten by a snake – a rattlesnake at that.

I smoothed him down and had his water fixed. I said if it ever happened again, he would have the whole of his stay with us on the house.

"That's a bet, Mr. Brown," I said. "No hot water; no cheque. Right?"

He snorted, stamped around, then finally grinned.

"That means I'll get hot water."

"You'll get hot water."

It seemed the way millionaires liked to be treated. He went around telling the story, and the other visitors came to me with their troubles.

"You go to Ricca," he said. "He'll fix it. That guy's a smart crook."

And they did come to me. They stopped me in the corridors or on the terrace or in the bar, and I fixed things for them. When they went to the office and I wasn't there, they said they wanted me and would be back.

Louis didn't pull any punches, either.

"Better let Mr. Ricca handle the staff, Mrs. Wertham," he said. "It works better that way. A man can handle this set-up better than a woman."

She was smart enough to see that the business would suffer if she continued to boss it, and she turned the office over to me.

"Go ahead, Johnny. You're in charge of the casino now. But don't get any big ideas. I'll keep the keys, and when you want money I'll open the safe."

She also kept control of Bay Street. They didn't know Paul was dead, and they were scared of her. She went over there three evenings a week to watch her interests, as she called it, and they needed watching. That suited me fine. While she was there, I was with Ginny.

It didn't take me long to find out I was in love with Ginny. After I had got over the scare of dumping Reisner, she was all I thought about. I knew it was the real thing. I knew I was gambling with my life even to think of her, but that didn't stop me. No other girls, Della had said, and that didn't stop me either.

A couple of days after I had first met her, I wrote to Ginny. I told her I was sorry about the way I had left her.

"I guess I must have sat in the sun too long," I wrote, hoping she would believe me. "I was feeling terrible, and I didn't want to scare you. I've been in bed, but I'm fine now. I hope you'll forgive me, walking out on you like that. May I come and see you and apologize?"

By the time she received the letter I had fixed up a three-room apartment on Franklin Boulevard, a quiet district in Lincoln Beach, and that's where I told her to write.

With a hundred dollars and all found I wasn't exactly broke, but I wasn't rolling it in. I did a little gambling now and then, playing on one of the crooked tables. The croupiers let me win, and every so often I picked up a couple of hundred bucks when I needed it most. But I didn't drive it into the ground. I was careful not to take too much off the house. I argued it was a good thing for the suckers to see the boss win now and then, and that was my story if someone tipped Della what was happening.

With my hundred bucks and the odd money I won I just about afforded the rent of the apartment and its running expenses.

I told Ginny I had been transferred from the Pittsburgh office of the insurance company I was working for, and had been given the job of starting an office in Lincoln Beach.

I made out I was working every hour of the day, trying to get things started, and she believed me. I hated lying to her, but there was no other way round it. I was in love with her. I wanted to marry her, but before I could do that I had to have money, and I had to have my freedom.

If Ginny hadn't had such a good job, it might have been easier. I felt I couldn't ask her to run off with me until I had enough money to take care of us both. I played it wrong. Knowing what I know now, she would have gone with me if I hadn't a cent. But you find out that kind of thing too late: anyway, I did.

Whenever Della went over to Bay Street, I'd skip into the Buick and beat it down to Franklin Boulevard. I'd call Ginny on the phone, and she'd either come over or I'd go over to her place. I heard a lot of music while I was with her, and when she was with me, we played chess. That's a game I had never played, and she taught me. Don't think I hadn't other ideas in my head when I was alone with her, besides listening to music or playing chess, but that's the way she wanted it to be, and that's the way it was.

Some evenings we went to Raul's. I figured we were safe there. It wasn't the kind of place Della would ever show up in, nor were we likely to run into anyone from the casino there.

I soon found out that Ginny was as much in love with me as I was with her. Her two weeks' stay at the beach cabin was coming to an end. That worried both of us.

"What shall we do, Johnny?" she asked. We were at the Franklin Boulevard apartment. "Just how soon do you think we can get married?"

We had got that far in eleven days.

I had been beating my brains out on the same problem. I had two things to do before I could marry her. I had to get my hands on a large sum of money, and I had to find some place where we could go where Della wouldn't think of looking for us.

When Della had dragged me into this set-up she had promised

me a quarter of a million. "Word of honour," she had said. I had carried out my part of the bargain, but she hadn't carried out hers. I now considered that quarter of a million was mine by right. If she wouldn't give it to me, I was going to take it. But before I could lay my hands on it I had to find out the combination of the safe, and that wasn't easy. There was half a million in cash in that safe, and it was a good one. Unless I found the combination I had no more chance of breaking into it than I had of swimming the Atlantic.

It was a problem, and I didn't know how to solve it. All I could hope for was to hang on and wait for a break. The other thing I had to do before I married Ginny wasn't anything like so difficult. I had that already doped out: where to go when the time came.

I figured I could lose myself in Cuba. The moment I got my hands on the money, I'd charter a plane, and Ginny and I would fly to Cuba. I reckoned we'd be safe there. Della wouldn't think to look for me in Cuba, and even if she did, and even if she found me, there was nothing she could do about it.

So when Ginny said, "Just how soon can we get married?" I had part of the answer ready for her.

I told her I thought in about six weeks.

"My boss has told me if I make a success here," I said, "he's going to give me the manager's job at our branch in Havana. It'll be a fine job, Ginny. We'll have all the money we need. You won't have to work any more. How do you like the idea of living in Cuba?"

She said she didn't mind where she lived so long as I was with her.

Every now and then I got scared, wondering how I was going to make good oh the lies I was telling her, but it was no good worrying about that. The things I had to worry about were getting the safe open and getting away from Della.

When I wasn't with Ginny I worked at the casino. I got a big bang out of running the place. Every morning I called a meeting with Della in the chair. I insisted that Louis, the head chef, the top croupier, the housekeeper and the wine steward should sit around the conference table. Della didn't like the idea, but she soon found I was right. We got ideas from these people. They had never been consulted before, and they liked being consulted, and they gave out ideas that meant more money in the kitty. I had ideas, too. I had a piece of ground cleared and had a helicopter landing-ground constructed. I fixed with a Miami airport for a taxi service of helicopters to fly a shuttle service from Miami to Lincoln Beach. If our people got bored with the casino they could hop over to Miami, and if the playboys and girls in Miami wanted a change, they could hop over to us.

I got that idea going in the first week, and it paid dividends.

Another idea I had was to hook up with the local television station and put the casino on the air. We had a good band and cabaret every evening, and I fixed it we had a nightly spot which I gave free in return for the publicity.

"I wouldn't have believed you had it in you, Johnny," Della said one night. We were together in her cabin. She had just got back from Bay Street, and I had just beaten her by five minutes from Ginny's place. "That television idea of yours is going fine."

"Yeah, it is. How about a token of appreciation? How about that quarter of a million you promised me – word of honour? I can invest it as well as you."

She gave me her silky smile. I knew it was a waste of time, but every so often I punched it home.

"Have patience, Johnny. You'll get it."

"When?"

"Come here, darling."

That was the part I hated. Making love to her when she crooked her finger. But I had to do it. I had to keep her away from Ginny. So long as I made out I was crazy about her I figured I was safe. So I made out I was crazy about her.

There were nights when I slept in my own cabin, and it was then, when I lay alone in the darkness, that I thought about Reisner. Della had said I'd forget about him after a week, but I didn't. I kept thinking of him. I even dreamed about him; imagining him outside the cabin with his cut eye and smashed face, looking at me through the window.

I thought about Hame, too. He knew the set-up. I could tell that by the way he looked at me. He knew the lions hadn't killed Reisner, although he didn't say so in so many words.

"It's a funny thing," he said to me on the morning after they had found Reisner's body in the pit, "but that guy had been dead at least eight hours before those lions mauled him. Isn't that a funny thing?"

I said it was.

We stood looking at each other for perhaps half a minute, then he turned and walked away.

I told Della.

"He won't do anything, Johnny," she said, completely unruffled. "It's too late now. He won't do anything."

And he didn't.

But whenever I met him I knew he knew, and he knew I knew he knew. He was getting seven-fifty a week from us now, and I wondered how long it would be before he wanted more. That kind always wants more sooner or later. Luckily for us we had more to give. Even if we gave him twice that amount, it wouldn't hurt us. We were coining money, or rather she was. I knew she was making much more than she expected, because every now and then she'd give me an expensive present.

"Conscience money, darling," she said. "You really are doing a job of work here."

A couple of weeks later Ginny moved out of the beach cabin. She was going to work at the store in Miami for a while, and then she was going to Key West to make sketches of the turtle crawls down there. She wasn't sure just when she would be going, but she promised to call me.

Well, that was the set-up nearly five weeks after Reisner had died. I was skating on thin ice, but up to now the ice wasn't even cracking. I was feeling pretty confident. I had got away with murder. I had out-smarted Della. I was in love with Ginny, and, more important, she was in love with me. On the face of it, it didn't look bad.

Then Ricca showed up from Los Angeles.

VI

Della and I knew, sooner or later, Ricca would turn up, and we were ready for him. We had already had a cable, addressed to Reisner, from Levinsky, saying Wertham hadn't arrived in Paris. We guessed a similar cable had been sent to Ricca.

Hoping to gain a little more time, we had cabled back that Wertham had broken his journey and was in London. We signed the cable Reisner. We had expected Ricca would telephone from Los Angeles, but he didn't. He must have suspected something was wrong, for he came without warning.

I was alone in the office working out a new idea I had for the swimming-pool. I planned to scrap the overhead lights and put in coloured lights in the floor of the bath. I reckoned that'd be a novelty, and Della agreed.

It was a half-hour after noon: a good time to work as the staff was busy preparing for the lunch rush, and the customers were busy in the bar.

I didn't hear him come in. I learned later he had a trick of moving around like a ghost. I looked up to find him standing a few feet away from me. He gave me quite a start. He wasn't anything like I had imagined him to be, but I guessed at once who he was.

I had formed a picture of him in my mind. I had imagined him to be big and tough the way I had imagined Reisner would be. But he was nothing like that. He was short and fat: like two rubber balls; one on top of the other. He was pot-bellied and his legs were thick and short. His shoulders were nearly a yard wide. He wore his thinning black hair long and plastered to his head, spreading it out carefully, but there wasn't nearly enough of it to hide the dark skin that showed between the strands of hair like the trellis work of a fence. His face was round and fat and mottled with small veins that stamped him a drunk. He had snake's eyes, flat, glittering and as lifeless as glass. His lips were thick and set in a meaningless and perpetual smile.

"I'm Ricca," he said. "Where's Nick?"

My foot touched a button under my desk that connected up with a buzzer in Della's room. We had agreed only to use the buzzer as a signal that Ricca had arrived.

"In a little urn on the shelf in the crematorium," I said, and eased back my chair.

His expression did not change, nor did his smile go away. He put a pudgy hand on the back of a chair and pulled it towards him, then he lowered himself into it and puffed breath across the desk at me.

"You mean he's dead?"

I said I meant he was dead.

"That's very interesting. And who are you?"

I opened a desk drawer and took out a box of cigarettes. I left the drawer half open. I had a ·45 Colt automatic lying in there. All I had to do was to dip into the drawer and grab it if there was trouble. We had Ricca's reception pretty well worked out.

"I'm the guy who's running this joint," I said.

"That's interesting, too." His snake's eyes went to the half-open drawer. From where he sat he couldn't see the gun, but that didn't mean he didn't know it was there. "And who put you in charge?"

"I did," Della said from the doorway.

"That's also interesting," he said without looking round. He kept his eyes on me. "Where's Paul?"

Della came around the desk and stood behind me, facing Ricca.

"How are you, Jack?" she said. "It's a long time no see. How's Los Angeles?"

Ricca crossed his fat legs. He was careful to keep his hands folded across his belly. It began to dawn on me he was dangerous. His smile was as wide and as meaningless as before, and his expression hadn't changed. He couldn't have known Della was here. He had just learned Reisner was dead. But neither of these items had dented him.

"Answering from left to right," he said, his eyes still on me. "I'm fine. It sure is a long time no see. Los Angeles is fine. Where's Paul?"

"He's dead," she told him.

His expression didn't change, nor did his smile shrink.

"And I always thought Lincoln Beach was a healthy town. Well, well, he had to die some time, I guess. What happened to him? Did he catch cold or was he helped off this earth?"

"He was killed in a car smash."

He raised his right hand slowly and examined his fingernails.

"So you got yourself a young man and took over the casino?" he said, as if he were speaking to himself.

"That's just what I did," Della said calmly. "And there's nothing you can do about it, Jack."

His smile widened.

"I always thought you were a smart girl, Della," he said placidly. "Anyone else beside you two know he's dead?"

"No. It's better it should dawn on them slowly."

Ricca nodded his ball-like head.

"Much better." He pointed a short, fat finger at me. "And who's this?"

"That's Johnny. For convenience he's known here as Johnny Ricca."

Ricca continued to smile. He nodded to me.

"That's very smart. Of course Nick was under the impression this young man was me."

We didn't say anything.

"You're a smart guy to get yourself on board this gravy train," he went on.

"And I'm smart enough to keep other people off it," I said. Even then his smile didn't fade.

Della sat on the edge of the desk. She lit a cigarette.

"Look, Jack. Let's put our cards on the table," she said. "Paul's dead. That leaves you, Levinsky, Johnny and me. Levinsky has the Paris set-up. You have Los Angeles. We have Lincoln

151

Beach. There's no reason why any of us should get in each other's way. It's a natural carve-up. What do you say?"

"I think you've worked it out pretty well," Ricca said. "Are you sure this guy can handle the job?"

I edged my hand towards the drawer. This could be the curtain-raiser to trouble.

"I'm sure of that, Jack. He has a flair for the job. He's like Paul."

That startled me, because she sounded as if she meant it.

Ricca nodded, his eyes on my hand.

"I guess that fixes it, then. I'm not complaining. I like smart people, and I guess you two are pretty smart."

Della relaxed a little, but I didn't.

"Mind if I stick around for a couple of days?" Ricca went on. "I'd like to look the joint over."

"Why, sure, Jack, we'd love to have you," Della said, before I could chip in. "Come on outside and have a drink. Coming, Johnny?"

"Right now I'm busy," I said. "Suppose we get together for lunch around half-past one?"

"Right."

Ricca got to his feet. Before I could shut the drawer he leaned forward and peered in.

"Smart fella," he said, beaming on me. "I like a guy who knows how to take care of himself. Be seeing you."

He held the door open for Della. I sat still watching him. It wasn't until he had shut the door that I slammed the drawer to. I found I was sweating a little, and my heart was beating faster than normal.

I trusted that guy like I'd trust a tiger. He was too smooth. That stuff about having no complaint was so much eye-wash. No one, especially his kind, was going to be gypped out of a joint like this without some come-back.

I sat thinking for some minutes, then I got up and went over to the window. From there I could see part of the terrace. They were out there. He was still smiling, but he was talking, too. He was talking fast and waving his fat hands, and Della was listening; her eyes on his face and her expression tense. I wondered what they were talking about.

Around half-past one I went into the restaurant. Most times I had meals in the office, otherwise as soon as I was seen I was pestered. It was surprising the number of people who wanted to

152

buy me a drink or to yap about their winnings or groan about their losses.

Della and Ricca were already at a table in a corner, away from the rest of the tables. Louis was taking their orders himself.

I sat down.

"This helicopter idea of yours is terrific," Ricca said, when Louis had taken my order and had gone. "I guess I'll try it in Los Angeles. I might hook up with San Francisco."

Della smiled at me possessively.

"I told you, Jack, he's a clever boy, and they like him here, too."

"I had a look at that lion pit," Ricca went on. "Della told me what happened to Nick. I guess you don't feed those cats yourself, do you?"

I matched his grin.

"I'm too smart," I said. "One accident's enough."

"Yeah. Had he been dipping into the reserve like Paul thought?"

"A little; not much," Della said.

"That's a big reserve. That's twice the amount I carry."

There was a moment's silence.

"We need every nickel of it," Della said, her voice hard.

He looked at her, then at me.

"It crossed my mind you might feel inclined to transfer say a quarter of it to Los Angeles. Just an idea, mind you. Paul was always switching lumps of his reserve. It was a smart move. He kept everyone satisfied."

I put down my knife and fork. I suddenly wasn't hungry any more. But Della went right on eating as if she hadn't heard.

Just for a moment the smile slipped, and I saw behind the fat, rubber-like mask, and what I saw I didn't like.

"Of course it's up to you," he said, smiling again.

"I said we needed every nickel of it, Jack," she said, without looking up.

"Maybe you do."

The waiter came and switched plates. Ricca started talking about the casino at Los Angeles. The moment had passed, but I wasn't kidding myself. He'd try again. How far he was prepared to push it remained to be seen, but he wasn't the type to give up easily.

We had coffee and brandy on the terrace. I was in the middle of explaining to Ricca my idea of lighting the swimming-pool when I saw him and Della look up and past me. I glanced up. There was a girl standing right by me. For a moment I didn't recognize her, then I saw she was Georgia Harris Brown, and she was drunk.

I hadn't seen her since that day we had parted on the beach, and seeing her again came as a shock to me.

"Hello, handsome," she said, and put her hand on my shoulder. "Remember me?"

She was wearing a pair of linen slacks and a halter. Her cute, pert little face was flushed, and the whites of her eyes were bloodshot.

I got up. Ricca got up too. Della watched me, the way a cat watches a mouse. I had an idea I was heading for trouble.

"Is there anything I can do?" I asked stiffly.

"Sure." Her fingers gripped my coat to steady herself. "That's why I'm here."

"You know Mrs. Wertham?" I said. "This is Jack Ricca. Ricca, I'd like you to meet Miss Harris Brown."

Ricca bowed, but she ignored him.

"I thought you were Ricca," she said.

"So I am. He's my cousin, on my father's side."

"It surprises me a louse like you had a father," she said.

The words hung in empty space. I didn't say anything. Ricca didn't say anything. Della lit a cigarette.

"Hello, bastard," Miss Harris Brown went on.

I was aware Ricca was watching me with interest. Della's face had gone pale, but she didn't make a move. They were my cards, and I had to play them.

"What do you want?" I said.

Della and Ricca weren't the only two looking at me now. Everyone on the terrace was looking.

She pushed her breasts out at me, and her red-painted lips curved into a smile that was as vicious as her eyes.

"I want to know who the whore is you're going around with," she said. "The pretty little trollop with red hair. The one you take to your rooms on Franklin Boulevard. The one you slop over at Raul's. Who is she?"

I went hot, then cold. My brain closed up. I opened my mouth, but nothing came out of it.

Ricca said, "She's his sister by his mother's side. Now go away, you drunken little fool. Your eyes are watery, your nose is red, and you've got a stinking, rotten breath."

Someone in the audience laughed.

Miss Harris Brown collapsed like a pricked balloon.

I watched her run across the terrace, down the steps and towards her cabin. Then I looked at Ricca.

"It was easier for me to do it," he said, "but if I spoke out of turn, I'm sorry."

"Thanks," I said. "She was drunk."

Then I looked at Della.

"Where's Raul's Johnny?" she asked, smiling, but her eyes were like chips of ice. "Or shouldn't I ask?"

"You heard what I said: she was drunk."

"We get them like that in Los Angeles," Ricca said soothingly. "You don't have to pay any attention to them. They are kind of crazy in the head."

Della got up.

"Jack and I are going over to Bay Street," she said, without looking at me. "We'll be seeing you."

She walked down the steps towards her car.

Ricca patted my arm.

"Women are funny animals," he said, "and she's no exception."

It might have been Reisner talking.

"Don't let it bother you, Johnny."

He went after her, and his smile was a mile wide.

VII

I sat at my desk, a cigarette smouldering between my fingers, my brain busy. The writing was on the wall. I didn't kid myself I could bluff Della. She was too smart. By tonight she would have found out about Ginny, my apartment on Franklin Boulevard and Raul's. Then would come the show-down.

She wouldn't have to give me away to Hame. She'd team up with Ricca and let him take care of me. This was my out. I had to skip before it was too late.

I twisted around in my chair and looked at the safe. Behind that heavy steel door was a bundle of money belonging to me. If I could get to it, I hadn't a worry in the world. But I hadn't a hope of opening that door without the combination.

For nearly four weeks I had sat around hoping the combination would drop in my lap. I now had three hours, possibly four, to get it if I was ever going to get it.

I wouldn't get it from Della: I was sure of that. Then who else knew it beside Della? For the first time I really began to bend my brains on the problem. Reisner had known it, but he was dead. The firm who made the safe would know it, but they wouldn't part with the information. Would Louis know it? There was a chance he might. I picked up the telephone and called his office.

"Louis? This is Ricca. I've got a problem. Mr. Van Etting is in my office. He wants to cash a cheque in a hurry. Mrs. Wertham's out. You wouldn't know the combination of the safe?"

I did it well. My voice was business-like, but casual.

"I'm sorry, Mr. Ricca, but I do not know it," Louis said, and from the sound of his voice he would have told me if he had known it.

"Aw, hell!" I said. "What am I going to do? This guy's getting in a rage."

"Maybe you could reach Mrs. Wertham," Louis said. "She may be at Bay Street."

"I've already tried. She's not around. You haven't three thousand bucks in your office, have you?"

He said he never kept big sums in his office.

"Okay, forget it, Louis. Sorry to have bothered you. I guess Mr. Van Etting will have to get into a rage."

I wasn't disappointed. It had been a hunch, and it hadn't come off. I was about to replace the receiver when he said, "If Miss Doering had been with us she could have told you."

Miss Doering? I stared at the opposite wall. Reisner's secretary! Della had given her the sack. She had been furious with her for calling Hame when Reisner hadn't shown up.

I gripped the receiver until my hand ached.

"Did Miss Doering know the combination?"

"Why, yes, Mr. Ricca. When Mr. Reisner was out she took care of the money."

"Well, she isn't here," I said, making out I wasn't interested any more. "Never mind. Forget it, Louis, and thanks."

I hung up and sat thinking for a moment or so, then I grabbed the telephone again and got through to the staff supervisor.

"This is Ricca. Can you give me Miss Doering's address?"

She asked me to hold on. The minute I had to wait seemed like an hour.

"247C Coral Boulevard."

"Got her phone number?"

Another wait.

"Lincoln Beach 18577."

"Thanks," I said, broke the connection, paused long enough

to wipe the sweat off my face, then got on the phone again.

"Get me Lincoln Beach 18577."

I hadn't had any previous dealings with Miss Doering. Della had handled her, and from what she had told me, she had handled her pretty roughly. I had seen her, and she had seen me. I had given her a smile now and then because she was a looker. I had no idea what she thought of me, and I knew I couldn't put this across over the telephone. I had to see her.

The line clicked and buzzed, then a woman said, "Hello?"

"Miss Doering?"

"I guess so."

"This is Johnny Ricca. I want to see you. I could be with you in fifteen minutes. How about it?"

There was a pause, then she said, "What about?"

"If I told you that I shouldn't see you, and I want to see you. Okay for me to come over?"

"If that's the way you feel about it."

"I'm on my way."

I walked out of the office, along the corridor to the elevator. I rode down to the ground floor and tramped across the lobby to the terrace. Someone spoke to me, but I didn't look to see who it was. I kept right on. The Buick was waiting at the foot of the terrace. I got in and drove down the carriage-way. The guards opened the gates as soon as they saw me. I was doing seventy before I hit the highway.

247 Coral Boulevard was a sprawling mansion that had been converted into apartments. I took a creaking elevator to the fourth floor and walked down a corridor to a door on which the numbers 247C were picked out in white paint against a glossy apple-green background.

I leaned against the bell-push. She had the door open before I could really get any weight into it: a blonde, slim lovely, with arched eyebrows that weren't her own, a figure you only see in *Esquire* and an invitation in her eyes.

"You must have moved," she said. "Come on in."

She was wearing one of those house-coat things. The way it set off her figure was nobody's business.

We went into a small room that was cluttered up with a settee, two armchairs, a radio and a table. You couldn't have swung even a Manx cat in it. She sat on the settee and I sat beside her.

We looked at each other. I had an idea she wasn't going to be difficult to handle.

"Have you found another job yet?" I asked.

"No. Want to give me one?" She crossed her legs, showing me a knee that might have interested me before I met Ginny, but which I scarcely looked at now.

"I want the combination of the safe in Reisner's office. Louis said you knew it. That's why I'm here."

"Well, you certainly don't believe in wasting time," she said, and smiled. "What makes you think I'll give it to you?"

"I'm just hoping. You don't seem surprised."

She leaned forward and dug a long finger into my chest.

"I'm surprised you haven't been before. I was expecting you, handsome. Your type doesn't sit in a room all day with a safe full of money without getting ideas. What do you intend to do – skin her?"

"She promised me a little dough, but she's changed her mind. I'm pulling out and I'm hoping to take what she owes me."

"What makes you think I'll help you?"

"I have no reason to think you will, but there's no harm in trying."

She leaned closer.

"Don't be so stand-offish. I could be persuaded. I was always a sucker for muscular men."

I kissed her. It was like getting snarled up in a meat-mincer.

After a while she pushed me away and drew in a deep breath.

"Hmmm, not bad. With a little tuition and patience you could be good."

I ran my fingers through my hair, wiped the lipstick off my mouth and took a sly look at the clock on the overmantel. It showed five minutes after five.

"I don't want to hurry this, but I'll have to," I said.

"Do you think you'll get away with it?" She had opened a powder compact and was restoring her face.

"I'll have a try."

"What are you going to do? Walk out with a bundle of money under your arm? The guards will love it."

"I'll take it out in a suitcase in my car."

"About as safe as jumping out of this window."

"Now wait a minute. Let's get this straight. Where do you come in on this deal? What's your cut to be?"

She laughed.

"Do I look all that crazy? I wouldn't touch a dollar of it. You may not think it, but I don't take money that doesn't belong to me. I have other faults, but that's not one of them. I'm going

158

to give you the combination because I'd like that black-haired, snooty little bitch to be well and properly gypped. I hated Reisner, and I hate her. It's my way of getting even for all I've put up with from both of them. Go ahead, Mr. Ricca, help yourself. The more you take the better I'll like it."

I looked at her. She wasn't fooling.

"Okay, let's have it."

She reached over, opened a drawer in the table near by and gave me a slip of paper.

"It's been waiting there ever since I first saw you. I knew sooner or later you'd want it."

I looked at the row of figures, my heart banging against my ribs. Talk about a break! I could scarcely believe it.

"Well, thanks," I said, and got to my feet.

"Going after it now?"

"Right now."

"Still going to take it out in your car?"

"Any better ideas?"

She leaned against me.

"You're learning, handsome. There's only one way to get that money out and be sure of it. Perhaps you don't know this, but at six every evening the railroad truck calls for luggage or empty crates, or whatever's going by rail. There's always something. Pack the money in a suitcase, address it to yourself at any station to be called for. The man will give you a receipt. You'll find him loading up at the luggage entrance. He handles the stuff himself. There's seldom anyone there. It's the only way, handsome. The guards don't check his stuff, and when you go, you'll go empty-handed."

I patted her on the shoulder.

"You're more than smart; you're brilliant," I said. "That's a whale of an idea."

She leaned more heavily against me.

"Show a little appreciation."

It took me ten precious minutes to untangle myself from her clutches, a quarter of an hour to buy a black pigskin suitcase with good locks, five minutes to buy a coil of thin rope and a big meat hook, and ten minutes to get back to the casino.

As I drove in I asked the green-eyed guard if he had seen Mrs. Wertham.

"Not in yet," he growled.

I drove fast around to the back of the casino. Twenty feet above me was my office window, overlooking a walled-in garden that was reserved for the management, and no one else. I set the suitcase down immediately below the window, ran back to the car and drove around to the front entrance.

I went up the steps to the terrace three at a time. People said hello, and tried to stop me, but I grinned at them and kept on.

When Della checked up on me she would learn I hadn't come in with a suitcase, only a small brown-paper parcel that contained the rope and the hook.

I got to my office, locked the door, opened the window and dropped the hook, attached to the rope, down on to the suitcase. I snagged it the first throw. I hauled it up, then went over to the safe. With the combination in my hand I turned the tumblers. I was working against time. The desk clock showed five minutes to six.

I came to the last number, turned to it and felt the tumbler fall into position. Holding my breath, I tugged at the handle of the safe. The door swung open.

I sat back on my heels and feasted my eyes on the contents. On two shelves were neat packages of one-hundred dollar bills: stacks and stacks and stacks of them.

I pulled the suitcase closer, opened it and began to pack the bundles in. Two hundred and fifty of them filled the case: it was the most awe-inspiring sight I'd ever set eyes on. There were still another two hundred and fifty bundles left on the shelves. But they didn't belong to me. I left them right where they were.

Before I slammed the suitcase shut I took three one-hundred dollar bills out of one package, folded them small and wedged them down the side of my shoe. Then I snapped the locks, turned the keys and put them in my pocket. I shut the safe door and gave the knob of the lock a couple of turns. Then I dusted the safe with my handkerchief and stood up.

I was panting with excitement and my collar was a wet rag. The hands of the clock showed six.

I took the suitcase to the window, leaned out and dropped it. Then I hooked the hook to the window-sill and slid down the rope. When I reached the ground I jerked the hook free, coiled the rope and hid it under a shrub. I picked up the suitcase and bolted across the lawn.

The trucker was just through loading up by the time I got there. He had signed off and was getting into his cab. There was no one else around.

"Just in time, I guess," I panted.

He looked me over, hesitated, then gave a resigned grin.

"Where to, mister?"

"Got a label?"

He found one.

I printed my name on it.

> John Farrar,
> Seaboard Air-Line Railway, Grt. Miami.
> To be called for.

He wrote out a receipt.

"Sorry to hold you up," I said, and gave him ten bucks. "Keep the change."

He nearly fell off the truck.

"I'll take care of this for you, sir. It'll be right there waiting for you."

I hoped it would.

I stood back and watched the truck drive away. It made me sweat to think of all that money going on that journey without me to guard every yard of it.

But she was right. It was the smart thing to do. If those two guards spotted the suitcase they would want to know what was inside it: especially the green-eyed guard. He had it in for me.

I folded the receipt the trucker had given me into a narrow ribbon. Right now that scrap of paper was worth a quarter of a million dollars. I took off my slouch hat and tucked the ribbon of paper behind the sweat band.

Things were working out better than I had imagined. I had got the money out, now I had to get myself out.

I remembered the ·45 Colt automatic I had left in my desk drawer. I might need that gun. I decided to get it.

It took me a couple of minutes to reach the office. I stopped short just inside the doorway.

Della and Ricca were sitting near my desk. Ricca had the Colt in his hand, and it was pointing at me.

VIII

"Come in, Johnny," Della said.

I closed the door and walked across the expanse of fawn carpet, somehow keeping my face expressionless, and cursing myself for coming back.

As I made for the desk, Della said, "Don't sit there. That's no longer your place. I want you to meet my new partner," and she waved to Ricca.

"So that's how it is," I said. "Did he talk you into it or did you talk him into it, and what's the idea of the gun?"

"Neither," Della said. "Miss Harris Brown talked you out of it."

I took out a packet of cigarettes together with the keys of the suitcase. Without letting them see the keys I let them slide into the side of the chair. I lit a cigarette and blew smoke at her. I could tell by the way she was breathing that there was going to be an explosion before long. She was only keeping control of herself because she wanted to prolong what she imagined was my agony. She was pale, and her eyes were deadly, and her breasts were rising and falling under the thin stuff of her dress as if she were suffocating.

"I told you at the time," I said, "that little mare was drunk."

"I know what you told me, Johnny," she said her voice going shrill. "But I haven't been wasting my time this afternoon. I have been making enquiries. You may not know it, but the guards log all cars that come to the gates. It didn't take long to find the number of the Lincoln that brought you back the night you killed Reisner. It didn't take long for Hame to find out the owner of the car is Virginia Laverick who has a beach cabin not far from here. Nor did it take long for me to find out she works at Keston's in Miami, and Raul under a little pressure told me you and she often go there for dinner."

I wasn't surprised. I knew she might dig out all this information as soon as she had left me after the scene on the terrace.

"Do we have to go into this with Ricca here?" I said. "It can't be much fun for him."

Ricca's smile widened.

"I thought it might be safer for you if I stuck around," he said. "Della's temper is a little uncertain. She wanted to shoot you as you walked in. I had trouble persuading her to change her mind."

"Maybe you'd better stay, then," I said.

"Do you deny you have an apartment on Franklin Boulevard, and this girl visits you there?" Della cried, leaning forward and glaring at me.

"No, I don't deny it," I said. "What are you going to do about it?"

She sat back, and there was a long moment of silence.

Ricca said, "Let's skip the next piece and go right into the last act. We're wasting time with this guy."

I was glad he was there. She looked ready to blow her top,

but his cold flat voice kept her under control.

"Yes," she said. "We'll skip the next piece. Well, Johnny, you've been warned. I told you to lay off other women."

"I know what you told me."

"Then you'll have to take the consequences," she said. "I'm going to throw you out of here the way I picked you up: a third-rate fighter without a dollar to your name. How do you like that?"

The least I expected was she would have me beaten up. I took a casual stare at the safe. It was shut. She couldn't know I had tampered with it!

"Now wait a minute," I said, sitting forward, "you can't get away with that. We made a bargain. I want my dough!"

If I didn't make out she was scoring off me, she might still decide to put a bullet in me. The rage and dismay I got into my voice even surprised me.

"We made another bargain," she said, "you're forgetting that, Johnny." Her eyes were bright with spite. "I said no other women – remember? You've gypped yourself out of a quarter of a million. How do you like that? Was Miss Laverick worth all that money, Johnny?"

I twisted my face into what I hoped was a mask of infuriated rage and started up.

"Sit down!" Ricca said, and the gun covered me.

I sat down.

"Throw me out if you like, but I'm going to have that money!" I snarled at her.

"You'll leave here without a dime and on your feet!" she said. "The guards have been told to let you out only if you are walking and you're not carrying a bag. You'll have a nice long walk ahead of you, and I hope you'll enjoy it!"

"Don't imagine you'll get away with this!" I shouted. "If you think you can gyp me . . ."

She was revelling in it now. I made out I was going to spring at her. Ricca stood up, threatening me with the gun.

"Empty your pockets on the desk," Della said.

"Make me!" I said. "I'd like to see either of you get close enough to make me!"

"That won't be necessary," Ricca said. "Do what she says or I'll shoot you in the leg and you'll damn well have to crawl out of here!"

I thought of those three one-hundred-dollar bills I had hidden in my shoe, and I had trouble in keeping a straight face.

"I'll fix you too!" I snarled at him, and began emptying my pockets on the desk.

When I was through she made me pull out the linings of my pockets to make sure I'd kept nothing back. I was glad I had stashed the keys in the chair. If she had seen those she might have looked in the safe. All the time I had been in the room I had kept my hat on. The receipt for the suitcase was burning a hole in my head, but neither of them thought to look inside my hat.

"Okay, Johnny," Della said, "now you're all set to go. I hope you'll be hungry tonight. I hope no one gives you a ride. I hope you rot in hell!"

"I'll fix you for this!" I yelled at her, and moved to the door.

"Better get going fast, Johnny," she said, and a cruel little smile lit up her face. "I said I'd throw you out as I found you, didn't I? Pepi and Benno are on their way over. They should arrive any moment now. They seemed very interested to hear you were here. So this is where you came in, darling. You're on the run again, and I hope they catch you!"

I started to say something when the door opened and Louis walked in. Ricca hid the gun behind his back.

"What do you want?" Della demanded. "Can't you knock?"

Louis's fat face looked startled.

"I thought Mr. Ricca was alone."

"Well, he isn't. What do you want?"

I went cold. I knew what he wanted. He had come to ask if I had managed to get the safe open.

"You talk to them," I said to him. "I'm clearing out. That fat boy's your new boss."

I shoved past him, jerked open the door as Della cried, "Wait!"

But I didn't wait. In three or four seconds she would know I'd beaten her to the punch. I had to get out and get out fast.

I jumped into the elevator and rode to the ground floor. Moving fast, I crossed the lobby, pelted down the steps and vaulted into the waiting Buick.

I shot away from the casino steps and down the carriage-way like a bat out of hell. Half-way down I lowered the wind-shield until it was lying flat. I crouched down in the seat. By the time I saw the gates ahead of me I was driving at sixty miles an hour.

The two guards were there. The green-eyed one had his gun in his hand. They had heard me coming, and probably she had phoned I was to be stopped, but I wasn't stopping.

Those gates looked big and impressive, but they had two weaknesses. They opened outwards and they were held shut only by a single bolt. Moving at this speed I didn't reckon they would hold me, and they didn't.

The guards jumped clear as I swept down on them. I held the steering-wheel as tightly as I could and lowered my head. The solid steel bumpers smashed into the gates, and they flew open. The car rocked and swerved, but I straightened it, shoving my foot down hard on the accelerator. I heard the bang of a gun, but I didn't care. I was through those gates and on to the highway. I went on feeding petrol into the cylinders: the speedometer needle flickered up to eighty. They would have to move to catch me!

A couple of miles down the road I came to the bends: the climbing switchback that led across the dunes to the Miami Highway. I had to cut speed, but that didn't worry me. They would take a few minutes to get after me, and they couldn't go faster on this road than I could.

Well, I had beaten her! I wanted to sing and yell. I had outsmarted her in spite of her smartness. I'd got the money and I was out, and before she could get things moving I'd be safely hidden in Cuba. I was riding higher than a kite!

After driving for fifty miles or so, I turned off the highway and got on to the secondary road. The Buick was an obvious car to spot, and I was less likely to be noticed on the secondary road than on the highway. Before long I would have to get petrol. I was running low.

As I drove I remembered Ginny was staying with a girl friend in Miami, and I knew her telephone number. I decided I'd stop at the next filling-station and call her. I'd get her to charter a plane this night, and if I could persuade her to go with me to Cuba, and I thought I could. I'd be sitting on top of the world!

About a couple of miles farther on I spotted a filling-station and I pulled in.

An old guy with a goatee beard came waddling out of the shabby little office.

"Fill her up," I said. "Have you a phone here?"

"Right in there, mister."

I suddenly remembered I had only three one-hundred-dollar bills on me. I bent down and flicked them out of my shoe.

"I got nothing smaller than a C. Can you give me change?"

"Sure. You go right ahead and phone. I'll get you change."

The phone was on a battered desk by an open window. I called Ginny's number. The light was fading now. It was getting on for nine. I could see the old guy pumping petrol into the Buick. On the desk was a packet of Camel's. I took one and lit up.

"Hello," a girl said over the line. It wasn't Ginny.

"Miss Laverick there?"

"No, she's out, but I'm expecting her any minute now."

I cursed silently.

"Okay. I'll call back in five minutes."

I hung up and went outside to see how the old guy was getting on. He was screwing on the cap.

"She's full, mister."

"Get me the change will you? I want to phone again in five minutes."

He got me the change and sold me a packet of cigarettes. I hung around and wasted eleven minutes before I finally got Ginny. By then I was getting a little uneasy. A fast car can cover a lot of miles in eleven minutes. I wasn't kidding myself they wouldn't be after me by now.

"Why, Johnny, darling!"

"Now, listen, kid. I've a surprise for you. I've got that job. Yep. I heard only just now. And I've another surprise for you. I'm on my way to you now."

"Why, Johnny, does that mean . . . ?"

"Yeah, it means just that, but hold everything and listen. I'm to start work in Havana tomorrow. I want you to call the airport and charter a plane to Havana to be ready to take off in four hours. I want to know if you'll come with me."

"Charter a plane? It'll cost a fortune."

"Never mind the money. I've got all the money in the world. Will you come with me, Ginny?"

"Tonight?" Her voice rose. "But I should have to pack and . . ."

"It's tough, but if you can't make it I'll have to go alone . . ."

"Not another word, Johnny. I'll make it!"

That's the kind of girl she was.

"As soon as we arrive, we'll be married, Ginny. Hold everything. I'm on my way!"

I slammed down the receiver and ran out.

The old guy was standing with his back to the petrol pump, his hands in the air and his goatee trembling. I pulled up short and spun around, my heart skipping a beat.

166

Della was standing in the shadows, by the window, a gun in her hand, the awful little smile flickering around her lips.

"Hello, Johnny," she said.

I knew if I made the slightest move she'd drill me. There was a look in her eyes that turned me cold.

"Get in the car, Johnny; you and I are going for a ride."

And I knew if I even hesitated she'd shoot. I walked over to the Buick and got in under the driving-wheel. She opened the rear door and got in behind me.

"Miami, Johnny," she said, "and snap it up!"

I trod on the starter, shifted into second and pulled away from the row of petrol pumps. The old guy still stood as stiff as a statue, his hands in the air. She had scared the guts out of him.

We drove for about a mile in silence, then she said, "Where's the money?"

I could see her in the driving mirror, the gun was pointing at the back of my head. Her face in the moonlight was as white as a fresh fall of snow, and her eyes scared me.

"Where you'll never find it," I said.

"We'll find it. Benno and Pepi are waiting for you in Miami. They'll make you talk, Johnny, and then they'll kill you, and you'll be glad to die."

I kept driving. There wasn't anything I could do about it yet, but I was working on it.

"So you thought you'd marry her," she went on, the words spilling out of her mouth in a vicious rush. "That's a laugh! She's in this, too. We'll pick up Pepi and Benno, and then we'll all go down to the airport and pick her up. You'll talk fast enough when you see those two working on her. I'll make her suffer! Don't think she'll escape. She's in this as much as you!"

That settled it. Only she had heard my conversation over the phone. Only she knew I had arranged to meet Ginny at the airport. It was as simple as that. Ginny wasn't going to fall into Pepi's hands. I had still the last word. The road was straight: on either side were mangrove thickets. It was as simple as that.

"Well, so long, Ginny," I thought. "This is the way out. This is the only way out," and I got a picture of her in my mind with her copper-coloured hair and her big, serious eyes and her lovely mouth as I pulled down hard on the wheel.

As I swung the car off the road, I shoved the accelerator to the boards. I felt the car leap forward. I didn't look where we were heading. My eyes were fixed on the driving mirror. I could see Della's face.

"Go ahead and shoot me," I thought. "If this is my end, it's your end too. You're not going to get your dirty claws on Ginny."

I saw the fear and horror in her face. I heard her thin, wailing scream. I saw the gun drop out of her hand as she threw up her arm to shield her face.

Then we hit a tree, bounced off it, shot into the undergrowth and smashed into another tree. I held on to the steering-wheel for dear life. Della had disappeared. I felt the car turning over.

"This is it," I thought, and I wasn't scared. I was thinking of Ginny as the car turned over, and I was still thinking of her when something crashed down on my head.

PART FIVE

CURTAINS

I

"COME on! Snap out of it!" a voice bawled in my ear, and a hand caught hold of my coat front and hauled me upright. "Wake up, louse!"

I got my eyes open with an effort, and stared into the fat, blue-chinned face of Benno. Instinctively, I tried to throw a punch at him, but my arm didn't respond.

Snarling, he slammed me across the mouth with the back of his hand, and I flopped back on the bed, scarcely conscious.

Dimly I heard a fat voice say, "Don't hit him like that, you fool! I want him to talk!"

"He'll talk!" Benno said viciously, and hauled me upright again. "Come on! Take notice or I'll yank your goddamn ears off!"

I opened my eyes again and looked around. I was lying bound hand and foot, on my bed in the bedroom of my apartment on Franklin Boulevard. Benno was sitting on the bed, and Ricca stood at the foot of the bed.

For a long moment I was confused and bewildered, then I remembered Ginny. Was she still in the apartment? Had I imagined she had been there? I remembered her coming to the door and the terror on her face.

"What have you done with her?" I croaked.

Ricca smiled.

"She's in the other room. You played your hand pretty badly. I wanted her as well as you, and you led me right to her."

I strained at the cord that bound my hands, but it didn't give.

"Better bring her in here," Ricca said to Benno. "It's time we started."

Benno patted my face with a hand that smelt of lavender water.

"You and me are going to have fun before long," he said.

He went into the other room.

Ricca continued to smile and puff breath at me. His snake's eyes were vicious.

Benno came back, dragging Ginny with him. She was gagged, and her wrists were tied behind her. There was a rip in her skirt, and she had pushed a knee through one stocking. She looked as if she had had a bad time. She stared wildly at me, horror in her eyes.

"Ginny!" I cried, struggling upright. "What have they done to you?"

"We haven't done much to her yet," Ricca said, "but we will unless you are ready to talk."

"Turn her loose and I'll talk," I said wildly. Just to see her in the hands of a rat like Benno drove me frantic. "But she's got to go free! She isn't in this. She's got to go free."

Ricca pulled up a chair and lowered his bulk on to it.

"You had your chance when I made my first offer," he said. "It's out of my hands now. Petelli's claiming you. All I want is the money, then I turn you over to him." He pulled at his thick lower lip. "Unfortunately she'll have to be turned over to him, too."

"That won't get you anywhere," I said. "Either she goes free or the money stays where it is, and it's where you'll never get your claws on it."

"Don't be too sure about that. I have an idea I can persuade you to talk."

"You heard what I said! Let her free or you don't get the money!"

Ricca lifted his fat shoulders.

"It's out of my hands. She knows too much. Benno's going to knock you off. She'll have to go, too."

I turned ice-cold. I had only to look at him to see he wasn't bluffing.

"She'll give you her word not to talk," I said. "I don't give a damn what happens to me, but you've got to let her go!"

"I happen to hold all the cards in this deal," Ricca said. "Ask yourself which would be better for her: a bullet through the head or to be worked over until you decide to talk. You'll see Benno at work. Better save her from that. What do you say – a quick bullet or Benno?"

Benno put his hand on the front of Ginny's frock and ripped it down to her waist.

I was licked and I knew it. Ginny would be better off dead than tortured by Benno.

Without looking at her, I said, "Yes. Don't let him touch her. I'll talk."

Ricca rubbed his hands.

"I thought somehow you would. Where's the money?"

"The Miami Safe Deposit."

I could see by the momentary blank expression in his eyes he hadn't expected this.

"I see. Very sensible of you."

Then suddenly I remembered the ·22 I had left in the suitcase. I felt a hot surge of triumph run through me. With that gun I could fix him and turn the tables on Benno.

"You will write them a letter . . ." he began, but stopped as I shook my head.

"Do you imagine I'm all that of a dope? I and no one else can get the money. I left instructions I was the only one to enter the strong room."

Ricca stared down at his feet. Then he glanced up and waved his hand at Benno.

"Take her away," he said. "Why doesn't Pepi come?"

"He doesn't know we're here," Benno said. "How many more times do I have to tell you?"

"Try to find him. We want him."

"Forget him! He might be anywhere. Can't you swing this yourself?"

"Take her away."

Benno shoved Ginny out of the room. As he reached the door he put his knee in her back and shot her forward. I heard her fall on the floor.

"If ever I get my hands on you . . ." I said, straining at the rope that held my wrists.

Ricca smiled.

"It's your own fault. How can you expect an animal like Benno to treat a girl decently?" He grimaced as he looked through the open door. "You and I will go and collect the money," he went on. "After that, Benno takes charge, but I promise you I will see he makes it quick. I owe you something. I am grateful to you for getting rid of Della. Now, of course, I take over the casino myself."

I stared fixedly at him.

"And when we get to the safe deposit, don't make trouble," he went on. "The money belongs to the casino, and I can prove it. Hame will play along with me. There's nothing you can do about it."

"I know when I'm licked," I said, thinking of the '22 in the suitcase.

He went into the other room and I heard him talking to Benno. While I had a moment to myself I tried desperately to free my hands. I might just as well have tried to tip over the Woolworth building.

Ricca came into the room again.

"If I am not back within the hour he will take her away from here. I needn't tell you what he will do to her. So no tricks."

He cut my ankles free.

"Stand up and turn round."

Benno came to the door, a snub-nosed automatic in his hand. He kept me covered while Ricca freed my hands.

"Okay," Ricca said, pulling a gun from his hip pocket. "Let's go."

I went first and he followed. We walked down the four flights of stairs. Drawn up outside the front door was a dark-blue Packard.

"You drive, Johnny. I'll sit at the back. And snap into it. I don't imagine Benno will keep his hands off her for long. She's pretty, isn't she?"

My sick fear for her turned to cold, vicious rage against him. I didn't say anything but drove fast until I reached Roosevelt Boulevard. Here the traffic was heavy, and it took me some minutes to weave the car to a standstill outside the Safe Deposit building.

A guard came over.

"I deposited a suitcase here this morning. I want to pick it up."

"You know the way, sir? Mr. Evesham will look after you."

I said I knew the way, and went up the steps with Ricca at my heels.

The princely Mr. Evesham looked surprised when he saw me, but he remembered his manners and stood up and bowed.

"My partner's arrived unexpectedly," I said, waving to Ricca. "I'll want the suitcase for a couple of days."

"Certainly, sir. Shall I come up with you?"

"That's okay. I know my way."

"I'll have the receipt for you to sign when you come down."

"Thanks," I said, and walked over to the elevator.

Ricca stood beside me, smiling, as the elevator took us to the fifth floor.

"They arrange things well here," he said. "Might be an idea to have something like this at the casino."

I didn't say anything. When the elevator stopped, I walked down the corridor with him just behind me.

The guard came out of the guard house.

"Let me have the key to room 46," I said.

He studied me, then went away. After a moment or so he returned and handed me the key.

"Third door on the right, sir."

I continued down the corridor and stopped outside room 46.

"Without your co-operation," Ricca said, "it would have been impossible to get the money. What a sensible young man you are."

I unlocked the door and pushed it open.

"Quite luxurious," Ricca said, looking in. He made no move to enter. "I think I'll wait here. Bring the money to me."

But I wanted him inside with the door shut.

"The door has to be closed before the safe will open," I said, entering the room. "Wait outside if you like."

He looked up and down the empty corridor, then pulled out his gun.

"In that case I'll come in with you. I don't trust you out of my sight, but don't make any false moves."

I had no qualms about killing him. Ginny's life and mine were worth a lot more to me than his. I knew the sound of a ·22 wouldn't be heard outside the steel-lined room.

I stood beside the safe and began to spell out the combination. I was calm and my hands were steady. I kept thinking of Ginny along with Benno. I knew I mustn't make the slightest slip.

The safe door swung open.

"Better keep back," I said. "There's a gadget somewhere that photographs when the safe is opened."

"They seem to have thought of everything," Ricca said. I could tell by his voice he wasn't suspicious. "Is the money there?"

"What do you think?" I hauled out the suitcase and dumped it on the table. There wasn't room for him to come around and stand by my side. He faced me. I snapped back the locks and threw open the case. The open lid was towards him. He couldn't see what was inside the case. I tossed a bundle of bills on the table as he began to move forward. He paused and looked at them, an oily smile spreading over his face. That gave me the opportunity to pick up the ·22 lying in the case.

I aimed through the lid of the case at his belly. A little gun like a ·22 hasn't much stopping power, but I knew a slug in his gut would paralyse him. I waited until he began to move forward again, then looking right at him, I squeezed the trigger.

The gun went off with a noise like the breaking of a dry stick. Ricca reared back, his face contorted with agony, his hands clutching at his fat paunch. Then he folded forward as if he had a hinge in his back. His gun dropped out of his hand, and he fell across the table, his face hanging over the upraised lid of the suitcase.

I gave the top of his head a hard shove, and he slid off the table on to the floor.

I was breathing heavily, and I began to shake as I watched him squirm about on the floor, his hands pressed to his belly, blood oozing out between his fingers.

I picked up his gun. Holding it by the barrel I bent over him. We stared at each other. There was a film forming over his eyes, but by the way his mouth twisted into a snarl I knew he could still see me. I hit him very hard in the centre of his forehead. The heavy butt of the gun crashed down, breaking the skin and driving a little hollow into the broad expanse of bone.

He stopped squirming and stiffened out. For perhaps a second or so I stood over him, then sure I had taken care of him I straightened up and stepped away from him.

I wiped the sweat from my face, dropped his gun by his side and shoved the ·22 into my hip pocket. I shut the suitcase and snapped down the locks. Then without looking at him, I stepped to the door and opened it. The corridor was still empty. I locked the door, dropped the key into my pocket and walked quickly to the guard room.

The guard appeared.

"I'm checking out," I said. "My partner's going through some papers. He may be some time. Don't disturb him, will you?"

"That's all right, sir."

"He has the key. He'll give it to you when he leaves. What time do you shut?"

"Six-thirty, sir."

I looked at my wrist-watch. It was now a quarter to four. I had nearly three hours in which to get clear.

"He'll be through by then."

I rode down in the elevator. Mr. Evesham was waiting for me.

"My partner's working up there. I've fixed it with the guard."

"Quite all right, sir."

"I'm taking the case. Do you want me to sign anything?"

He gave me a couple of forms. I signed where he indicated.

"I'll be back in a couple of days."

"You are very welcome, sir," he returned with a stately bow.

A guard opened the door of Ricca's car as I came down the steps. I slung the suitcase in the back and got in under the steering-wheel.

"Thanks," I said as he closed the door.

I drove fast to Franklin Boulevard.

II

I parked the car outside the back entrance of 3945 in a narrow alley that ran parallel with Franklin Boulevard. I put the suitcase in the boot of the car, then pushed open the garden gate and entered a wilderness of trees, shrubs and overgrown flowerbeds. I made my way from tree to tree until I was within sight of the back of the house.

Against the wall, built between two steel shafts, was an outside dumb-waiter, which tradesmen used to haul up the groceries to the various apartments. I planned to haul myself up to my apartment in it, and take Benno by surprise.

The chances were he was still in the front room with Ginny. If he was, and I could get into the apartment without him knowing, I was sure I could take him. There could be no shooting in that house unless I wanted a hoard of policemen swarming around me, and I didn't.

As I stood looking up at the windows, a big white cat came out of the shrubbery and rubbed itself against my leg. It belonged to the janitor, and used to come up to my apartment when Ginny and I were there, and Ginny would feed it.

I had too much on my mind to bother with it, and I gave it a little nudge with my foot, but it didn't take the hint. When I began to dodge from shrub to shrub, working my way to the dumb-waiter, it followed me.

I squeezed myself into the box. It was a tight fit, and I wondered if the rope would be strong enough to take my weight.

The cat jumped on to my lap, and rubbed its face against mine. I was about to push it off when an idea struck me. It might be useful in the apartment to create a diversion, and I decided to take it up with me.

I caught hold of the rope and began to haul. The box moved creakily upward. In spite of the system of pulleys I had a lot of weight on my arms, and my progress was slow.

I was panting by the time I reached the third floor, and I

stopped to get some breath back. The cat kept bumping its face into mine. It didn't seem at all perturbed that we were hanging in space. After a minute or so I began to haul again. Inch by inch the box crawled upwards until finally it came to the wooden trap leading to my kitchen. I jammed on the brake and thankfully let go of the rope.

I sat with my legs dangling while I massaged my aching arms. As soon as my heart had stopped jumping like a freshly landed fish, I turned my attention to the trap. I pressed gently, and it swung open. I looked into an empty kitchen. The cat jumped from my lap on to the floor and started twining itself around the table leg looking up at me hopefully.

I took off my shoes, then slid soundlessly to the floor, crept over to the door and opened it half an inch. For some seconds I heard nothing. Then I heard Benno humming to himself. He was in the front room.

I closed the door again, then I picked up the cat and holding it under my arm, I opened the china cupboard and took out a couple of plates. I pitched them into the air. The crash they made when they hit on the floor was enough to raise the dead.

Still holding the cat I stepped back and flattened myself against the wall by the door. I waited. Nothing happened. All I could hear was my quick, light breathing and the faint purring of the cat.

Minutes ticked by, and I began to wonder if Benno was coming. Then suddenly I noticed the door was opening.

I bent down and gently put the cat on the floor. I gave it a little shove sending it away from me. Then I straightened up, every muscle in my body tense.

The door continued to open inch by inch. The cat stood still, staring at the door. Suddenly it growled, and its tail bushed out.

The door swung wide open.

"Goddamn it!" I heard Benno mutter. "A cat!"

I held my breath, praying he would come in, but he didn't. He remained just outside the door. I could hear his breath whistling down his nose.

The cat backed away.

"How did you get in here?" Benno demanded. "Here, come here."

But the cat didn't seem to like the look of him. It spat at him, continuing to back away.

Benno wandered into the kitchen. He had a gun in his right

hand. He came in slowly, snapping his fingers at the cat.

"Here, pooch, come here," he said.

He was within three feet of me before some instinct warned him of his danger. He swung around as I struck at him. That quick, unexpected movement spoilt my aim, and instead of landing on his jaw, my fist caught the top of his shoulder. The force of the punch sent him flying. He crashed against the wall, made a frantic effort to regain his balance, and at the same time aim his gun at me.

I flung myself at him, my right hand clamping down on his gun hand. I crushed his fingers against the gun butt and pinned him against the wall.

His fat, vicious face was only inches away from mine. He tried to grab my throat, but I slammed over a punch that caught him on the side of his head, stunning him.

I tore the gun out of his hand and threw it away, then my fingers sank into the fat flesh of his neck, my thumbs digging into his windpipe. As I exerted pressure, his face turned blue and his eyes started out of his head. I held him against the wall and throttled him.

Only the whites of his eyes were showing when I stepped away from him and let him slide limply to the floor. My hands ached, and my heart thumped as I bent over him. I put a finger on his eye: it didn't flicker. I touched the artery in his neck: no pulse answered me.

I straightened up, flexing my aching fingers and then with an unsteady hand I lit a cigarette. Reisner, Della, Ricca and now Benno, I thought. I could feel no pity for any of them. If I hadn't killed them, they would have killed me.

The cat came over and sniffed delicately at Benno's dead face. It put out a paw and patted his nose.

I took two or three hurried drags at the cigarette, then dropped it and put my heel in it. Time was running out. There was still much to do.

I put on my shoes, shoved Benno's gun in my hip pocket and went along the passage into the sitting-room.

Ginny lay in the armchair. Her hands were tied behind her, and she was still gagged. Her head lolled forward and she seemed to be in a faint.

I ran to her, slashed through the cord that bound her wrists and gently eased the gag out of her mouth.

"Ginny, darling!"

She moaned softly.

"Ginny, it's me. Come on, darling, we've got to get out of here!"

Her head dropped back and her eyelids lifted. Recognition slowly came into her eyes and she touched my face.

"Where have you been, Johnny?" she said huskily. "I waited and waited. I moved in here, hoping you'd come back. It's been so long."

"I'll tell you about it later. Come on, kid, we've got to get out of here. We've got to get out of town. I have a car outside."

"Where are we going?" She sat up, her land going to her torn dress.

"We can decide that as we go. We've got to hurry."

She shivered.

"Where is that awful little man? Who is he?"

I pulled her to her feet. Her knees buckled and she would have fallen if I hadn't supported her.

"Don't worry about anything. I've taken care of him. Let's get out of here."

"No!" She tried to push away from me, but I held her. "I'm not going with you until I know what all this means. Why do we have to leave? Send for the police, Johnny. Get the police here. Why should we run away?"

"You don't understand, Ginny," I said, trying to control my impatience. Every second we wasted now made our getaway more difficult. "We can't go to the police. The police captain is in this too. We must get out of here!"

Sudden fear jumped into her eyes.

"What is all this talk of money about?" she asked breathlessly. "What money, Johnny?"

I knew at once it would be fatal to tell her about the money. Later, perhaps, but certainly not now. She might not understand that it was mine by right: she might even think I had stolen it.

"He's mistaking me for someone else," I said. "Now come on, Ginny. I'll tell you about it in the car."

"He kept asking me about the money," Ginny said wildly. "He said you had stolen it from the casino."

"He's lying. Now, come on, darling. He may be back any moment. He's dangerous. We must get out of here!"

"Johnny, did you steal it?"

"Of course I didn't."

"Word of honour?"

"Yes, word of honour. It's all a mistake. Come on, Ginny, let's go."

"You'll have to help me. I can't walk far."

I drew in a quick gasp of relief.

"You're not going to walk at all. I'm going to carry you," I said, and took her in my arms.

She put her arms round my neck.

"I've been so frightened, Johnny. I've missed you so."

"It's all going to be all right," I said. "In a week, darling, you'll have forgotten this ever happened."

I went to the front door and opened it.

Captain of Police Hame stood just outside. He had a ·45 in his hand and he rode me back into the room, his blue eyes like chips of ice.

III

I set Ginny down in the armchair and raised my hands as Hame moved into the room, closing the door with his foot.

"Looks as if I've caught up with you at last," he said. The ·45 centred on my chest. "Ricca lived long enough to tell me you killed him. You're getting as dangerous as a mad dog, Farrar."

I heard Ginny catch her breath in a horrified gasp.

"Now look . . ." I began, but Hame stopped me.

"I got proof you killed Reisner and the Wertham woman, and now Ricca," he went on. "That's one murder too many. Back up against that wall!"

I knew what he was going to do. I could read it in his eyes. He couldn't afford to let me stand trial. I knew too much about him. The easiest out for him was to put a slug into me while resisting arrest.

My eyes went to Ginny. She was staring at me: her face was white and horrified.

Hame followed my glance.

"And you too," he said to her. "You're in this. Back up against the wall with him!"

She would have to go, too. He wouldn't want a witness to my killing.

"Wait, Hame!" I said. "We can do a deal."

"Back up against that wall!" he snarled at me. "I'm not making any deals with you. I don't have to!"

"You don't have to, but you will," I said, speaking fast, knowing any second he might shoot. "I've got half the casino's reserve: a quarter of a million dollars!"

179

That held him, as I knew it would hold him. His eyes flickered.

"You don't bluff me, Farrar," he said in a grating voice, "and you don't talk yourself out of this," but there wasn't any conviction in his voice.

"Turn us both loose and I'll split it with you. A hundred and twenty-five grand in cash!"

"Where is it?"

"Where you won't get your hooks into it without my sayso," I said. "This is cash, Hame. Money that can't be traced. All I want is three hours to get clear. Is it a deal?"

"I wouldn't make a deal with you unless I saw the money," he said.

"You can see it, but I want your word you'll turn us loose with a three-hour start when you get the money."

A thin, sneering smile came to his sun-burned face.

"I take the lot, Farrar. You haven't a thing to bargain with. I'll take the lot and you can have an hour's start."

"No! I'll give you two hundred grand. I've got to have something. I've got to have a getaway stake, and I want three hours."

"The lot or I'll put a slug into both of you and take a chance of finding the money." He was grinning now. "Please yourself. I told you you have nothing to bargain with, and you haven't."

I had intended to play with him. I was ready and willing to buy Ginny's and my freedom for half the money, but he wasn't taking the lot. I'd worked too hard for that money to part with all of it. There was only one way out of this. I had to catch him off his guard and kill him.

"Give me five grand," I said, making out I was frantic. "I've got to have a getaway stake."

"Maybe," he said, still grinning. "Where is it?"

I realized he'd shoot me the moment he got the money. Once again I was being jostled into murder.

"I'd be a fool to tell you, wouldn't I? As soon as you know what's to stop you shooting me?"

He tried to keep a straight face.

"My word."

"What's the use of that to me?"

He grinned then.

"Well, suggest something."

I nodded to Ginny.

"She can get it and bring it here."

"Suppose she doesn't come back?"

"She will. She loves me. Do you think she wants me to get shot?"

All the time I was talking, Ginny had sat motionless, staring at me. Now when I turned to her, she flinched away.

"Go on," I said to her. "Get the money and hurry." I reached forward and offered her the key of my car. "The car's around the back. It won't take you long."

She crouched in the chair, and the look she gave me sent a chill up my spine.

"Ginny! Please do what I say. This is the only way out for you. Get the money, and it'll be all right." I tried to make her understand I was offering her escape.

"No," she said. "I'm not having anything to do with it. You did steal that money, didn't you?"

"It belonged to me, Ginny," I said desperately. "I can't explain now . . ."

"Of course he stole it," Hame cut in. "It's money belonging to the casino."

"Oh, Johnny, how could you?" she said, wringing her hands. "How could you get me into a thing like this? You've lied to me all along. When you didn't come to Miami as you promised, I phoned the insurance people you talked about and they said you'd never worked for them. Ever since we first met you've lied to me." She pounded on the arm of the chair with her fist. "I'm not going to be dragged into this! And don't talk to me of love!"

I was sweating now.

"You've got to get that money! Don't you understand he'll shoot both of us if you don't go? Take this key and get out!"

"Oh no," Hame said. "Not if that's the way she feels about you. She stays here. We'll start from the beginning again."

Around the half-open kitchen door I saw the white cat come in.

"Then let me go," I said my muscles tightening. "She means everything to me. I'll come back. You can trust me to come back."

"No woman's worth a quarter of a million. We'll all go."

The cat brushed against his trouser leg. He hadn't seen it come in, and feeling something against his leg startled him. He looked down with an oath.

I was waiting for that moment. I sprang at him, my right hand grabbing at his gun arm, my left at his throat.

181

The gun went off with a crash that rattled the windows. Hame staggered back, then went down with me on top of him. I fastened on to his wrist and smashed his gun hand down on the floor. The gun went off again, but it fell from his hand.

For a minute or so we fought like a couple of animals. He was as strong as a bull, and knew every dirty trick in the box. We rolled to and fro, upsetting the furniture, while we punched, kneed and butted each other. It was like getting tangled up with a buzz-saw, trying to hold him.

He got his hands on my throat and began to squeeze. He had a grip like a monkey-wrench, and the air was cut off from my lungs. I clubbed him on the bridge of his nose and flattened it, crashing the back of his head on the floor. For a second or so he was dazed and the strength went out of his hands. I tore his fingers from my throat, twisted clear, crawled up on hands and knees. He was up on his feet a shade after I had straightened up. His face was a snarling mask of blood which poured from his broken nose.

At long range I knew I could take him, but hugged in those iron muscles he could lick me. I had to keep clear of him.

Maybe he had forgotten I was a boxer. He didn't act as if he thought I knew how to fight. He rushed at me, his arms reaching out for my waist, to bring me down into another murderous clawing wrestle on the floor. But I had had enough of that. I slipped to one side and jolted my right in his face. That hurt him, but it didn't stop him. He was tough. It'd take more than a slam in the face to put him down.

He came at me again, and this time I went in at him. We met like two charging bulls. I felt his hands grab my coat front. I grinned into his savage, blood-soaked face, then I brought over the left hook: the same punch that had broken MacCready's jaw, that had floored Waller, that had put paid to the Miami Kid. It landed flush on the side of his jaw, and I felt the jar run up my arm. I didn't care. He was out long before he hit the floor.

Gasping for breath I turned to look for Ginny, but she wasn't there.

"Ginny!"

I rushed into the passage. The front door stood open. Turning, I ran back into the sitting-room and to the window.

I saw her running down the long drive towards the gates. She was staggering as she ran, and she was holding her hands in her face.

I leaned out of the window.

"Ginny! Wait for me!"

But she didn't look round, although she must have heard me. She kept running, and beyond her, at the gates I saw two prowl cars swing to the kerb. Two cops tumbled out of the first car and started up the drive. She ran slap into them She was falling as she reached them, and one of them caught her and lowered her to the ground. Two more prowl boys spilled out of the second car and came pounding up the drive.

They looked up and saw me. I was looking at Ginny. There was a tightness in my throat and a sick, empty feeling inside me. I had a premonition I was looking at her for the last time. Then I turned and ran into the kitchen.

Benno lay stiff in death, his fat, vicious face seemed to snarl at me. I jumped over him, climbed into the box elevator and loosened the brake.

Seconds later I was running down the weed-covered path to the back gate. No one fired at me. I jerked open the gate and scrambled into the waiting Packard. I was shooting down the narrow alley that led to the boulevard when I heard police whistles. At least I had a car under me, and a fast car at that.

Where was I to go? The general alarm would be out in a few minutes, and every patrol car would be looking for me.

Who would hide me from the police? I thought of fat Zoe Elsner who ran the Liberty Inn on Bay Street. If I could reach her I might buy a hide-out.

I headed for Bay Street.

Half-way down Lincoln Avenue that runs parallel with Lincoln Beach's main street, I spotted a cop ahead, looking towards me from the sidewalk. He began waving at me. I shoved down the accelerator and the Packard surged forward.

The cop ran out into the street. He had a gun in one hand and a night-stick in the other. The people on the sidewalk stopped to stare. He was a pretty brave cop, but at the very last second he jumped aside. His night-stick came hurtling at me, and instinctively I ducked my head. The stick smashed a jagged hole in the windshield. I heard shooting behind me and felt the thumps of slugs as they made holes in the back panel of the car.

I kept on, switched the car around the corner and came out on to the wide boulevard that runs the length of the promenade and terminates at the gates of the casino.

I wouldn't get far now with a smashed windshield. Already people on the sidewalks were staring at the car as I shot it towards the big underground car-park.

I pulled up behind a line of parked cars at the bottom of a brilliantly lighted ramp. I was out of the car and opening the boot when a white-coated attendant came up. I saw his eyes go to the smashed windshield.

"What happened to that?" he asked.

"Hit a bird," I said, hauling out the suitcase. "I'll be back . . ."

I saw his eyes light on the bullet holes in the back panel. I closed my fist and smashed it at his jaw. He went down, his head bouncing off the fender.

I looked to right and left. At the far end of the park three white-coated attendants stood around a car, talking. They didn't look my way. There was no one else in the park to pay me any attention. I walked rapidly up the ramp. The suitcase weighed a ton. I wouldn't be able to travel far with this burden hanging at the end of my arm. But I wasn't going to ditch it. With all that money I might still buy my life: without it I was done for.

As I reached the top of the ramp I spotted two prowl cars coasting along the boulevard, and heading in my direction. Across the way a cop stood on the edge of the sidewalk. On the corner, fifty yards farther on, was another cop.

I had to get under cover, and at once. There was no hope now of reaching Liberty Inn.

Within ten yards of the cop opposite me was the imposing entrance of the Lincoln Hotel, a forty-storeyed skyscraper that dominated the promenade.

I crossed the street with a crowd of sun-worshippers as the traffic lights turned red. I kept in the middle of them, rubbing shoulders with a fat man in a beach wrap and on the other side a blonde in halter and shorts. She looked curiously at me.

The bulk of the crowd were headed for the hotel. I went with them. As I was pushing through the revolving doors I looked back over my shoulder: a mistake. The cop on the side-walk caught my eye. He stiffened, stared, then started towards me.

I kept pace across the lobby with the blonde in the halter and shorts. She and a couple of tanned lounge lizards got into the elevator. I got in with them.

The starter looked sharply at me.

"Tenth," I said curtly, before he could open his mouth.

The cop came through the revolving doors like a jet-propelled rocket. He was charging towards the elevator as the doors swished to. No one in the elevator had noticed him, except of course, me.

Not so good. In a few minutes the hotel would be teeming with police.

The car stopped on the fifth floor and the two lounge lizards got off: nobody got on. That left the starter, the girl and myself.

"Twenty-second, please," the girl said, and ran her thumb along the length of the halter, just inside.

The starter goggled at her, his eyes shifting to her suntanned legs.

"Yes, miss," he said. He looked at me as he closed the doors. "What's your room, mister?"

"I'm making a call."

"Sorry; against the rules. You have to check at the desk first."

"A little late for that, isn't it?"

The blonde was staring at me now. She dug her thumbs into the elastic top of her shorts, pulled it away from her waist and let it snap back again. She seemed full of cute tricks.

"I'll have to take you down, sir," the starter said, his mind more on the girl's shorts than on me.

"Please yourself," I said, shrugging.

The car stopped at the twenty-second floor and the doors swung open. The blonde got off. She began to walk down the long corridor. The starter paused to watch her go. Her behind jiggled as she walked: it seemed to fascinate him.

I tapped him on the shoulder. As he turned my fist connected with his jaw. I hit him so hard I nearly tore his head off his shoulders. He folded down on hands and knees and stretched out. I picked up the suitcase, stepped out of the car and pressed the outside button, closing the doors. Then I set off down the corridor after the blonde.

I caught up with her as she was putting a key into the lock of a door marked 22/4454. She was opening the door when she became aware of me standing behind her. Her eyes popped open and she took a hasty step forward that took her inside the room. I had Benno's ·38 in my hand and I touched her naked midriff with it.

"No screaming," I said pleasantly, and rode her into the room, closed the door with my heel and set down the suitcase.

"What do you want?" she asked, in a strangled voice.

"Sit down and take it easy," I said. "Nothing's going to happen to you. The cops are after me, and I am staying here until they go away."

She sat down. She seemed glad to.

I lugged the suitcase to the open window, and looked out. It was a long, long way down to the promenade. Already there was a big crowd gathering outside the hotel. As I looked three prowl cars with wailing sirens came rushing towards the hotel entrance.

"In ten minutes or so," I said, turning away from the window, "the cops are going to call on you. Please yourself what you do. I'm wanted for four murders: one more won't make any difference to me, but a lot to you. Tell them you haven't seen me. If you try any tricks you'll get the first bullet. Okay?"

She blanched.

I was sorry for her, but I was in such a jam I couldn't afford to pull any punches. I kept by the window. The crowd grew every second. More prowl cars arrived. The cops started to shove the crowd back, leaving a wide space before the hotel. There must have been three thousand people down there, and their numbers were growing every second.

I heard sounds in the corridor. No cop can walk quietly, and when there are a number of them, they sound like a herd of buffalo moving around.

They were going from room to room as I guessed they would. Well, it was up to the blonde now. If she let me down I was sunk.

"They'll be here in a minute," I said, trying to make my voice tough. "You know what to do," and I waved the gun at her.

She sat as still as a waxwork; her eyes growing bigger, and her face the colour of old parchment. She didn't look pretty any more.

Then there came a rap on the door.

For a long moment of time nothing happened. I looked at the blonde and motioned to the door with my gun. She stared at me, horror mounting in her eyes.

The knock came again: louder this time.

"Go ahead," I whispered, sure now she wasn't going to do it. I was right. She suddenly gave a wailing scream and slid off the chair on to the floor.

"Open up!" a voice bawled, and a shoulder thudded against the door panel.

IV

There was no future for me now. Once in their hands, with Hame in charge of the investigation, I was as good as dead. But that didn't worry me. All I could think of right at this moment was the money in the suitcase. If I couldn't have it, then I was determined Hame wasn't going to have it. Nothing else mattered to me now except how to keep that suitcase away from him.

The voice again bawled through the door panels. "Open up, Farrar! We know you're in there!"

Once again a shoulder crashed against the door which creaked, but held.

I went to the window and looked out. Running the whole length of the building below the window was a footwide ledge Leaning out, I could see the ledge terminated about thirty yards away to my right by a bulging piece of floral carving, overlooking the corner of Roosevelt and Ocean. If I could reach that bulge I would have excellent cover from a shot in the back.

I looked down. Three hundred feet below me the promenade teemed with people, staring up at me. It made me feel a little sick as I looked at the narrowness of the ledge, but it was either that or to be shot down when they broke into the room.

Again the shoulder crashed against the door. I swung my leg over the window-sill and got out on to the ledge. I held on to the framework of the window, groped inside and hauled up the suitcase.

A tremendous roar of excitement came from the crowd below, but I didn't look down. I stood for a second or so, staring straight ahead, my heart hammering and my knees weak. It would have been bad enough to take that walk without the suitcase, but with it, pulling me off balance all the time, it was going to be a nightmare.

Bracing myself, my shoulder rubbing the face of the building, I began to move forward.

I put one foot directly before the other, like a tight-rope walker, not attempting to move fast, and keeping my eyes fixed on the bulging corner stone ahead of me.

I crept past a window, moved on, aware of an urge to look down. I struggled against it, knowing if I did, I was done for.

Ahead of me was another window, then wall space, then the corner stone. When I was within six feet of the window a man's head appeared. I stopped short, my breath whistling through my clenched teeth.

He was a fair, tanned man in a fawn sports jacket and a bottle-green shirt. He gaped at me, his mouth falling open. Very slowly, so as not to disturb my balance, I slid my right hand into my hip pocket and pulled out Benno's gun.

"Mind you don't fall," the man said in a horrified strangled croak. "Hadn't you better come in here?"

"Get back and shut the window," I said, and pointed the gun at him.

He gave a gasp and jerked back from the window. Once again the crowd roared at me.

I started to move forward again. When I reached the window I peered in, the gun pushed forward. The room was empty. The door stood open.

I had twenty feet to go before I reached the shelter of the corner stone. I moved more quickly. Behind me I heard a shout, but I didn't look round. I kept on, expecting to hear a shot and feel a bullet smash into me, but nothing happened.

I reached the corner stone and gripped hold of one of its projections. Even then I wouldn't look down.

For a moment or so I stood there, trying to get my breath looking at the buildings opposite: the windows crammed with staring faces, not more than fifty yards from me.

"Get back you fool!" a man shouted at me. "What do you think you're doing?"

I put the suitcase down on the ledge behind me. Still holding on to the projection I began to climb around it. A woman screamed. The roar of the crowd surged up and submerged me in sound. Satisfied I had a good hand and foot-hold, I reached down and pulled the suitcase to me. Then, clinging on, I lifted it. For perhaps three or four seconds I remained pressed against the projecting corner, my foot wedged into one of the ornate carvings, the fingers of my left hand dug into a crevasse of stone, the suitcase dangling from my right hand in space. Its weight upset my balance, but I managed to hang on while the people at the windows opposite yelled and screamed at me.

I remained like that for some time. Then slowly, inch by inch, I began to edge into the hollow made by the two ornate projections either side of the corner stone. It took time, and once or twice I thought I wasn't going to do it. Without the suitcase it would have been easy, but having to work only with one hand

and to counter-balance the drag of the suitcase made it terrifyingly difficult. I got into the hollow without quite knowing how I did it. I had quite a bit more room once I was inside, and no one could get at me either from the right or from the left.

I was so exhausted I could no longer stand upright, and still clinging to the suitcase I sat down, my back firm against the hollow in the stonework, my legs dangling into space.

For the first time since I had been out on the ledge I looked down.

Roosevelt Boulevard and what I could see of Ocean Boulevard were packed solid with gaping faces. From this height they looked like a white-checkered carpet spread out below me. I could make out the tiny figures of cops and patrolmen trying futilely to clear the street. In the distance a mile-long traffic block hooted and honked. I could see people leaving their cars and making their way on foot to the hotel.

At a guess I had only a few more minutes before the police started to try to rope me or send some courageous harness bull along the ledge to grab me. My time was running out. But I couldn't grumble. At my side I had a quarter of a million dollars. Below me I had some five or six thousand people who were concentrating on me, and me alone. The next move was obvious.

I opened the case and took out a packet of hundred-dollar bills. I broke the elastic band and tossed the packet high into the air. The notes broke loose and spun to the ground in a fluttering little cloud.

The crowd below me stared up, watching the bills as they floated down to them. The bills took some time to reach them. A man jumped high in the air to be the first to grab one. Then they realized what I was throwing down to them. A yell went up that seemed to split the air and shake the buildings.

A man leaning out of a window opposite yelled, "He's throwing money away!"

I was working fast now, splitting the packages open and tossing the bills out as fast as I could take them from the suitcase.

The windows opposite began to empty of faces. Those who at one time had the better view were now rushing to the elevators to get them to the street in time to horn in on this rain of money.

Well, I had promised myself if ever I got hold of real money I'd go on the biggest spending bender ever. I was keeping my promise, and I was getting a tremendous bang out of it. Right at this minute I was the most powerful and the most important man on earth.

The scene below defeated imagination. People fought, trampled on each other, screamed, yelled and clawed. Even the cops were flaying with their night-sticks to get their hands on the bills as they floated to the ground. The wind spread them far and wide. I could see people fighting on the beach. I watched a girl cramming crumpled bills down the front of her dress, only to have the dress torn from her by a yelling, greed-crazed old woman, old enough to be the girl's grandmother.

A man with a handful of bills was being pushed against the side of a car while four women beat him with their handbags. A policeman was trying to turn a woman who lay on the sidewalk while she screamed like a train whistle.

I tossed the last of the bills down to them, and then sat back to watch. My breath was coming in great heaving gasps, and I had sweated right through my clothes. I would have gone through all I had gone through to have had those ten-minutes of power all over again.

But the money was gone – a quarter of a million gone as Della had said it would go: like snow melting in the sun, and now I had nothing to show I had ever owned it. My one supreme moment was over, and it would never be repeated.

No one in the street below was paying any further attention to me. They had forgotten me in their mad, greed-crazed scramble for the money, and they were still fighting and yelling amongst themselves.

My time was running out. Before long the police would organize a means of reaching me. I had two alternatives: I could either give myself up or I could anticipate my destiny and slide off the ledge into space. I was sure there would be no out for me once Hame got his hands on me.

If it hadn't been for Ginny I wouldn't have hesitated. I would have ended it there and then, but I remembered how she had looked at me when Hame had said I had stolen the money. I remembered, too, she had said she didn't believe I had ever loved her. More than anything else in the world now I wanted her to know how much she had meant to me, and still meant to me. I wanted her to know my side of the story, sure that if she knew the facts, and how I had been drawn into this mess as inexorably as a swimmer gets sucked into a whirlpool, she would realize, after I had gone to the chair, that I wasn't quite so bad as Hame had painted me.

And because it was essential to me that she should know the truth, I decided to give myself up. Before they brought me to trial I would have time to write down my story just as it had happened, and if the verdict went against me, Ginny would at least have my written record.

Having made the decision, I got cautiously to my feet. I looked back along the ledge. A policeman was leaning out of a window about twenty yards away from me. Reluctantly, his eyes popping and his face shiny with sweat, he swung his leg over the window-sill.

"Stay where you are," I said, waving him back. "I'm coming in."

As I walked towards him, moving slowly, steadying myself against the side of the building and keeping my eyes fixed on him, I heard the deep-throated roar from the crowd below. It reminded me of the noise the lions had made when I had dropped Reisner into the pit. At least he hadn't known what was coming to him.

I did.